AFTER
DROWNING

We gratefully acknowledge the support of the Canada Council for the Arts and the Ontario Arts Council for our publishing program. We also acknowledge the financial support of the Government of Canada through the Canada Book Fund.

Cover design: Val Fullard

After Drowning is a work of fiction. All the characters and situations portrayed in this book are fictitious and any resemblance to persons living or dead is purely coincidental.

Library and Archives Canada Cataloguing in Publication

Mills-Milde, Valerie, 1960–, author
       After drowning : a novel / by Valerie Mills-Milde.

(Inanna poetry and fiction series)
Issued in print and electronic formats.
ISBN 978-1-77133-285-9 (paperback).-- ISBN 978-1-77133-286-6 (epub).--
ISBN 978-1-77133-288-0 (pdf)

              I. Title. II. Series: Inanna poetry and fiction series

PS8626.I4568A38 2016   C813'.6   C2016-900306-X
                                                       C2016-900307-8

Printed and bound in Canada

MIX
Paper from
responsible sources
FSC
www.fsc.org   FSC® C004071

Inanna Publications and Education Inc.
210 Founders College, York University
4700 Keele Street, Toronto, Ontario M3J 1P3 Canada
Telephone: (416) 736-5356   Fax (416) 736-5765
Email: inanna.publications@inanna.ca Website: www.inanna.ca

AFTER DROWNING

a novel

Valerie Mills-Milde

inanna poetry & fiction series

INANNA PUBLICATIONS AND EDUCATION INC.
TORONTO, CANADA

For Michael,
always.

Her finely-touched spirit had still its fine issues, though they were not widely visible. Her full nature, like that river of which Cyrus broke the strength, spent itself in channels which had no great name on earth. But the effect of her being on those around her was incalculably diffusive: for the growing good of the world is partly dependent on unhistoric acts; and that things are not so ill with you and me as they might have been, is half owing to the number who lived faithfully a hidden life, and rest in unvisited tombs.

—George Elliot, *Middlemarch*

PROLOGUE: ANNIE, 1986

THERE IS A FIRESTORM over the water. Flames shoot upward, like firecrackers, and illuminate the harbour. The silhouettes of the buildings emerge from the dark, their windows alive with the flames.

The fishing tug *Dolly* is burning.

Annie watches from her vantage point on the bluff. The trees make a tangled screen here, dead-looking limbs of black and grey. She and Keaton have come to this spot many times after roaming the backstreets of Port, after sitting on the beach or walking the pier. They always took the path beside the old trolley rail that climbed from the shore.

From up here, it's possible to see the entire town, the east and west beach, the length of the harbour, and beyond that, the lake. Her eyes range over the fiery boat and then search the docks.

There is nothing to do, but wait.

Below, a handful of people have gathered on the street. They press together in groups of twos and threes. A man, short and squat, flings his arm and points toward the burning tug. "Andy Ruddell's gone in after the Beau kid." There is a horrible whine, the sound of metal giving way. "Christ, the gillnets and part of the rigging are down."

People clasp their hands over their mouths in horror, some stepping back, turning, taking a few running steps toward home.

"The Beau kid's gonna blow all the tugs to hell."

Andy emerges from the enclosed deck of the *Dolly* with Keaton slung across his back. When they were all kids together, the others used to chant monster, monster when Andy lumbered onto the field, twice the size of anyone else; he was graceless then, his arms hanging from him like a pair of wooden paddles. He's a hockey star now, a rare talent. Clusters of admirers wait for him at the end of his games, and from the stands, scouts slyly follow him with video cameras.

Staggering, Andy carries Keaton from the deck of the tug, away from the reach of the flames. He drops and sways and then lets Keaton slip to the ground. For several long moments, he stays on his knees, Keaton lying next to him like he is sleeping. A sleeping child.

When he finally pulls himself to standing, Andy's movements are clumsy. His first steps falter and then he propels himself back to the burning *Dolly*. Annie's gaze follows him only as far as the boat's railing and then her eyes return to Keaton. She feels the pull of him. She could pick her way through the dark and then rush along the few streets to where he is. She sees herself do it.

Earlier that day, sitting next to her on the cold cement curb outside of the school, he had said, "No matter what happens Annie, you stay away. You leave me alone." She had been shivering, her long arms cradling her knees. She didn't look at him. When he took her face in his hands, his fingers were hard against her chin.

"It can't be helped now."

She knows where it lives, that collision of desires: the longing for action and the longing for release. For Keaton it had taken shape around the time of his father's disappearance. It has wrapped itself around him, and squeezed.

A woman in a bulky bathrobe breaks from the group on the street and runs to Keaton. She crouches over him until a new rush of heat and smoke drives her back; she presses an arm across her nose and mouth to keep from choking.

Retracing the steps he took from the boat to the dock with Keaton, Andy has emerged from the *Dolly* with someone else. He looks almost furious, his movements lurching and ungainly. He drops Terry Spar, and then collapses.

Annie scrambles to a place slightly down the incline and closer to the harbour, where she has an unobstructed view of Keaton. He lies on his back, his head falling to one side. A couple of feet away, Andy lies strangely twisted, his torso at an odd angle to his legs. By the light of the street lamps she sees that Andy's clothes are smoldering. Close to him, Terry Spar thrashes, his left leg bending and straightening, then bending again.

Orange emergency lights approach from the north, where the main highway leads into town. Like acrobats, five firefighters jump out of a truck. They run to the prone figures on the dock, their hands searching for pulses. One reaches for his radio. The *Dolly* begins to belch ever larger plumes of black smoke and the firefighters, moving quickly now, shift Terry Spar, then Andy, and finally Keaton, to the far side of the dock. One of the firemen turns to the harbour and with a broad sweep of his arm, he takes in the entire line of boats that are tied aft and fore of the *Dolly*. The fire hasn't jumped yet but it might.

There is a commotion of orders, directions and then a large circular canister with a hose attached is lowered from the side of the truck. Two of the men wheel the canister close to where the *Dolly* burns. The canister whirrs into action, the men rolling it further forward, and then taking hold of the hose, directing it toward the narrow opening of the boat's enclosed deck, into the hidden heart of the blaze. Soon, the *Dolly*'s deck and pilot house are filled with a pulpy foam that oozes down her gunwales, catches on fragments of her rigging and the charred remains of her nets.

When the ambulances arrive, the paramedics move quickly, carefully, checking wrists, placing oxygen masks over mouths.

They hose down blankets with water from the fire truck and place them at the foot of the stretchers. Terry Spar screams when he is lifted, making Annie flinch. When they lift Andy, he doesn't make a sound.

Two police cruisers pull in behind the fire truck. The man from the street, the one she heard holler, runs to the officers and gestures toward Keaton. The kaleidoscope of pulsing emergency lights, orange, blue and red, makes Annie's head swim. Focus on Keaton, she tells herself. Stay with him. Keaton, having torn off his oxygen mask, sits up, his head hanging against his chest. One of the officers squats next to him and speaks and Keaton slowly nods his head. The officer points directly to the back of a waiting ambulance.

Keaton is on his feet, tall officers on either side, his face tipped up, head moving as he scans the bluff, and then his gaze locks on to where she is, crouching, and Annie knows that he sees her.

1.

O N THE DAY BEN VASCO DROWNS, the lake is graduating shades of greys, browns, iridescent greens. No white caps. The sky is a definite blue, with slow, cheerful clouds pinned above the beach as if to a child's felt board. A summer sky over a brooding lake, a coarse, sandy beach curled around the rim of the town, beginning at the painted oil tower and ending where the high, wind-eroded bluffs rise abruptly from the lake's edge.

Pen watches Maddie scamper from the nearby gully, a plastic pink watering can clutched in her hand. She has on a purple two-piece bathing suit and her belly protrudes, round and tanned. She is small for a four-year-old, and still delicious, thinks Pen. A piece of fruit. Maddie has collected an odd assortment of beach objects: a stick, a seagull feather, five stones varying in size and colour, a worn piece of green glass. She has laid them out in a pattern, with the stones making a circle in the centre, and now she waters the strange collection as though watering a row of pansies, for the moment preferring this to wading.

Pen has chosen a thinly populated spot on the beach, close to where the grasses start, and a distance from the waterline where many families splash in the shallows. The beach, she notes, remains remarkably unchanged since she grew up in this small fishing town. She makes the calculation: fifteen years of living away.

She leans back on her elbows, and focuses on the density of

people at the water's edge. This beach was never her family's summer playground. She and her brother Keaton had never properly learned how to swim.

A father walks a bare-bottomed toddler to where the waves lap and whistle over a line of stones. He lifts the kid up and then dips him down; "*Voom, voom.*" His voice becomes the engine of a plane and the baby squeals, his delight irrepressible.

For a few short hours, under a generous summer sun, the adults have become kids again. Pen points her foot, makes circles with her ankle and feels some tension drain. The sun has made her drowsy, her limbs heavy. The beach is littered with people who have surrendered themselves completely to the day, and although she feels seduced by the heat, the sound of the waves, Pen does not belong to the scene. Maddie does though, her active little body leaving an array of footprints in the sand. Maddie will soon be eager to go to the water, drawn by the colours, the waves. Pen has never had a love affair with this lake. It is too familiar, too treacherous. She couldn't wait to leave it when the opportunity came.

Maddie, caught by the glimmer of Pen's ankle bracelet, has descended on her, her small fingers scrabbling at the clasp, her face tight in concentration.

"Maddie!" Pen is laughing but trying to pull her leg away.

"I just want it for a little while," says Maddie. "Just to add to the other things." Pen eyes Maddie's treasures, recognizes that there are still gaps, a few breaks in the pattern.

"You can have it if you put it on top of something, like my shoe, so that it doesn't get lost in the sand." She bends over and loosens the clasp, places it into Maddie's waiting palm, and as she straightens, she sees that to her left, close to the change facilities and the parking lot, gulls have gathered over a knot of people. Most of the group stay away from the water, rooted to beach towels; some eat while others stare impassively at the lake. A man in billowing swimming trunks, his ball cap askew, drips relish on towels and hovers around a cooler.

Beside him is a young woman with straightened blonde hair. She stands with her hands on her hips, not looking at the man, examining instead her painted toenails. Another woman kneels and rummages through the cooler's contents. Matching oversized T-shirts cover the women's bathing suits, with the word "Woodside" printed in black against an orange background. The kneeling woman shuts the lid of the cooler and wipes her brow with the back of her hand.

"Sal, this is your *second* one. You had one already today. You just don't remember, that's all."

"No me," the man is saying, his head roving in a determined arc. From behind, a large gap-toothed woman starts to laugh, her hands clapping, her shoulders rocking as she watches Sal, who is still saying "no me, no me."

Most of the group are middle aged, their limbs heavy, their movements slow. Pen has never seen people from a group home in Port before. Several feet away from the group a man stands shin-deep in the shallows. His arms make the breast stroke in the air, his legs stomping up and down, as if imagining himself to be swimming. He wears a stretched and inviting grin, open to the lake and sky, and a few fine wisps of his hair float across his round, balding head.

Sal, still holding the hot dog, takes a few steps toward the man in the water, bellowing something. A name: "BEN-NY!"

His head lifts with the effort of pronouncing each letter. Pen hears affection in the call. Benny doesn't turn. His face opens like a peeled orange to the shine of the lake, to the yellow sun.

Pen pulls her gaze away from Sal and Benny and the Woodside group and sees that Maddie has put the bracelet on top of a long, flat stone, coiled like a snake that she now places in the centre of the circle of stones. She stands back and studies her handiwork, her hands slapping at her thighs in excitement.

"There!" she says.

"Done?" yawns Pen.

"No!" says Maddie.

"Well, what is it, exactly?" Pen asks, knowing that if Maddie were to explain it, Pen wouldn't understand. Like all true collectors, Maddie's motivations remain a mystery.

Maddie looks up, her eyes squinting. "Some of the stones are sparkly," she says, "and the feather belonged to a bird."

Pen rests her chin on her knees. "And the stick?"

Maddie doesn't answer. She is distracted by the sound of someone close by ripping the flip-top off of a can. Maddie has located the source and she cocks her head. Pen tracks Maddie's gaze back to three men who sit in aluminum armchairs planted in a straight line beside a reedy clump of birch trees. The men wear jeans and T-shirts, mirrored sunglasses that give them an aloof, proprietary look. One of them wears a black leather vest. All three hold beer cans sunk deep in Styrofoam cuffs.

Bikers have been coming to Port for years, swarming the tavern, scouring the shoreline that connects Port to the other small fishing towns. When they were kids, she and Keaton had seen them in town, loitering outside of the Fish and Fry, sitting on their Harleys, their long-toed cowboy boots stretched out idly, like reptiles sunning themselves on the black asphalt. She remembers feeling curious. She wanted to move closer, but Keaton, four years older than Pen, resolutely held her hand.

She frowns, questioning the veracity of the memory, wondering if she has invented the hand-holding, the protection Keaton offered. After their father disappeared, it was different between them. Keaton pulled into himself and became relentless about making money, careless and hard with her feelings.

Pen looks over at the bikers sitting on the beach, a couple of them showing signs of a burn, a delicate pink spreading over white arms below black T-shirts. And they must be hot, sweaty in those ridiculous boots, those heavy jeans. Pen has become paranoid about sunburns since having Maddie. Maddie is fair, not like Pen. Maddie is more like her father. If Jeff were here, Pen is thinking, he might be playing with Maddie in the water, tossing her about in the shallows, pretending he was a crocodile and delivering Maddie into a delirium of terrified giggles. For a moment, she wishes he was here, but then the wistfulness passes.

Maddie studies the bikers, interested in them, Pen can see by the way she is stalk-still, her green eyes not moving from the spot where they sit. Suddenly, she turns back to her collection and grabs a feather, a piece of glass and the stone with Pen's ankle bracelet. She half-hops, half-creeps over to where the men are sitting.

One of the men, the one in the vest, looks over at Maddie and raises his eyebrows. A granite profile, no smile, a contracted sharp eye above a mounded cheekbone; a deep trench from nose to chin, pocked skin.

Maddie stretches out her hand to him, bowing ever so slightly as if presenting a gift to nobility. She moves her body back and forth, fidgeting with excitement or nerves.

"I found these," she says, coy and smiling. "Maybe you wanna look?"

Since Jeff and Pen separated last fall, Maddie has been interested in all sorts of men, chattering at them in line-ups at grocery stores. Pen has never seen Maddie so intent on making contact as she is right now. The man is still, except for an encouraging opening up of his right palm, which he rests on the arm of his chair. Maddie moves in and leans her head in close, carefully dropping the treasures into his hand. He pauses and then reaches into his vest. He replaces the sunglasses he was wearing with reading glasses, and then scrupulously studies what she has given him, his lips clipped and prudish. He nods in silent approval, which elicits from Maddie a short and joyful dance.

"Do you like them?" she asks.

Determined not to provide an audience, Pen looks away and picks up her novel, a flat-toned Scandinavian mystery that she pretends to read.

"What do *you* think of them?" the man asks Maddie, something almost courtly in the tone.

This is a game, like Jeff might play. Pen can feel Maddie's anticipation mounting. "Well, I think they are all *pretty* things," she says. "Lots of things on the beach are pretty. But you would have to walk and walk and walk to find all of them." She shakes her head, almost sadly. "*We* could walk."

"We *could* find more," he says, stroking his goatee that is mostly grey. "But these things you got here, these are pretty nice!" He says this with reverence, with conviction. A man looking at a '66 Mustang convertible. He has entered into the spirit of things. Now Maddie is looking at his boots.

"So how come you wear boots on a beach?" She has a finger in her mouth and the other hand is opening and shutting behind her back.

"'Cause I want to."

Maddie titters. "You can keep those treasures. I can find more. Do you want to see them if I do?"

Biting down on her lip, Pen wants desperately for Maddie to stop. She *wills* Maddie to look over at her. The man raises an eyebrow and then knuckles his eyeglasses up the wide bridge of his nose. He studies the treasures in his hand for a long time. Pen can see how he catches Maddie's eye, how he encourages her with a look that is just short of a smile.

"Beautiful things," he says, as though giving a valuation. "Likely important stuff. I'd hang on to them if I were you."

Maddie will keep on and on with this and there will be no end. Pen drops the book onto the blanket and puts her hand over her eyes like a visor.

"Come back over here, Maddie." She pats the beach blanket enticingly, like she might encourage a cat to come to a treat. Maddie doesn't turn to look at her. It is an awkward moment, Pen losing the thread between herself and Maddie, her Mother instinct disappearing down a rabbit hole. There are gaps in Pen's maternal radar. Dead spots.

The man still has his hand out with Maddie's treasures and Maddie isn't moving.

"Maddie!" Pen is cranky now.

At last, giggling, Maddie faces Pen with a *come-and-get-me* expression. When Pen doesn't stir from her blanket, Maddie turns to the man and takes his hand, tipping its contents into her own small palm. The man's head tilts appreciatively.

"Goldilocks," he says, studying Maddie. "That's what I'm gonna call you!" He looks over at Pen. "Goldilocks your kid?" With his sunglasses off, his eyes are penetrating, clever, full of a concentrated interest. He is probably trying to size Pen up. She is wearing only her bathing suit and the tattoos on her collarbone and ankle are visible. She has a piercing in her brow with a silver ring, acquired in her years before Maddie. People often assume that Pen, who is slight and dark, is younger than she is, but she is almost thirty-two.

"I have to plead guilty," she says, smiling.

He pauses, his eyebrows raised, surprised or chiding, Pen can't tell. "She's a great kid."

"Mostly," Pen forces a laugh. "Until she isn't."

Maddie makes a little jump, her neck outstretched, her eyes opened wide, her gaze glued to the man. "Listen," she says, her finger pointed up to the sky, inspiring, commanding, "I'm *not* Golidlocks. My name is Maddie."

Now she's serving up her name, thinks Pen. An invitation. And to a biker. Pen stands and puts her hand out toward Maddie, gesturing insistently like she is directing traffic. Maddie has no *reason* to want more attention, she thinks irritably. The custody arrangement she has with Jeff is informal, fluid. No written agreement is in place. When they are home, Maddie sees Jeff almost every day.

"It's okay," the biker says, his gritty blue eyes looking right into Pen. "I don't care."

Pen brushes the sand from her thighs and peers over at Maddie and the men.

"I had a kid once," he says, the revelation having surprised him, a sudden awkwardness flashing across his features, the look of someone caught. Pen holds his gaze and churns in her own discomfort, feeling his unmasking as her own.

One of the other men, the younger of the two, shifts in his chair and reaches for another beer in the cooler. "Hey, T, I didn't know you had any kids."

The man called T tips his chin toward the lake and scans the shoreline where people move and settle like insects. There are no words, only the sound of the hungry gulls. Pen frowns at Maddie.

"Maddie, I've *asked* nicely."

"Mommy, you should walk with me. To find stuff." Maddie's green eyes are serious, challenging and Pen trudges over to her, reaching out her hand.

"Okay. Maybe. But come back over to where our things are first, Maddie. Please?"

Back on the blanket, Pen puts both of her hands on the sides of Maddie's face, then smoothes Maddie's hair. She puts her lips to Maddie's ear, which is no bigger than a sea shell.

"You shouldn't talk to strangers, Maddie."

Maddie takes a long and exaggerated drink from the can of coke she has mostly buried in the sand. "You *let* me talk to them," she says.

Pen sighs heavily and puts an arm up over her eyes. "You shouldn't say your name."

"Now you're mad," says Maddie sounding unconcerned. She rummages through the bag of food.

"No, I'm not mad."

"Chips?" Maddie grins up at Pen. "Daddy always brings lots—" she adds.

"First we put some more lotion on." Pen squeezes out the white lotion onto the palm of her hand, spreads it over the child's back, liking the economy of skin and muscle, the perfect diminutiveness of Maddie.

"Can we *now*?" asks Maddie.

"Sure," says Pen, opening a bag for Maddie who sits cross-legged on the beach blanket. A little Buddha. Out in the lake, the growl of a Sea-Doo makes Pen drag her eyes away from Maddie and the beach, and out toward the water.

Maddie is up again, walking with the watering can, mesmerized by the gulls who now sweep mawkishly over the Woodside group at the water's edge. They are no more than twenty feet away. She throws out a chip from the bag, then another. One gull floats down not far from her, cocking its head, opening its beak. Maddie, spell-bound, tosses out another chip.

"Stop that, Maddie," Pen laughs. "We won't be able to get rid of them."

Maddie is jumping up and down, delighting in her success with the gull. The gull watches her, then hops forward and squawks. Its insistence is unnerving, and Maddie draws in her little arms, and her head shrinks, turtle-like, into her shoulders.

Seconds later, she drops the bag. There are dozens of gulls, screeching and calling, wings flapping too close. She backs away, not crying at first, but whimpering. The gulls peck at the sand and beat each other off with their wings while Maddie stands frozen, and then runs, tripping and scrambling to Pen, slamming hard into her chest, burrowing.

T is watching them. Pen can feel it. "Goddam rats of the air," he says. Then, "Scary little shits."

One of the men says, "I think those are pigeons, T. *Pigeons* are the rats of the air."

Pen ignores the men. Maddie's momentary need for her is reassuring after the months of sea-sawing with Jeff. "He's right, Maddie," she whispers. Maddie giggles, already struggling for release.

It is only then that Pen sees the activity at the water's edge. A ruffle of disturbance is moving over the Woodside group. Two or three have struggled to their feet. Someone, maybe Sal, is making a baleful sound.

One of the female staff looks anxiously out at the water, her manicured hands cupped over her sunglasses. The other staff struggles up from her knees and makes a heavy little jump in the air. She shouts, "Ben. Benny!"

Pen scans the lake and sees him. He is much further out now than he was when she first noticed him. His head seems to float above the water, but every few seconds it goes under, then bobs back up.

His head goes down and Pen waits for it to resurface again, but it doesn't.

The older of the Woodside women, the one who was on her knees, now takes charge of the group. "Stay back. Stay away from the water."

Sal is already lumbering toward the lake, bellowing. "Benny, Benny. COME HOME."

The woman catches him and places her hands on his shoulders, pressing him to the ground the way a dog is made to sit. "Sal, don't move. Do you understand me? I said, don't move, not one inch."

The younger staff sprints down the beach, her orange T-shirt neon in the bright afternoon light. She is heading for the nearest of the five lifeguard towers, her step slowing with the recognition that the chair is empty, a relic against the sweep of a summer blue sky.

Along the beach, people are startled, necks craning, hands cupped across foreheads to sharpen their eyes. Women pull their children back from the water. A man is poised to run toward the lake but he doesn't. Instead, he looks nervously around, as if waiting for direction.

Out of the corner of her eye, Pen sees movement. T is peeling off his vest, his jeans sagging, his long grey hair falling spidery and limp down his back. He has both boots off now. He dashes magnificently into the water, making a shallow dive, his head turning back to the bystanders. "Make a line — join hands and come toward me," he commands.

A mother holding a toddler, the child Pen saw earlier, is stumbling, half-running down the beach. "I can't swim," she calls out, "but I'll stay with your children." She trots toward Maddie and Pen. "I'll keep her with me — at the van. Go. Go join the line." Pen says nothing and the woman hurries on.

Pen feels herself moving further out from the crisis, from the people in the water, watching as though she were somewhere above, in a balloon. She can barely feel Maddie, who is still in her arms, facing the water. Maddie points.

"He should come out now. He's gonna get cold." Pen doesn't know if she means the man who went under or T.

New arrivals join the people already in the lake, the line is moving forward with precision. T calls out their steps, urging them on, his voice compelling.

"One." Pause. "Two." Pause. "Three...." With each pause their heads sweep to the left, to the right, looking for any sign of the lost man. Pen hears the biker's calls like a beating drum. Like a dirge.

A group of opportunistic gulls have begun to feast on abandoned chips and hot-dogs, and a golden retriever plunges toward them and makes them scatter. The younger of the Woodside women has joined the line, while the older one stays with the group on the beach. She is gesticulating while talking on her cell phone. The group is strangely quiet now.

A couple of the people in the line stumble, splashing and struggling to regain their footing.

"Stop!" T holds his hands out to his sides, still clutching the hands of the people next to him. "It's too deep here."

From down the beach, where the oil tower sits beside the whitewashed pier, a young man is running with a life ring. His frame is tight and muscular, his hair sporting wide-blond streaks. He has a whistle around his neck, and he is running as though he is in a race, his movements well oiled, everything calculated for optimum speed. His entry into the lake has greater flourish than the biker's had, but somehow, it is less convincing. He takes up the centre position of the group and begins to call the steps.

T punctuates the air with a middle finger.

"Where the hell were you, asshole?"

The shorter members of the line have their chins splashing in the water. "Hold the line," the thin, high voice of the lifeguard calls out. He leaves a gap in the chain, giving the life ring to T who throws it over his shoulder.

Diving along the edge of the line, back and forth, the young lifeguard's body is lithe, his shoulders and hips arching in dazzling flashes. A dolphin, trained for a show. Pen watches, mesmerized, like Maddie had been watching the gulls.

"They're in a row," says Maddie. "The people—" Then, "I could go," she says. "The man went in with his clothes."

"No, Maddie. You have to *stay* here, with me." She is gripping Maddie, and Maddie is trying to pull away. The lake has changed colour, more pea-green now than brown. Pen can see a sailboat, far off, and against the horizon. Other boats turn toward the pier, which marks the entrance to the harbour and the mouth of the river. Commercial fishing boats line the high, cement docks, some gunwales painted white, like her father's was, others painted orange, yellow, red. In her mind she traces the view from the end of the pier, where the lighthouse is, up the river, past the fishing boats and under the lift bridge, into the cozy harbour, leisure boats nestled against low-lying docks, some with drying tea-towels, bathing suits hung from their railings, shirtless men in cockpits drinking beer.

Two small leisure boats are moving toward the chain, slowing, but the lifeguard is motioning for them to stay back. "Cut your motor," he yells, but his voice is too thin, too young, to rise above the motor. T makes a gesture of cutting his throat and he glares at the boaters until the engines sputter into silence.

The people in the chain have stopped looking out at the lake. They are looking at each other. A man lifts a wrist to his nose and rubs it.

Maddie has pried herself away from Pen now and she is off the blanket, inspecting her collection while new people have arrived on the beach, from cottages, from cars and vans. The retriever has found another stick and he is trotting up and down, looking out at the lake for his master.

There is a wail of sirens, and some in the Woodside group put their hands over their ears. Their heads shake back and forth, and a few begin to rock. The rescue boat growls and slaps across the water from the harbour. From somewhere down the beach, whistles are blowing. Pen knows these sounds. She has been expecting them. She holds her breath.

After her father's boat had been found capsized, empty — a floating husk on the green-brown water — there was nothing to do but brace herself, to suck in air and hold it deep, wait for things to right themselves so she might breathe again.

The man in the water will not come back.

Her eyes stay on the lake, her toes dug into the coarse sand. Her stomach is filling with something sour, the bitterness reaching up into her throat, stealing her voice.

"Mommy! Mommy, I'm talking and talking and you don't *listen*. I'm hot. I want you to go looking with me. For stuff."

Pen struggles up from the depth of her thoughts, suddenly frantic to take Maddie away from this place. She feels a cold sweat come on, simple fear now crawling over her skin.

"No. Not now, Maddie. We can't go down the beach now," she says, shoving Maddie's watering can, her book, her lotion, and the plastic food containers into her beach bag. She'll have to carry the rest unpacked.

"Come on, Maddie. Quick, quick." Maddie is scrambling to gather up the collection, trying to hold it all in her hands but wanting to hold onto Pen. She stumbles in her pink flip-flops, whines a little when her bare feet touch the hot sand.

"Maddie. Hurry!"

"Hot. It's way too hot! My feet are burning.... "

"We'll get ice cream. At Nan's. Come on, Maddie."

They cut through the parking lot where people stand, leaning against vans, talking, shaking their heads.

They walk toward the centre of town, past the Harleys angled in a gleaming line of blacks and golds outside of Pirates Bar, past the geraniums that mark the beginning and end of the lift bridge. Maddie has her hands cupped protectively around the treasures. Her hands are too tiny to hold them all, and every few steps, an object falls. She stops to retrieve it, stooping down, her protruding spine like something embryonic.

"Mommy, stop. Stop! My things are getting lost. They'll get stepped on." She holds up a feather, greasy and gapped. "Okay," she says to herself, "okay, okay," and then something else falls.

Beyond, people are walking on the sidewalk, licking ice-cream cones, gazing in the shop windows with no notion of what has happened at the beach. No one notices Pen and the chattering, limping Maddie as they plod back to the house Pen's mother still lives in, on a little street set away from the lake, not far from the muddy river.

2.

L ONG BEFORE THE BODY is pulled from the water, T leaves the beach. He climbs out of the lake, puts on his vest and tells the other two guys, Solham and Blue, to get back to the farm. He doesn't need any interviews with cops or EMS people. He just wants to be left alone, to chill. When he walks into Pirates, Big John sees he is wet, and kind of messed up. Big John is sympathetic in the way T thinks gorillas might be to lesser, dumber animals. Like kittens. He presses a beer into T's hand.

T has known B.J. for years. B.J. started out as a bouncer, a natural because of his size, but B.J. is smart, a born entrepreneur. And he had kept himself a free agent, avoiding patches and affiliations, keeping his mouth shut. He'd bought this place from one of the clubs years back and now it is known as neutral territory. B.J. has a blue-striped tea towel draped over his arm and his ugly mug looks curious, even concerned. "Have another one on the house."

Yes, he certainly will. The air conditioning is on and T feels strangely still, his wet jeans, his shirt cold like a compress against his skin. He thinks about how, not long ago, he was heating up like an egg in a pan.

It had started off a sweet day. Sitting in the sun on the beach earlier, he'd had that heavy, lazy feeling. After the fifth beer there was a static buzz in his head, a small softening of his edges. A pleasant progressive numbing.

The kid, Goldilocks, dropped into his dream. Out of the

corner of his eye, he'd watched her hone in on him, her little body shifting this way and that, navigating the sand, her eyes, bright. Happy eyes that were locked on to his. She dumped her cache of treasures into his hand and he felt himself light up like Yankee Stadium. To kick-start an old crank like him takes some power, T thinks with dawning admiration. He looks around Pirates at the collection of dissolute sad sacks, bikers and wanna-be bikers, mostly guys whose time is running out.

T has a pull on his beer that is warm and flat. A disappointment. He thinks of Goldilocks' mom, pretty, listless, her face closed over like a book. He had a kid once who was beautiful, with brown eyes the size of walnuts. T had known, in some far-off part of his brain, that the kid, who was a boy, quiet and watchful and soft, was a once-in-a-lifetime chance.

If he had the kid still, he would like to go to the beach. The kid would play, make sandcastles and T would help. Funny, his life inside the club has taken him to more beaches than he ever would have gone to as a civilian. It's expected that members be on parade, to cruise up and down the strip, make noise. T pushes bedraggled strands of hair from his face. Exhausted, he shivers and coughs. He's been afflicted by bone-wracking fits for months now. The coughing subsides and T spits up some nasty stuff into a napkin.

B.J. arrives with another bottle and puts it down.

"You swallow half the lake today?" B.J. asks, eyeing T's sodden clothes.

T shrugs. "Some guy drowned in the lake. I went in. End of story."

Lost in his thoughts, T arranges the events at the beach in the same way he would construct a report for headquarters. Reporting is a habit, like everything else T does. He had been taken up with Goldilocks, but even then, his eyes were in scan mode, a practiced sort of autopilot that he had perfected since the club had taken him on as a bodyguard back in the eighties.

There were a lot of people in the water, their bare skins shiny and wet, cold maybe. He doesn't like water and he hates bathing suits. The guy was a few feet out and standing shin-deep. He was kind of goofy-looking, his swinging arms pointlessly making circles in the air.

When he moved out further, T tracked him, catching the instant when he dropped, as if pulled, the big head slipping under the water. The tension had drawn together in T's chest, in his belly, his limbs, the way it always does before something big happens. He kept his eyes on the lake. And then he counted: one, two, three. Now he wonders, who taught him water-safety? Christ, he doesn't even remember who taught him to swim. After the count of five, he was up and out of his chair, vest off, and flying into the water.

"You get to him in time?" B.J. is still standing next to the table with his arms crossed and a quizzical look on his face.

"Nope."

Not for a moment had he expected to find the guy, pull him to safety, revive him. What took T into the lake, what kept him moving forward with the others, holding hands, counting out the steps, was an intense feeling of possibility. When the search and rescue people ordered them all out of the water, T, dripping wet and feeling pathetic, looked up toward the cottages where Solham and Blue were sitting, but they weren't who he was looking for. It was instinctive, that look. It made him think of how people are at the end of a long bus ride, how they scan the platform for a particular face. Then he had caught sight of them, the mother walking ahead of Goldilocks, the woman's body small, quick, pushing hard against the sand, labouring with the stuff she was carrying, and the kid doing her best to keep up. She's running, he thought. He watched them until they rounded the corner and then they were out of sight.

B.J. is waiting to see if T wants to talk. He doesn't.

"What were you doing on the beach, T?" A light goes on behind B.J.'s pebble-small eyes. "For that matter, what the fuck are you *doing* around *here* at all?"

With his back to the bar, B.J. leans across the table, tilts his head and looks directly into T's eyes. His voice is low, and it sounds to be coming from somewhere deep in his boots.

"I've been hearing that shit's going down, T. Didn't know *you* were wrapped up in it. Watch your back." B.J gives T a hard and lingering look and then nods for emphasis. T holds his gaze. He can't talk to B.J. about what he's doing down here. For the last several days, he's been kicking around the shitty farmhouse they'd taken over for the job, waiting on final orders from Winnipeg. This morning, he told Solham and Blue they were coming with him to town for supplies, and that he thought it was a good day for the beach. Solham had laughed, but T meant it. "Get the fuck in the truck, bonehead," he growled.

He wonders if the sun is low now, sunk down behind the western bluffs. He can't tell sitting in here. It's perpetual twilight in Pirates. The EMS will call off their recovery effort, once the darkness rolls in, but maybe they've got the body by now anyway. The booth he sits in is next to a window. He adjusts the louvered blind and light pours over his knuckles.

The door to Pirates opens and shuts with a bang and every one inside looks but pretends not to. B.J's planted behind the bar again. He's wiping it down with that tea towel of his, his movements professional and thorough. When he catches T's eye he glares back, not wanting an audience, and T looks out the window instead. Even with the blinds open, he can't see the lake from here.

When he was just a kid, before all the foster homes and the tight-assed social workers, his mom had talked to him about beautiful things: that lake up north and the way her people used to cook geese over open fires and hunt deer, shit like that. She took him there once. A lake with water the colour of New Mexican turquoise. It's where her people were from. He was naked, running, splashing, trying to swim to a tiny island where there was a black and white dog waiting, wagging its tail. He had panicked, gulped in water, and then he had ended up on the warm rocks, chest hurting with the effort, panic eased by the warmth, the dog curled into him, his mother somewhere on the shore, not far away. This might not have happened. She might have told him it did. She wasn't reliable. She wasn't really up to the job of raising him. In his mind though, when he thinks of being up there, with her, she is happy, a wide bright grin on her face, a look that is for *him*. When he thinks of *beautiful* he thinks of that place, that feeling. Beauty, T has decided, is rare and it can't be kept. He has never held on to one beautiful thing in his life. Not one.

T finishes his beer and then grunts something in B.J.'s direction. Some of the other customers look up at him as he leaves. He's still wet and washed-up, looking every single one of his fifty-three years. He couldn't care less.

3.

IT IS SUNDAY AND THE DAY after the drowning. The weather in Port has continued to be fine, dry, clear air, blue sky. Pen is in Irene's kitchen, wiping down the counter with a dishcloth that has a hole in it the size of Maddie's hand. There is a dull rasping vibration behind her eyes and she feels disconsolate and glassy. Being back in Port has that effect on her, but it's worse today.

The kitchen is a true galley, and Irene and Pen move tentatively around one another, careful not to touch. Pear-shaped, Irene is Pen's height, her body luxuriantly puddled around her hips; there is a sweet beatific smile on her face, and an ominous shine about her. She stirs batter in a mixing bowl, the skin on the chafed fingers stretched to a bloodless white. For years she has worked at the Fish and Fry, her hands hovering over the deep fryers, her fingers scalded by hot water in the sinks. The resulting scar tissue is ugly and revealing, a frank declaration that everything in Irene's life has been healed.

Pen gives a side-long glance at the stove-top and wonders when it was last de-greased. Irene has remained casual about housekeeping, and the house wears an attitude of benign disregard, an otherworldliness that Pen finds irksome.

"I don't really want pancakes, Mom. Neither does Maddie."

"I *do* want them." Maddie is sitting at the counter, a wooden spoon poised in her hand. Irene has dressed her in a cornflower blue sundress and slipped sparkly barrettes into her hair.

"You *won't* once they show up on your plate," says Pen. "Why don't you have some melon first?"

A small eater, Maddie is more interested in the production of breakfast than in the eating of it. The batter is too thick and lumpy for her to stir. Gripping the spoon, she pulls on the batter, the ceramic mixing bowl rocking, and then skidding dangerously close to the counter's edge.

Irene steadies the bowl and adds a dollop of milk into the mix. "I haven't got melon." With her wrist, she sweeps back a lank of silver-black hair and beams brightly, steadily into Pen's eyes. "What I have is bananas," she says definitely. "And blueberries."

"Well, let's put those out first," says Pen, opening the fridge door and peering inside. "Which do you want, Maddie? Banana or berries?"

Maddie ignores the question. She has dedicated herself to the loosened batter; she stirs furiously now. "A boy at the beach went into the water and didn't come out, Nan. His friends were upset, but the man with the boots went in to help him. It's cold when you stay in too long. You get goose bumps."

Wiping her hands on a tea towel, Irene gently takes the spoon from Maddie and rests it on the counter. "That boy drowned," she says. "He won't feel cold. Not anything."

Maddie cocks her head to one side, thinking, and Pen tries to catch Irene's eye. She wants to send Irene a warning, prevent her from saying too much or saying the wrong thing, but Irene is absorbed with stroking Maddie's cheeks.

After Pen's father Rod disappeared, Irene offered nothing. No hint of what might have happened to him. Pen steps between Irene and Maddie and sets down a bowl of rinsed blueberries. "When a person drowns, it means that they are *gone.*"

Maddie's green eyes narrow. "When do they come back? In the ambulance?"

"Not really," says Pen. She opens the cabinet door under the sink, hoping to find some spray cleaner, longing suddenly to clean the stove before Irene uses it to fry the pancakes. She finds a bottle at the back and emphatically sprays down the stovetop.

"I *saw* an ambulance," Maddie says.

"Yes, there *was* an ambulance. But whether or not the person comes back depends on if the person *really* drowned."

"Mommy, people don't stay in the water. You have to hold your breath in the water and your breath runs out."

"Not if they drown. Breathing is over." She makes a final pass over the oven door with the gummy cloth and tosses it into the sink. From the corner of her eye, she can see Maddie, bothered and watching, her elfin face intent on extracting an answer.

"That's what I *asked* you. About *drowning*."

"Maddie, I—"

With the tips of her fingers, Irene sweeps delicate circles on Maddie's back. Now she drops her face close to Maddie's. "When he drowned, he became something else," she soothes.

"But the man jumped into the water to bring him back." Maddie will cry now, thinks Pen, her own chest tightening, a prickling heat spreading across her forehead.

"And if the man *saved* the boy, then he could make him breathe again."

"*No* Maddie, that was the end of the boy's breathing."

With her face set in refusal, Maddie slithers down from the counter and opens the cutlery drawer. "It's hot in here," she says, her tone suddenly deflated. She pulls out spoons, two yellow corn-cob holders, ferrets out a couple of chopsticks that are still in their packages. She lays them out on the counter.

Pen inspects one of the yellowed chopstick packets, prodding it with her finger. She's relieved to have moved away from the subject of drowning. "It *is* hot," Pen says looking instinctively for a window where she knows there isn't one. "Hey Maddie. It's a funny kind of day for Nan to choose to make her pancakes, isn't it?"

Pen eyes Irene who is oblivious to the heat and stirring the abandoned batter.

"We can open the door. *Then* we can have pancakes," Maddie says, her face beaming again.

Maddie finds no fault with Nan. Maddie possesses an abundance of loyalty and Pen loves her dearly for it, although Pen can be jealous of Maddie's fervour for Irene, and even Maddie's devotion to Jeff. In the main room Pen opens up the patio doors and a frail morning light tumbles in. Her eyes sweep over the room; a beat-up sofa, two ancient over-stuffed chairs that Irene has covered with African–looking throws. Witches' balls and crystals. On the coffee table is a blue and white bowl, brimming with stones. Pen knows intuitively how the flat, smooth sides of the stones will feel between her fingers. Beach trophies. Irene has written on each one in cheap black marker: *hope, joy, faith,* the printing uneven and childish. In the midst of the New Age stones and the twelve-steps books, Pen looks for some vestige of her father, but can't find him.

Outside, a glint of light sparks from the rigging of a boat on the river and Pen follows it with her eyes. *Rod* — in her memory, he is quiet, tensed, colourful expletives bursting from him, and his sighs — eruptions that came from his deepest parts. He had a particular way of rolling his jaw, sliding it from side to side, forcefully working it. He liked wooden toothpicks and sugary store-bought doughnuts. It was his nightly ritual to watch the suppertime news, and then read the newspapers, Rod darting out to the deck every half-hour for a smoke.

Wiry, a frustrated energy just below the surface, everything about Rod was quick. Pen likes to think of him as smart. When he spoke, his words were packed tight with affection. *"Missed you today, my little Pea."*

What she remembers most was his smell: spicy, cold air mixed with fish and cigarettes, and the smell of lake water. Sometimes, there was the smell of beer, though she never saw him drunk. Once or twice a week, he drank with the other men, still in his work clothes, home early enough to be out by five the next morning.

She was only ten when he died. A little girl.

Over the years, Pen has tried to hold onto the idea of him but she can't. He is made up of pieces, Polaroid images on the brink of vanishing: Rod wearing a red and black plaid jacket and crouched down on his haunches with a net stretched wide on the dock, a torn and gaping hole in its centre, his expression perplexed.

She runs her eyes over the house, Irene and Ed's house now. A breath of air comes in from the open door, lifting the dust and cat fur to a perfect frenzy. The cats in Pen's childhood were like phantoms, half-starved and nameless. Now, Irene's cats loll around like porn stars and have the names of dead celebrities; *Marilyn, Tony, Frank.*

"Hello Gina," Pen says evenly to a glossy black beauty stalking through the patio doors. The cat looks at her with green-eyed insouciance. "Want my pancakes, Gina?" Gina blinks indifferently and Pen sighs, bends down and strokes her.

In the kitchen, Irene and Maddie are scooping batter into a fry pan, Maddie using a gravy spoon, lumps of batter falling into the sizzling oil. Irene has Maddie's hand in her own, making sure she doesn't get too close to the heat. When Pen was a child, Irene had vacillated between verbal savagery and a cloying desperation. Memories of Irene's boozy hugs, her sloppy kisses, Irene's unhappiness, come to Pen's mind. Pen knew no remedy, no response. She was too young to escape to the docks or onto the *Isobel*. In that regard, Keaton had been spared, spending most of his time outside of school with Rod.

A run this morning would have cleared her head, chased away the old and tiresome ghosts. Her running gear is in her bag, folded tidily beneath the journal article she brought to read. She might have time to run before breakfast, she might even manage to *miss* breakfast altogether; the idea brings on a surge of guilty anticipation.

She slips into Keaton's old room where she stays now with Maddie, closing the door, pulling up the blind. The room is unchanged. A battered dresser between twin beds, an orange shag carpet on the floor. She sits on the end of the bed that was Keaton's and eyes Maddie's stuffed animals, lined up at the headboard, her picture books strewn over the tangle of Disney princess sheets. Keaton never objected to Pen spending time in here with him, her belly flat to the floor, the carpet itchy on her bare legs, Keaton on the bed, drawing. Cartoon characters, action figures; his back curled against the wall, his head bent over his sketchpad, a spare pencil tucked between his teeth. It was the outline of the figures he liked to draw most, the muscled backs, the over-sized feet, strange helmets, heavy armour. He was fast. The figures were strong, drawn with conviction. What seems strange to her now is that he left them unfinished, either abandoned completely and crumpled, or flung over the side of the bed for her. His drawings sailed down, the figures featureless, naked. She carefully gave them eyes, coloured in their clothes, gave them hair and mouths. Keaton was older and the better artist, but she was detailed, meticulous. She had more patience then. More patience than Keaton.

Together, they made up stories, added captions. Pen drew the speech bubbles and Keaton printed the words. The figures took on names: *Dumpster, String-Man, Crank.*

"Crank's gonna hammer on String-Man."

Pen giggled. "A dog's gonna bite Crank in the butt and then the hammer's gonna fall on his head." Silly, ridiculous storylines. She and Keaton were conspiratorial, gleeful.

"Draw a dog now, Keaton." And he did. A beautiful dog with fur like a flowing lion's mane.

No more than three months after Rod disappeared, Irene took Ed in as a boarder. The house was overrun with broken-down furniture, rescued cats. And people. Irene would drag home people who were down-on-their-luck from the bar. Ed took Pen's room at first, and then, after three months he moved in with Irene. For years, rumours were floated about Ed and Irene, that they were lovers long before Rod drowned.

And then Keaton was gone too and Pen stayed alone in this room, Irene remote, still drinking, nursing the dual hurts of Rod's abandonment and Keaton's later defection. Now, when they visit, Maddie takes Keaton's bed, a small reassuring lump under a stained white coverlet.

There is a knock on the door and Ed peeks in his head, a round-faced man wearing a ball cap, with watery eyes that sink behind half-moon glasses. He looks like an ex-priest or a washed-up boxing coach. His features have collapsed into a worn perseverance. "Breakfast's on." Almost an apology.

Following him, Pen sits in a chair and watches Irene slip around the crowded room, putting butter, syrup, cutlery out on the table. She takes a bowl of sugar from the cupboard and places it in Maddie's hands and Maddie walks ceremoniously with it to the table.

Ed is silently dolling out the pancakes. When Pen looks at Ed now, she finds not a trace of the drunk he had been. Twenty years of sobriety. Irene likes to tell people that, her hands on Ed's shoulders. She tells it like she is proselytizing, her voice pretty and hushed and urgent. Ed has become her evidence of miracles. When she runs her palms down his cheeks her bracelets collide, releasing an insistent tinkle.

Ed sits at the table with Maddie on his knee. He wordlessly puts his cap on her head.

"Papa Ed, you said maybe I could go out on the *Irene* with you. To catch fish." Maddie has twisted her body around and she is bracing herself against his thigh, looking up into his face.

Ed gazes at Pen with something of an appeal. "I don't think your Mom thought that was such a great idea."

"Why?" Maddie asks.

Pen says. "Boats aren't safe, Maddie."

"Then Papa Ed shouldn't go on them," Maddie says.

"You can do other things with Papa Ed."

Pen wants Maddie to have Ed and Irene in her life. Months go by and Ed and Irene don't make the trek to Toronto. "You should come to Toronto," she has told them in winters past. "There's nothing in Port when it's cold and there are piles of things to do in the city. The Science Centre, a kid's play. Maddie would like it if you came."

"Roads are bad, Pen. And that car...."

She knows, even as she asks, that they won't climb into the ancient Taurus, scrape the ice off the windshield, and travel the three hours in a car that doesn't have a working heater. Port is their bubble, their universe. It shouldn't seem selfish of them to not leave it, but to Pen, it does.

Ed has the paper spread over a corner of the table and on the front page is a piece about the drowning. Irene sees Pen eyeing it.

"Town's been quiet about what happened. Not much said at The Fish and Fry last night except that Search and Rescue hung around the beach, long after their job on the water was done." Pen knows that The Fish provided free coffee and sandwiches for EMS. Unasked, Irene is pouring more coffee into Pen's mug.

"Why would they take people to a beach when they can't swim?" asks Pen, pushing the mug away a little, thinking of the Woodside residents parked by the water, hot and sweaty, nothing to do but eat bad food.

"People like the beach," says Irene, "even if they don't swim."

"That guy was *in* the water," says Pen pointedly. "I have to wonder about supervision."

"Nobody sayin' what happened yet." Ed's tone is cautious, reasonable.

"Nobody says *anything* openly here. They must think it's bad for tourism."

Irene reaches out and loops a strand of Maddie's hair around her index finger and smiles. She won't engage with Pen when Pen is edgy. Ed looks steadily at her, a mixture of sadness and sternness in his round walrus eyes, magnified now by his

Walmart reading glasses. Pen feels sobered, just looking at him. The locals don't talk about their lake's cankered history. The extinction of fish, the hardship of trying to make a living here. She thinks of watching the Lake Erie tugs leave the harbour when she was a child, slipping out in the quiet of the morning, graceful despite their lumbering hulls, the chipped paint. They kept going for fish even when the fish weren't there anymore. The blue pike, herring, white fish, bass: already all but disappeared, and the rainbow smelt was in decline. But there was still yellow perch, walleye, white bass for the tugs to go out for.

Pen looks at Irene now, appearing so content in the inspirational clutter of her sitting room, the dirty river lapping at her back door. "They'll have to talk about this," Pen says. "That man was part of a government-supported group home or something. There will be inquiries."

There had been an inquiry after Rod drowned. Long after his death had been a flat out and accepted fact, they had waited on the findings. Keaton told her that it came down to money. The insurance. They really needed it. It was important that the drowning be viewed as an accident. An act of God.

4.

IT IS LATE AFTERNOON and Pen is on the deck, talking on her
cell phone with Jeff. She imagines him sitting on the futon in
his bachelor apartment, probably in his workout clothes, black
T-shirt and grubby sweatpants. Short and stocky, full-sleeve
tattoos, a shaved head and goatee, Jeff wears a tough-guy
image. His undergrad students joke that he is a closet white
supremacist, but nothing could be further from the truth.
He is an avowed pacifist and a PhD in Peace Studies, a great
scholar, an elegant writer. As a kid, back in North Bay, he was
into heavy metal, fantasy novels, and Taekwondo. Despite the
intellect, his eagerness makes him seem younger than he is. Jeff
is excitable, committed, the general amiability in his nature
punctuated with an intense need for her. His expectations of
her are a hazard for them both. Holding the phone, he'll have
his elbow cocked sharply into his knee; the call will cause him
pain, *is* causing him pain.

"So tomorrow. You guys are coming back?" He's trying to
sound casual, though she can tell how much he misses Maddie.

Pen lowers her voice so Maddie won't hear and tells him for
the second time that there was a drowning at the beach and
that she and Maddie had seen it. "The OPP has put out a call
for witnesses. They'll want statements."

She can hear him suck in a breath, weighing what he wants
to say and what he can say.

"So you couldn't have gone this morning?"

She feels a familiar resentment blooming in her chest, a dislike of having to explain. "It's nice here, Jeff. Maddie's having a good time."

"I'd like to see Maddie."

She *would* ask him to come down, she tells herself, but it's summer session and Jeff is teaching to make up for the shortfall in their income so he can pay the rent on the apartment he took last September. Besides, he hates coming to Port, even though he's never actually said so. "I burn," he's said when they've come down to the beach together in the past. "I'm from the *North*. We can only take direct sun when it's minus 15°C out or lower." He used to make her laugh with remarks like that.

And the near-arguments they've had about Port, how Jeff and everyone else believe that the lake is dying. She was furious at him for saying it; she felt herself clutching the place bearishly. A confounding reaction, she knows, because in truth, Pen believes that it is dying too.

She kicks the peeling baseboard with her toe. The drowning, the police, and their inquiries have awakened a kind of dread in her. There were police inquiries after Rod disappeared, and then later, there were questions about Keaton, about the *Dolly*. There were charges laid.

"I don't like the idea of giving a statement. Maybe I'm putting it off."

"Just procedure, Pen"

"Maybe," she says. "But what I say might have something to do with who's seen as responsible."

Jeff pauses, holding back. "Pen, it was a drowning. Accidental."

"What was he doing in the lake in the first place? And then there was the rescue attempt.... A biker was first in the water..." She can see Jeff, thoughtful, a little impatient, intelligently putting all the pieces together. She pulls her arm around herself and looks down at her bare toes.

"Anyway, I'll figure it out," she says.

Maddie comes out. She has changed into one of Irene's tie-dyed T-shirts, a flowery silk scarf tied around the waist. When Pen hands over the phone, Maddie's face changes into a play face, antic and stretched. She can hear Jeff's voice, boisterous, booming on the other end.

"Bye" Maddie blurts and waits for Jeff to say "bye" and then she says "bye" again. Maddie won't end it of course, and finally, laughing, Pen takes away the phone.

The afternoon light slants from the west. Pen wants to take Maddie away from the confines of the house. "Come on. Scoot and get your bathing suit, Maddie." Pen is up from her deck chair, the lemonade she was drinking abandoned. "It isn't good to stay inside all day," she says.

"Mommy, I *wasn't* inside all day. I was on the porch." She is a strangely logical child, and Pen doesn't always understand her.

"Right. But don't you *want* to go to the beach?"

Maddie changes into her suit, and then she plants a fat kiss on Irene's remarkably smooth and smiling face before racing for the door.

Once they are close to the beach, the sidewalk ends. Maddie insisted on riding her tricycle, something that Ed picked up at a garage sale and the rigid wheels don't manage the sand that is banked in the potholes and gullies. Dismounting, Maddie stands with a look of studied refusal on her face.

"This is a dumb bike. It doesn't work."

Pen looks at the faded plastic tricycle and wishes that she had made Maddie leave it behind.

"If you feel that way about it, let's leave it here for some other kid," she says. "Someone who will *appreciate* it."

Maddie lets her arms drop and looks over at Pen, her face long and solemn. "You're very mean to say that." She points at the tricycle. "You could carry it?"

Pen sighs and carries the trike over to the side of the parking lot where she dumps it behind a garbage can. "We'll pick it up after." Maddie doesn't look convinced. "We will, Maddie." It isn't the first time she has thought of Maddie as a tyrant. Pen is not quick to resolve each of Maddie's small grievances, to soothe and to cajole in the way she imagines most mothers do. People, she believes, recognize this deficiency in her. Jeff, Irene, Ed.

The parking lot is already starting to empty, women shaking beach blankets into the air, slapping at sand-covered feet with towels. The sand will be everywhere. It will travel with these summer people back to the city, to the quiet cul-de-sacs, places that are far inland from the lake.

The beach holds onto nothing of the day before, no security tape, no rescue devices. A lifeguard sits high up in one of the chairs. Not the young man who sprinted down the beach yesterday. What will happen to *that* lifeguard? she wonders.

Maddie, not wanting to put her feet in the water, takes a stick, and makes squiggly lines in the wet sand. She is humming a song, one that she has been taught in nursery school: *I'm going to Kentucky, I'm going to the fair, to meet a senorita, with flowers in her hair....*

They are walking west on the beach, into the sun, and ahead of them are the bluffs. The colour has gone from the water's surface, but still it prances mischievous, self-preoccupied, in the angled light. Pen slips off her sandals and walks at the water's edge where the coarse sand becomes pebbly, her feet feeling the bite of ancient fossil and stone. She didn't used to wear shoes at all in the summer. The soles of her feet had toughened and become rough as tree bark.

It's hard to walk purposefully on a beach. There are so many treasures, much that is mesmerizing, even here, without the advantage of tides or the abundance of sea life. Driftwood, abandoned junk, the carcasses of fish, and the occasional dead seagull. And fossilized stones etched in pink and ivory. Maddie, with her collector's impulse, cannot go far without tossing away her stick, snatching up some small item, dropping it into the middle of the Micky Mouse baseball cap that she holds.

Pen finds some bits of coloured glass, one the shape of a dog or a rabbit. "Here, Maddie," she says, holding it out. "Come see."

Maddie looks at it and plucks it from her hand. "That's a *different* green from the one I have," she mutters. "It's not like the one I gave to the man. The man with the boots. He took the boots off when he went in the lake. But not his clothes."

Pen peers thoughtfully at the remaining pieces. "I used to collect glass like this," she says. She thinks of the biker telling Maddie the glass was beautiful. "It's made from old bottles that have been washed over and over by the water, so much there aren't any edges left." She kept the glass in canning jars, sorted by the colours: blues, browns, greens, the edges smoothed and blunted, the surfaces opaque.

They have been a family of collectors. In the fall season, Keaton and Rod used metal detectors to find objects, sometimes coins and jewellery left behind by the summer people. They did it more out of curiosity than necessity. She supposes now it was a kind of sport Keaton and Rod shared.

When she was old enough to join them, Pen carried a coffee can that she used for the glass. At the end of the scavenging, Rod peered into the can and admired the contents, his finger shifting the pretty bits. Then he and Keaton compared what they found, laughing at the ridiculous nature of lost things. Stuffed-monkey key chains, kewpie-doll penknives. One afternoon, after they were done, Rod took Keaton down to the docks. Pen went home, her can weighty, her mood elated. She emptied the can onto the carpet, and began sorting the glass into piles. Placing each piece in the pile where it belonged was far more satisfying than doing a jig-saw puzzle. She didn't bother to count the pieces. What was important was seeing the piles of glass growing, evolving into tiny islands on the yellow green carpet. She was kneeling over the glass, her back to the door, when Irene came in, her face flushed. "Where are the boys, Pen?"

"The *Isobel*," said Pen, not looking up.

"You've been gone all day." Irene's voice was loose, whiney.

"I'm home now," said Pen, still lost in the tiny glass mountains.

"Leave that. Come here." Something between a shout and a cry. A broken sound. Pen was startled, scattering the glass across the floor.

She had tried to give Irene comfort. She rested her forehead on Irene's chest, but she couldn't bring herself to put her arms around her. After Irene finally let her go, Pen went down to the docks, to wait for Keaton and Rod. She left her treasures behind.

Maddie has a puzzled look when she examines the piece in her hand. Pen smiles, realizing that for Maddie bottles are plastic, not weighted like the glass she holds. "It's made from glass, Maddie. Lots of things were made from glass before."

Maddie goes ahead, and Pen finds another piece, a sliver of deep blue. Without thinking, she bends and reaches into the water, takes the glass from amongst the pebbles, then holds it out to the light.

She is standing, holding the glass, when she sees a figure walking east. The sun is behind, and she sees the figure in silhouette. The long legs and the collection of mannerisms seem vaguely familiar. There is something slightly off-kilter in the gait. The rhythm is only a suggestion, circular and inevitable. Recognition comes: Andy Ruddell. Keaton's friend.

He slows down, unhooks his thumbs from the waistband of his jeans, extends one large hand in her direction.

"Penny Beau" he says.

Andy's face is a paradox, and not what she remembers. The left side is covered with a light etching of scars, zig-zagging like streams and tributaries on a map. The eyelid is stretched tightly, hooding the left eye, and when he smiles, only the right side of his face is changed. His hair, which was always a crimped sandy brown, is receding, showing even more of an ample forehead, freckled skin.

Keaton's friend since elementary school, Andy had been a giant, burdened by an out-sized body too large to manage with any speed or dexterity. When he was in grade five, a posse of boys had waited for him beyond the ball field, ensnared him with some fishing line and taunted him with "*monster, monster, freak.*" Keaton had gotten into the middle of it. The rumour was that he threatened the others with a gutting knife that he later used to cut Andy free.

Andy grew into a good-looking kid, a gifted hockey star, who inspired loyalty and admiration in team mates. Hockey scouts had talked to his parents about a "future." There were pictures of him in the St. Thomas newspaper: local talent always makes for good copy. All that talent had evaporated the night that Keaton burned Terry Spar's boat.

Pen hasn't seen him since. She heard that he had been in hospital for a long time and then he had moved to London, to live with an aunt where he finished high school. He ended up at a university somewhere close by.

The scarring, the awkward movements, are hard to reconcile with Andy's earlier incarnation. She feels a shock, a queasiness. Andy either doesn't notice or doesn't care that Pen is staring.

"And this," he says with a theatrical flourish, looking at Maddie, "is mini-Pen." The laugh is warm. "She yours?"

"Yeah," Pen sees that Maddie's eyes are screwed up and she is looking at Andy with her head cocked to one side.

"*You* had an accident," Maddie says simply.

"That's true," says Andy.

"I got a scar." Maddie points to a tiny scar in the middle of her forehead, a remnant from a fall on a stair when she was two. Andy bends down to take a careful look.

"Nice." He says appreciatively.

Maddie looks proud and thwacks her stick against the sand.

"Mine's not at as big." She adds. "And it isn't all over."

"Size isn't everything," says Andy. When he laughs, the good side of his face takes on an exaggerated expression, like someone performing in mime.

Frowning with exertion, Maddie tries driving her stick into the stubborn sand.

"Same determined look in the eyes as all the Beaus," Andy says, looking at Pen.

His good eye travels over her face, takes in the single piercing in her eyebrow, the tattoo on the inside of her wrist. She wonders if she is very much changed since they last met.

"I guess," she laughs. "You living down here now, Andy?"

"Actually, old neighbours of ours are celebrating an anniversary. Big party weekend. So I came for that, and to see the place, I guess. You?"

"Just visiting Mom," she says, her toe drawing a circle.

Andy says nothing. He was always easygoing, quick to laugh, a large, reassuring presence. Keaton and Andy were a study of opposites: Keaton was like something small and dangerous, something dark next to Andy.

"What's your name?" Andy is asking now, kneeling down next Maddie.

"Maddie."

"Maddie for what?"

Maddie giggles, anticipating a game.

"What do you think of Port, Maddie?"

"I like Nan's," says Maddie with certainty.

"Yeah, your Nan's cool," he says easily.

"She's got cats," says Maddie, jumping away, running a distance, and then turning back. "Do you? Have cats? There are some wild ones by the dock. Papa Ed gives them fish heads and he lets me leave some milk sometimes. You could *have* one," she says.

"Hmm. Got to be honest, Maddie. I can see myself visiting those cats sometime, but not taking one home."

Maddie seems satisfied with this. She nods her head. "Well, I can show you," she says, "when you want to meet them."

Pen starts to walk in the direction Maddie has gone, and Andy, with his lilting gait, falls in beside her.

"Heard your mom is doing good."

Pen shrugs. "She still goes to meetings."

Years before, when Irene was swept up in recovery and working her steps, she'd told Pen she was sorry. She knew the damage she had done, and she knew there was no way to explain it. Still, would Pen be willing to let her try? "I didn't feel like I mattered," Irene said simply. "Not to Rod. Not to anyone. And I didn't care enough about myself." She seemed earnest enough, a hint of a quiver in her voice, her eyes naked, drawn down. A passing sorrow, Pen concluded. Like a brief rainshower on the unreadable blank surface of the lake. In the end, Irene was nothing if not self-indulgent.

When Andy's face shifts toward the shimmering lake, his head swings in a slow arch, his vision interrupted by the wall of scar tissue that arcs over the eye, his head over-rotating to compensate. Everything about him makes her think of a precise system of balances and counter-balances. She follows his gaze out to the lake, where there is a steady stream of boats heading into the harbour, like ants at the end of a picnic.

"*This* place isn't so different."

"Not in some ways," says Pen. "But of course, it *is* different."

He picks up a rock and throws it at the water. It looks as if it should go a long way, as far as the horizon. But it drops short, the trajectory halted by the expanse of the lake beyond.

"Good throw," she says.

"I've seen better...."

"You and Keaton used to have tossing matches. The loser had to get thrown into the lake. But you were so much bigger. He used to have to take a run at you." Remembering this, she turns to him and beams.

Andy shifts his weight a little, his face unchanged. "I suppose you high-tailed it out of here some time ago?"

She struggles with what to say, not sure how to explain where she has ended up: an uncommitted academic, newly separated. A single mom. "I live in Toronto," she says.

"Yeah? And you work?"

"At the university."

"Teach?"

"And study. I'm trying to finish a degree."

"Well, that doesn't surprise me," he says. "You were smarter than the rest of us."

Because she doesn't argue this, she feels complicit in a lie. It has taken her four years longer than it should have to finish her dissertation. She is studying human geography and is now an expert in Diaspora, the scattering of people away from their roots. When she attempts to define it for other people, especially down here, she suspects she comes off as pretentious.

He is looking out at the water, and he doesn't ask her more about her life in Toronto.

"You, Andy?"

"Real important stuff," he says, his voice sunk deep in mock seriousness. "You'll be impressed. Really. I sell things. In large quantities," he looks a little amused. "I work for an auto parts supplier outside of Woodstock."

Sales suit him. Except for the scars. She wonders if his disfiguration is a deficit.

"You see what happened here yesterday, Pen?" He means the drowning but he doesn't say the word because of Maddie.

"We were here," she says, pushing up her sunglasses with the back of her hand, "sitting back a bit, but we saw him just before."

"That must have been kinda rough..."

"I don't know what happened." She looks out at the water, her eyes taking in the late-afternoon brightness. "One minute he was there. And the next he wasn't. Just like that."

They have walked almost as far as the parking lot now, and Maddie is looking for her tricycle, running back and forth like a squirrel looking for what it has buried. She tries to drag it with one hand, the other hand holding on to the hat, full now with her beach finds. Andy goes over to her and takes the trike.

"Nice wheels."

Maddie holds out her hat for Andy to inspect, a smile on her face. She points at the trike: "Can you take it to over there?" She asks, running to a spot where the ground has been flattened by parked cars.

"You here for a while?" Pen asks him.

"I'm taking a few days. Making a bit of a vacation out of it." He lets out a kind of restrained sigh and grins, then slides on a pair of sunglasses from inside his top pocket. They do a good job of covering much of the damage to his face and she has to wonder why he wasn't wearing them before. "It's been a horrible year." He's still smiling but not necessarily at her.

A feeling of shame creeps over her, like she's somehow responsible for his misfortune, all of it, whatever it is because of Keaton. It makes no sense. She looks away and tracks to the spot where yesterday Ben Vasco disappeared in the water.

"I have to make a statement tomorrow. About what happened."

He follows her gaze and then turns toward her, something reassuring in his posture. "Probably be good to talk. You know, about the statement. Other stuff. Maybe after you are done tomorrow, we could get something to eat."

She brushes the sand from her arms thoughtfully, slowly. She knows he wants to ask her about Keaton. When she looks at Andy now, she sees Keaton standing there too, his hands ground deep in his pockets, impatient, his mind wound around some plan.

"Okay. Why not? You have a number I can call?"

"I'll give you my cell number." He reaches into his wallet and pulls out a business card.

He grins and it comes off lopsided. "Don't have much of a personal life these days."

Pen laughs and they walk together. Maddie is waiting for them, sitting on the railway tie and laying out the treasure beside her. She hums something.

"Come on Maddie. I'll carry the trike until the sidewalk starts, then you'll ride again"

Maddie places the treasures back in the hat and they trudge along. They can see the harbour from here. Most of the boats have made it in now and people lean against masts, looking relaxed and mellowed by the day. Andy turns to Pen and one side of his face opens into a smile.

"I'll see ya'," he says.

"See you, Andy." They go in opposite directions: Andy disappearing behind the line of condos that rise jauntily beside the parking lot; Pen and Maddie slowly making their way to the centre of town.

Maddie makes small grunts as her feet push against the pedals. This time, she doesn't ask for help. Lifting her, Pen parks her on her hip and drags the trike behind. It's time to go back to the house, put Maddie in a bath, pour herself a glass of wine. Except there won't be any in Irene's refrigerator. The house is dry.

She'll buy some tomorrow. A big, cheap bottle with a screw cap. Something to look forward to after she has made her statement about the drowning. She'll get up in good time, have breakfast, and then leave Maddie with Irene while she drives over to talk to the police some twenty kilometers from Port. A trip she is dreading: too many associations with Keaton, with the torched *Dolly*. On the way home, she'll stop nearby for the wine and pick up some groceries. Things that Maddie likes: sweetened cereals, raisin bread, chicken noodle soup. She wouldn't allow that kind of food in the city. She would chastise Jeff for feeding Maddie "junk."

5.

THE HIGHWAY PEN TAKES away from the lake goes through restless hills that hug the river, then rises to where the land flattens into an expanse of golds and greens. This is fertile country. She passes blank-eyed farmhouses, their front lanes swelling with summer phlox, snap dragons, lupin. All of this is an ancient flood plain. All of it, at one time, covered by water.

The car is air-conditioned, a concession for Maddie. As a kid, Pen was prone to car sickness, particularly in summer, the heat making her thighs sticky against the vinyl seat, her stomach riding up into her throat. It wasn't that Rod didn't like stopping. He was most often lost in thought, tapping his fingers on the over-sized steering wheel, "greatest hits from the fifties and sixties" playing on the radio. From time to time, he lit up a cigarette, Irene leaning into him, cupping her hands around the burning ember to light her own. Irene's manner of smoking was deliberate, needy, a theatrical intimacy in the meaningful looks and the inhalations. Sometimes she would rest her left hand close to his thigh while he was driving. Rod never took his hand off the wheel to touch her. Now, Pen cannot imagine that Rod and Irene were ever together, they so seldom touched, though Pen has a memory of Irene brushing her knuckles over the scruff on his chin, teasing him with a chaste downward look, her lips pushed out in a comic pout.

Their windows would be rolled part way down, and the smoke

and the ash from the cigarettes would drift to the backseat, making Pen gag.

Keaton squished himself into the far corner of the backseat. "If you think about puking, you will," he'd warn. He would engage her in games of eye-spy, and animal-vegetable-mineral. There would be Chinese skin burns and pinching games, sometimes painful enough that tears would come to her eyes and she would forget. He grew bored before she did.

If they were in the car for long enough, the car sickness, the clenching in her stomach, the acid bitterness, always caught up to her. Keaton must have known by her sallow colour that she was about to be sick. He leaned over the seat and put a hand on Rod's shoulder.

"Better stop..."

One look in the rearview and Rod would know.

"Hold on, Pea." The car would be over to the side of the road, sitting in a cloud of dust.

It might have been Irene who got out with her, whisking Pen to the ditch, swiping the sick off her chin with a Kleenex. What Pen remembers is Irene's head snapping back as soon as Rod began to slow the car down, her eyes boring into her.

"It's always a *fuss* with you, Pen."

Rod would shoot her a look just short of contempt. "*Jesus*, Irene."

Maybe Irene felt guilty after. She would get Rod to stop at a corner store, and when she returned to the car she was all smiles, ginger ale and salted chips for Pen, a chocolate bar for Keaton. They could never tell with Irene; one thing didn't necessarily lead to the next.

The outskirts of St. Thomas come into view, the town where she will find the OPP station. The building is not far off the highway. She turns in toward a grey, concrete building with a couple of dwarfed evergreens at the entrance. It is a modest-looking place. The glass entrance doors are tinted a smoky brown.

Years before, Pen had stood in this very same reception room, next to Irene, who wore a blue nylon ski jacket, streaked a little with mud. Pen had on a pair of running shoes that had soaked through, and her socks were clammy on her feet. It was March 1986, and the weather was rainy and cold.

"Where's my son?" Irene had asked at the window. "Where's Keaton Beau?" Keaton, they were told, was in a holding cell somewhere at the back of the building. Irene, who was probably mostly drunk by then, had swayed a little, but had kept her eyes fixed defiantly on the clerk.

"You have to wait," she'd been told. "He's in with the officers."

They later learned that there was no question about Keaton's guilt. A resident in one of the houses, close to the docks, had seen Keaton climb on board the *Dolly*. The man recognized Keaton as the kid who crewed for Terry Spar. When the plumes of smoke started rising from the *Dolly*, he called the police. Keaton didn't deny that he set the fire, nor did he say why.

Now, standing in the quiet and filtered light of the reception area, Pen feels a familiar numbing, a separateness which is laced with an insistent urge to bolt. Despite this, she walks over to the window, and fishes inside her bag for her ID.

A heavy-set woman with glasses sits at the window, a pen poised between her fingers, her OPP jacket looped over her chair.

"I'm here because of the drowning yesterday," Pen explains. "The one on the beach at Port." She slides her driver's license over the counter toward the woman, who doesn't look at Pen.

"Don't need that." Instead, she hands Pen a clipboard. "Just fill this out: name, address, contact information and a brief statement about what you saw. Then give it back to me. Someone will be out shortly."

Pen has almost finished filling out the form when a glass door behind the reception desk slides open. A man with dark hair and bleached-looking teeth, wearing a jacket and slacks, walks out. A policeman in civilian clothes. Behind him is one of the group home women from the beach. It is the younger one, her blue eyes round, her white-tipped nails brushing away tears from her tanned face. The police officer is quiet, almost gallant, walking with her to the front door with his head bent close to hers. "Thanks for coming in, Danielle. It's hard to talk about, but it's important."

"What's going to happen now? To me and to Deb?" She nervously picks at the seam of the flaking pleather bag slung over her shoulder.

"Look, it isn't really a criminal matter."

"*Criminal*?" She grips the bag's strap, her eyes welling.

"We'll be in touch," he says gently. "If you think of anything more, please let me know."

Shoving on a pair of sunglasses, she leaves quickly; with her head down, she slides into the passenger side of a waiting Ford Explorer. At the wheel is a polished looking woman, with blonde bobbed hair, a crisp-looking blouse, probably Danielle's mother.

The officer is leaning, relaxed, amiable, at the window where the clerk sits, the two exchanging a few quiet words, and then he turns toward Pen. His faced is smoothed over, professional. His mouth, although he is young, is already thickening into early middle-age, and his dark hair is thinning. "You're here to give an account of what you saw at Port Saturday? Around the time of Ben Vasco's drowning?"

Although she had read the name in the paper, it is the first time she has heard his full name spoken out loud. Ben Vasco. The image of the head floating, then vanishing from the surface of the water, comes unwelcome into her mind.

"Yes. I am. I'm Penelope ... Pen, actually. Pen Beau."

At first, the officer says nothing. He seems to be considering something, and then thinks better of it. "Good," he says finally. "We've been hoping to get as many statements as possible. I'm Detective Sinclair." He holds out his hand and smiles. "I'm the lead detective. Come on back and we'll talk."

Following him, the glass doors swallow her just as they had

recently disgorged Danielle. Detective Sinclair's walk is casual, his chat with the other personnel easy and familiar. There is no sense of urgency about him. Ben Vasco is already gone. They come to a small room with a single window, the blind pulled against the outside light.

Detective Sinclair fills the small metal chair across from where Pen sits. He is unhurried as he reads over the paperwork.

"Sad," he offers, "What happened there."

"Yes," says Pen.

"You mind if we do a witness statement, Pen? It means I record what you say, and later it will be transcribed for the record."

"No. I don't mind."

Detective Sinclair has her sign another form, allowing him to record their conversation, and after he has witnessed it, he clicks on a small device that sits on the table between them. He speaks slowly, saying the date, the time, her name.

"So you were on the beach yesterday, July 12?"

"Yes. With my daughter Maddie."

"You were on the beach or in the water?"

"I was on the beach."

"How old is your daughter?"

"Four."

"Did you see the victim go into the water?"

"He was already there when I first saw him. But just standing in the shallows."

Detective Sinclair nods.

"What was he doing?"

"Well, he was kind of pretending to be swimming."

"Pretending?"

"I guess, just sort of practicing."

"With his body in the water?"

"Just his shins."

"And the water was?" Detective Sinclair puts a thick hand on his shin and looks over at Pen with his eyebrows raised."

"Something like that," says Pen.

Detective Sinclair bends into the recording device: "The witness has just indicated the victim was standing in approximately fifteen centimeters of water."

He nods again at Pen.

"Was there anyone else close to him in the water?"

"Not very close," says Pen.

"And what were the counsellors doing?"

"Making lunches for the others, I think."

He nods again.

"And did you see him swim out further?"

"No."

"No, you didn't see him swim out, or no he didn't swim out." Detective Sinclair is smiling broadly, trying to be less officious than the questions make him sound.

"No, I didn't see him swim. I guess I was busy with Maddie. I saw him a few minutes later. His head. That's all. It was up and then under, then up again. And then I didn't see it at all."

"How long from the time you saw him in the shallows to when you saw him further out?"

Pen remembers the confusion of the gulls, Maddie's terror.

"A minute, or two. I don't know. I don't know about time."

"Okay. And how many times did you see his head come up to the surface?"

"Two times, maybe."

The detective nods again. "Okay. And when did someone see that something was wrong?"

"A few people did, I guess. People kind of realized it all at once, and then one person went in, and others followed, to form a line."

"Did you join the line?"

"No."

"What did you do?"

"I stayed where I was. With Maddie."

"Okay. So, did you see the lifeguard?"

"After the line started. He was running down the beach."

"How long after?"

"I don't know. I don't know about time. I'm sorry..."

"How long were they in the water, searching?"

"I don't know..."

"Did you see the search and rescue operation?"

"No. We left before that."

"Okay. And can you tell me what you saw the counsellors doing through all of this?"

"They were trying to call him in. One of them ran for help, and the other stayed with the group. When the one came back, the other one went into the water."

"Did you ever hear them tell the victim to get back to shore, before he went out further?"

The gulls had been screeching, she remembers. And Maddie was crying so hard.

"No. I mean, I don't remember that. Maybe they did."

"And the lifeguard. Did you see him?"

"Yes." A flash in her mind of a young man running down the beach. Too late, thinks Pen. He was too late. "He joined the others in the water. The others who had joined the line."

Detective Sinclair smiles at her, and then leans over and clicks off the device. He crosses his legs and reads over Pen's statement again. "You're from Port, right Pen?"

"Yes. But I don't live there now."

"Must have been upsetting, to have seen all that." He says it directly but not without kindness.

"I've known people who have drowned in Port before." She feels she should be more upset, more visibly shaken. She needs to explain. "My father drowned out there when I was ten. A fishing accident."

"I'm very sorry."

She rubs the palms of her hands on her jeans back and forth, as if she is trying to encourage circulation. "He fished. Commercially."

Detective Sinclair nods his head, looks down at his papers.

She knows the gesture, a hint of awkwardness.

To make up for the disclosure, she goes back to Ben Vasco's drowning. "It's always worse when it happens on such a calm day." She looks at Detective Sinclair. "No one would have expected it."

"Can happen," he says, "even on the nicest day possible."

"There is often an undertow in that lake," she says.

"He couldn't swim. There didn't need to be an undertow for him to drown."

She remembers Ben standing in the shallows, his arms eagerly sweeping the air. He didn't realize how hard it could be, once his own weight began to drag on him, and he hadn't discovered the knack of floating. She knew from what she read in the paper that it hadn't taken them long to find Ben. He was pulled from the water, just east of where he had vanished. The rescue team worked on him a long time and then he was transported to the hospital. But he was pronounced dead there. The truth was though that Ben Vasco died in the water.

When the interview is over, Detective Sinclair walks Pen back to the reception area. He studies her for a moment, as if he has forgotten to say something important, and then he holds out his hand.

"Thanks for coming in," he says. She asks if he knows about Ben's funeral arrangements.

"Ben's been at the group home for years, and since the mother died, there isn't anyone in the area. There is a sister, I guess. She lives in the States. Once the Coroner releases the remains, the family will have to make arrangements." He pauses, then looks at Pen. "I can let you know, if you like. Will you be staying in Port?"

"Yes," she says simply. The answer comes out more definite than it should have. She hasn't spoken to Jeff. But it is what she needs: to stay longer.

6.

THE NEXT MORNING, the fourth day after the drowning, Pen wakes early to go for a run. Maddie is still asleep and will be for at least another hour. Watching her, eyelids fluttering, mouth-breathing like a little bird, Pen feels a tug so strong she wants to cry. She had not been prepared for motherhood when it came, not that Maddie was unplanned.

The pregnancy was a curiosity, as though she were wearing someone else's set of clothes. She was both fascinated and appalled by the alterations to her body, the expansion of her belly, the elephantine swelling of her ankles. Her body was alien. She read the recommended books and went to Yoga-For–Pregnancy classes but she remained skeptical that any of it was useful.

Maddie arrived two weeks early, an eagerness for life there from the start. Pen was euphoric, completely taken over by her achievement, but within a week she began a kind of rapid descent. The smallest demand defeated her, a pile of unfolded laundry, a sink brimming with dirty pots. To make matters worse, Maddie was colicky, fussing and squawking for most of her waking hours. Feeding didn't seem to help, nor did putting the baby on top of the drier, or driving her around half the night. When he was home, Jeff was helpful but he had gone back to his teaching duties by then, leaving the house by eight in the morning and seldom home before six.

She doesn't remember if she thought of walking away. She occasionally reads about the dark compulsions of women in the grip of postpartum, although her own experience is blanketed in a partial amnesia now. Some memories persist, memories of closing the nursery door on the inconsolable Maddie, lying down on the dusty hardwood in the hall, curling herself around one of Maddie's stuffed bears and shutting her eyes tight. She found that she could produce no tears. Not even a sound.

Jeff, besotted with the baby, adrenalin-charged, tried at first to lift her mood. He found a jogging stroller at a neighbourhood garage sale and, happy with himself, he presented it. "Now you can run *with* Maddie!"

Nothing was more appalling than the prospect of pushing a wailing, protesting baby and enduring the sympathetic looks of strangers. *Can I help? Would you like me to try?* She had relegated the stroller to the basement where it is still, next to three rubber bins that are full of Maddie's baby clothes.

They stood on the decaying cement patio behind their rented downtown house. Jeff was rocking Maddie, his movements attenuated, a strong man resolutely holding onto a fragile bundle. All through the long afternoon, Maddie cried and Jeff sang to her: blues, rock, everything in his expansive repertoire.

The baby's eyelids were heavy now, the rigidity in the small body almost gone.

"Just about there, Baby Girl" Jeff whispered, drawing the baby closer to him. "Into the arms of Morpheus."

It seemed to Pen that Jeff was holding the baby as if to *shield* Maddie from her, from the dark funk she had fallen into.

"Never in my life have I felt so alone."

Jeff widened his stance and then leveled his gaze on Pen. "Maybe we need to get someone in here. Maybe Irene," he said.

Startled by the thought of Irene, she shook her head, her eyes widening. "It's just the crying." She drew the back of her hand across her nose, spreading slick mucous across her cheek. She was disgusting, now. "Forget it," she told him. "I'm okay."

He stopped rocking Maddie. "You don't shower for days on end. You don't eat and you don't go outside." His head tilted

forward, combative, challenging. "Stop lying. You *aren't* okay."
Lying? She stared, disbelieving. He was bullying her now,
which was so unlike him. Before Maddie came along, if they
argued, he would leave the house for a few hours, go to the
dojo, or go to the bar. While he was gone, on the edge of fury,
she washed the floors, scrubbed the bottom of the garbage pail,
wiped door knobs. It was ridiculous that an adult, a *grown
man*, would need to disappear in order to cope, she told herself
Her fury would then sink into churlishness. *Screw you Jeff.
Why don't you call?* Soon she would be looking out the front
window and checking her phone. She could have called him, of
course, but she wouldn't allow herself that kind of desperation.

Jeff always came back. He would slide a beer from the door
in the fridge and then sit beside her on the couch, his hands
clasped tightly around one knee. His posture was tight, his
tone, searching. "I just don't get why you *want* to fight, Pen?"
She didn't want a fight. At least, she didn't think she did, and
she didn't want him to leave. He wanted to talk things out.
She would stare at his gym bag, dumped thoughtlessly on the
floor, the stacks of unsorted papers on the coffee table, and
silently surrender to relief.

After Maddie arrived, Jeff dropped the dojo, preferring
to give the baby her baths, singing, putting her chair in the
kitchen while he cooked vats of curry, and trays of bullet-proof
muffins. Fathering was a solace to him, a joy. He and Pen were
continents apart. She determined to hide what was going on
in her head. She deluded herself that no one, including Jeff,
would see how undone she was.

"Things will get better," she protested.

"Not on their own, they won't."

"Babies don't cry like this forever. They *can't.*"

"So it's a contest of wills, then." He looked exasperated.
"If *you* won't try and feel better for yourself, then do it for
Maddie."

Pen's eyes had drifted to Maddie, asleep in Jeff's arms. She thought she saw a ghost of worry hovering over Maddie's minute features, the suggestion of neglect or fear. By then, Pen had spent years hiding from Irene's neediness, terrified of the void she saw there. She wouldn't impose that on Maddie. She went to the doctor the next day and agreed to a course of anti-depressants.

Even now, long after the post-partum has disappeared, the essence of her love for Maddie is a mystery to her. At times, she is in Maddie's shadow, separate from her, alone on the dark side of the moon. But there are other times, like now, when a life without Maddie is simply incomprehensible.

The running gear is the same every day, more or less, depending on the season. In summer, Lycra running shorts, a tank top, a pair of tired Saucony running shoes. Although brittle with age, she has been unable to part with the shoes. With each step of her run there is a tiny jolt, a perturbation, which helps her to feel the ground. Pen shoves in the earphones of an Mp3, and chooses a playlist that is esoteric, with not many lyrics. Storytelling in songs is like a weight when she runs, particularly songs about lost lovers, endless nights. She stretches her arms over her head and decides to run in the direction of the centre of town.

Her gait is clipped, restricted at first, unsure of direction. She lived in Port for eighteen years and yet there is an uncertainty that climbs into her muscles here, a persistent questioning of herself. She takes in a deep breath and shakes out her hands, determined to find her rhythm, imagining the route she will take to the other side of the bridge, and then up the winding hill out of town. She thinks of herself at fifteen, sixteen, a sullen, withdrawn kid who found solace in schoolwork. After Keaton left, Irene and Ed were taken up with their first shaky steps toward sobriety, attending meetings, sharing their inspirational books. Pen could barely stand to be in the house.

The sun is delicate at this hour. It touches her skin but she doesn't feel the warmth. The light is almost translucent, the brightest, hottest part of the day still hours away.

Her pace is lengthening, swallowing up the pavement. The lift-bridge is down. She strides across, enjoying the look of the road ahead of her as it curls away from Port. Just past the bridge, streets angle down to the main beach and to the water but she isn't interested in going there this morning. She veers right, preparing to take the hill.

"Hey!" A command for her attention. Gruff, not unfriendly. She hears it through her music. It takes her a few steps to stop. To her left, a third of the way down a narrow street is Pirates Bar, the parking lot empty except for a Harley and a man who sits on the steps, a thick white mug in his hands.

"That's you, right? The girl from the beach." He has to call out to her because she is still too far away to talk. "The girl with Goldilocks," he adds, nodding his head, pleased that he has recognized her.

She stops and puts an arm over her eyes and peers down the street. She knows him at once. She stands for a moment, considering whether to wave and nod, turn, readjust her ear buds, and keep running. She sees herself do it.

He sets down his mug and rests his forearms on his knees, the palms up and open, like he is expecting to receive; — the gesture makes her think of Maddie.

"I don't bite," he says, glancing briefly over his shoulder and then looking at her again.

She takes out her Mp3 player and walks the half block down to him. She pulls her right elbow across her chest and dips sideways into a runner's stretch and then does the other side.

He gives her a sharp look. "Where's Goldilocks? Sleeping?"

"It's only just past six in the morning," she says, laughing.

They look at one another, wondering who will say something next. He pulls out a cigarette from his vest and holds it out to her, then shakes his head. "*Course* you don't." He lights it and takes a puff. He peers at her, frowning. "You saw it too. When that guy went under," he says.

Pen nods and slides her eyes away.

"Your little girl, Goldilocks, she *know* what happened?"

"The drowning incident, you mean?"

"Yeah. The *drowning incident*." He annunciates each syllable of *incident* as though the word amuses him. With wide fingers he combs wisps of greying hair from his face.

She pulls up one knee and stretches her thigh. "Maddie doesn't know that he died. Just that he drowned."

"There's a difference?" He picks up the coffee cup again, turns it with his hands and then sniffs loudly. "You're going to tell her, right?" he asks.

"It's a question of timing," she says.

He snorts and then shakes his head. "A dodge. People take the easy way out with kids."

"She's *only* four."

He shrugs and then looks behind him, at the lake. The sparseness in their conversation is intimate and strange. She is mesmerized, suspended in the moment with him. When he looks directly at her, his eyes are an exceptionally pale blue, though his skin is dark. His face is animated as if his thoughts have caught on something important.

"Goldilocks *has* asked about him." Not a question.

Pen doesn't tell him about Maddie's questions. "She'll forget about it, once we go back to where we live."

He shrugs and cocks an eyebrow.

"Well, everyone has their own way of dealing with things," she says, faltering.

He is looking at her with a mixture of disappointment and irony. From behind them, she hears the sound of a speed boat accelerating out of the harbour. T rubs his chin on his shoulder and takes a puff of his cigarette, coughing a little after. "These things will kill you," he says, holding up the cigarette. "You can tell Goldilocks that!"

She smiles. She used to smoke, years ago, before the running. Before Maddie.

"Sure will."

She shifts her weight from leg to leg, jogging on the spot. It's a little theatrical, but she needs to pull away.

"Don't let me keep you," he says, his voice now openly sarcastic.

She starts to run, turns, half-waves. When she gets back to the main street, her face is as flushed, her pulse as rapid as if she had already done ten K. She looks back and sees him on the step, his cell phone in his hand. She realizes that she didn't say anything to him about his part in the rescue effort. She didn't tell him what she saw.

7.

FACT AND DATE OF DEATH
DEATH BY DROWNING
CHIEF INVESTIGATOR'S REPORT SUBMITTED TO
THE CLAIMS REVIEW BOARD.

New World Insurance,
October 17, 1984.

The following report summarizes the progress of the investigation into a claim connected to an insured individual, a Mr. Rodney Beau, who disappeared during a storm while fishing on Lake Erie in a commercial vessel, *M/V Isobel.*

Irene Beau filed an application in June 1984 for mother's insurance benefits for herself, and child's benefits for her two children. The life insurance policy had been taken out by her husband, Rodney Beau, who disappeared on May 15, 1984, and who, she alleged, had perished in a boating accident. The purpose of this investigation is to establish whether Mr. Beau's disappearance, and presumed death, falls within the parameters of the policy, and whether a payout can be made to Mrs. Beau on the basis of eligibility.

The known facts of Mr. Beau's disappearance are as follows: on the morning of May 15th, 1984, Mr. Beau apparently rose at 4:30 a.m., dressed, and left his home for the dock, as was his custom.

That morning, Lake Erie was reportedly running five-foot swells, with a 35 knot wind blowing from the northeast. A gale warning had been posted by Environment Canada. Several other operators of fishing vessels were also on the dock, and a discussion ensued regarding the deteriorating weather conditions on the lake. It should be noted here that two individuals present on the dock that morning strongly advised Mr. Beau from leaving port. Both insist that when asked directly, Mr. Beau provided no explanation for ignoring the gale warning. Furthermore, although it was normal practice for Mr. Beau to have a crew member aboard to assist him with operating machinery specifically related to the nets, he did not make any arrangements for a crew that morning.

A short time past 5:00 a.m., Mr. Beau left the Port Horner harbour in *M/V Isobel,* a vessel generally referred to as a Lake Erie tug. This particular exemplar was built in 1955 by Dorrit Boat Manufacturers with a gross registered tonnage of 79.72 tons, length overall of 16.34m, beam of 5.79m and draught of 1.25m. The vessel's hull and main deck were constructed of 3/16' steel plate and her superstructure was constructed of aluminum sheeting. The vessel was powered by a Cummins 855 Diesel engine, producing 400 peak horsepower and a twin disc MG5114HD. *M/VIsobel's* top speed was 9 knots per hour. A single fuel tank of 200 litres capacity gave *M/V Isobel* the ability to operate at a lesser cruising speed for up to 48 hours. The vessel's navigation equipment included a two-way marine mobile, VHF radio with 25W power output, a 4kW surface-radar with a range of 25 nautical miles, a depth sounder, a magnetic compass and an electronic auto-pilot system connected to the vessel's rudder post with a hydraulic actuator. *M/V Isobel's* fishing gear was located on the main deck and shot off the stern as is typically seen in these types of vessels: hydraulic drums for the storage and deployment of gill nets and secured storage for floats, weights, lines etc.

The deck was enclosed by solid walls with no interior divisions, a feature unique to type and intended to protect the crew from the elements. *M/V Isobel* had a single-compartment hold for storing fish, below the main deck and forward of the engine compartment. The main deck hatch that provided access to the fishing hold was not water-tight, and, true to type, had exceptionally small scuppers for the conveyance of water.

M/V Isobel was inspected by Transport Canada in June 1981. The inspection report indicates that *M/V Isobel* met the safety regulation applicable under the Small Commercial Vessel Regulations. These regulations, however, pertain only to safety and firefighting equipment on the vessel. We have no definitive information about the seaworthiness of the vessel itself: *M/VIsobel* did not carry hull and machinery insurance and, therefore, no marine surveys of the vessel are available.

Mr. Beau failed to return to harbour by dusk. Around 8:00 a.m. the following day, and approximately 28 hours after leaving port, *M/V Isobel* was about 5½ miles from the southeast entrance to Port Horner harbour. The vessel was capsized and Mr. Beau was not on board.

M/V Isobel was salvaged and brought into Port Horner. There, the vessel was inspected by local police and by Transport Canada. The fuel tank contained no diesel fuel and several litres of lake water had found its way into the tank. The coaxial cable between the vessel's radio transmitter and antenna had pulled away from its PL 259 connector at the antenna end. One of the vessel's gill nets was missing and the starboard superstructure hatch and the engine access hatch were open. *M/V Isobel* suffered no other major and apparent damage.

The *M/V Isobel* was equipped with a heavily-galvanized steel lifeboat, or "Tilbury," which was typically secured by lashings upside down behind the wheelhouse.

As to Mr. Beau himself, an extensive search of north-central Lake Erie and its shoreline was conducted by the Ontario Provincial Police, the Canadian Coast Guard, and the United States Coast Guard for 84 hours after the vessel was found, with no result. His body has not been recovered. At this point in the investigation it can be surmised that Mr. Beau was either thrown or was self-propelled into the water and thus met his death by drowning. The unique design of the Lake Erie tug should be noted here; if Mr. Beau was in the hold when M/V *Isobel* took on water, causing it to capsize, he would have been trapped inside. His body would have been recovered with his vessel.

As noted above, Mr. Beau had allowed his policy around hull and machinery to lapse several years before. Our investigation is therefore not primarily concerned with the state of the M/V *Isobel* or any concerns about maintenance etc., outside of the determination of a probable cause for loss of life. There were no apparent defects in the vessel's hull, and no obvious problems with the vessel's engine to suggest a failure of the vessel.

Where there is no obvious accidental cause and where a weight of evidence points to a disturbed state of mind, (uncharacteristic or impulsive judgments, disregard for common safety practices) and there are antecedent factors including lifestyle, finances, and a stressful domestic situation, then investigators must remain open to the possibility of suicide.

There is at this point, an absence of any clear indication as to why the M/V *Isobel* floundered. Since there was a total of $70,000 in insurance payable upon Mr. Beau's death, we (the insurer) have undertaken an extensive investigation into Mr. Beau's habits, background, health, and character. Please note that while the investigation remains open and ongoing, some preliminary observations can be drawn at this time. First, it appears that while Mr. Beau was a devoted father, his wife Irene Beau suffered from a moderate to severe alcohol problem, and was observed by neighbors to drink to excess on a daily basis. This led to unsubstantiated suspicions that Mrs. Beau was a negligent parent. Second, there is evidence of serious financial difficulty that threatened Mr. Beau's livelihood and his capacity to provide for his family. Mr. Beau's vessel had twice been refinanced by the bank and was now at risk for repossession. Third, there is some suspicion in the community of marital infidelity on Mrs. Beau's part. This perception may or may not have been shared by Mr. Beau.

Puzzling questions remain around Mr. Beau's mental state, and it remains unclear whether death in fact occurred by his own hand. If that were to be the case, all claims by the beneficiaries would be necessarily null and void, and this insurance company released of any obligation to Mr. Beau's dependents. It is strongly recommended that on the merit of that question alone, a settlement be deferred until such time as the investigators can satisfy this committee with further evidence.

Respectfully Submitted by Mr. Everett B. Cooke
Chief Investigator, Claims

8.

GENTRIFICATION HAS BEGUN to take hold in Port, a tentative creep of bistros and cottage shops, mostly confined to the one block radius leading to the lift bridge. Pen feels disoriented by it. Perturbed even. When she first met Jeff, she had described Port as a kind of Bermuda Triangle where hope had fallen away from the world, an intractable fatalism hanging over the place. Strange that she now experiences an aversion to the changes she sees. A fundamental mistrust.

The restaurant where Andy has suggested they meet for dinner isn't the kind of place either of them would have frequented in the old days. They are on a stone patio, adjacent to a gabled, yellow brick house that has been turned into a small inn. The gables are a wistful blue and the wicker on the front porch has been painted the same colour. Overhanging the patio are three ancient willows, their large limbs languid in the summer heat. Pen has worn a sundress, a jean jacket over her shoulders, her hair let out of its usual hurried bun. She has on her sunglasses, even though the sun has already lowered itself behind the taller buildings, and the harbour is in shadow now.

She watches Andy slide his long legs out over the patio stones, his shoulders resting easily on the back of the chair. He appears relaxed, his sunglasses off, no hint of self-consciousness.

At first, they talk about Port, all the people who have left, made lives elsewhere. It surprises her that their names swim easily to memory. Growing up, Pen had not made lasting friends.

There were a couple of girls, nerdy school band members, who appreciated her because she was smart. She hadn't adopted her Goth persona then. That came after, springing to life in her undergraduate years, an education funded by bursaries, student loans, and a job serving drinks in a student pub. Though she has shed most of her Goth, she still has the eyebrow piercing, the tattoos. They give her an inverted smugness when she is at the university. Pen is not a typical academic, with privilege buried beneath wrinkled clothes, poor haircuts. She stays clear of the grad student culture; she feels she doesn't belong.

Their pretty server has brought them a bottle of Pinot gris, and she cheerfully pours a little for Andy to taste. He gives her a smile that is crooked, unreserved. His good eye twinkles appreciatively, but whether for the wine or for the service, Pen doesn't know.

He tells Pen that he does a lot of travelling for work, North Carolina, and Michigan of course. Mostly, down to Texas because the company's biggest client is there. There is something off in Andy's self-confidence, the apparent ease, the charm. There is something he leaves unsaid.

At first he didn't like his trips to Texas. "All that brash American stuff was hard to swallow. Remember how we hated the rich yachting people who came over from the other side? That's how I felt." But then he had come to appreciate how *easy*, how sensible and frank negotiating could be. One minute, he was sitting across from a bunch of guys in a boardroom, chins squared, shirtsleeves rolled up. "To use a hockey metaphor, like trying to get the other guy up against the boards." The next minute, he was at a fancy restaurant eating steaks and pushing back martinis, talking sports and cars.

"Business as sport. Once I figured that out, I realized I could do it. It's just natural, a language I understand."

He'd travelled to Europe too, he said, topping up her glass. He'd had to go over a few times. France, once. And Switzerland. He didn't mind the travel. He hadn't really put down roots anyway; "Not until recently, and that hasn't worked out," he says looking thoughtful. "I haven't got the hang of long-term relationships yet."

Pen ponders this for a moment. "So is this job it? The life-time plan?"

He smiles. "You ask like it sounds pretty bad."

"It's probably not what you expected, that's all."

He is waiting for her to say more but she doesn't.

"So what about you, Pen? You pretty settled now?" The server is coming around, placing small tea lights on the tables. Pen waits until she has stepped away, and then plays a little with a leaf of salad orphaned on the side of her plate.

"I'm separated from Maddie's dad and trying to finish a hard-ass degree. So not settled. I don't know if the separation is permanent yet. Still trying to figure that one out."

Saying it flatly like that, with no explanation strikes her as a betrayal. Jeff loves her. What she doesn't know is whether he can *stay* with her. She thinks back to how their story had started, in a downtown Toronto club, Jeff sitting at the bar and talking with a thin, weedy-looking girl whom Pen took to be his girlfriend. He was talking intensely, excitedly, his leg moving, pumping to the beat of the music, his fingers frenet-ically drumming on the counter.

The girl liked him, Pen could tell by the way her face was a little flushed. She was flirtatious, joking, a hand coming up to his chest and giving him a little push. The remarkable thing was that Jeff carried on talking as though he didn't notice that the girl wanted him.

He must have seen Pen watching. When the band took a break, he introduced the girl to the band's bass player and brought Pen a beer. There was a barely contained enthusiasm about him, something boyish and eager. When the band start-ed again, he was reabsorbed into the wash of insistent vocals and driving instrumentals. Every inch of him looked happy. It was contagious, that kind of enthusiasm. She was in the presence of someone guileless. Someone strangely put-together, someone safe.

She looks over at Andy who seems completely at home. She can't imagine Jeff sitting with her in a place like this.

"One thing about the hard-ass degree," Andy is saying, feigning seriousness, "it builds hard-ass life-summary skills. That's the briefest description of somebody's life situation I've ever heard."

"Succinct, you mean," she says, smiling. "I guess I have a talent for brevity."

"That's probably what I mean."

"Jeff, my ex, is a good guy," she adds. "Just a little intense."

"A Beau who has trouble with intensity. Now that *is* something new." Andy is beginning to eat with enthusiasm. He has ordered pork medallions in a ginger sauce, served with a large mound of creamy, mashed potatoes. Pen has ordered stir fry which arrives beautifully arranged on her plate.

"That's quite a meal for a hot summer's night," she says, watching Andy.

"Never let the climactic conditions get in the way of your appetite, Pen."

Around them, people sit, glowing from a day on the water, their laughter a little loose, a little self-congratulatory. The frank look of affluence. Andy sits on an angle, with one arm draped over the back of his chair. The candlelight has both raised his scars and softened his face, the scars now appearing intricate, as if by design.

Their plates are cleared and he orders coffee. Pushing his cup and saucer away from him he levels his strange, stretched gaze on Pen.

"You ever hear from him, Pen?"

She feels muscles in her throat tighten, a prohibition of words. She has no idea what she can say to Andy about Keaton.

"It's okay. Maybe you don't want to talk about him. To be honest, he really was a little shit for taking off like he did."

Andy is leaning back in his chair, smiling to himself, like he is watching a movie of all the crazy stuff that he and Keaton did together. He suddenly passes a hand over his forehead, rubbing at his temples.

"He could have stuck it out. It probably would have turned out okay." It's almost as if Andy is talking to himself.

"I've heard from him twice," she says, surprising herself. She so seldom talks about him. "The last time was just a few months ago."

Keaton called in the winter, a snowy February afternoon, a Sunday, she knows because Jeff was over. He was outside shovelling, a multicoloured hat pulled over his shaved head, the ear flaps hanging down. He looked like an exotic South American rodent. She was grateful that he was taking care of the snow, even a little amused and touched by how happy he looked out there. He had an Mp3 player plugged into his ears and she knew he was in a rocked-out galaxy, a rational and honest sort of place. Jeff's idea of heaven.

Maddie had refused to get out of her pajamas and Pen had decided not to care. There was a Disney movie burbling in the background, but Maddie wasn't really watching it. Instead, she had a kitchen pot on the floor and she was busy mixing: flour, laundry soap, a dollop of soya sauce, some liquid hand soap from beside the sink.

"Maddie, what are you making with all of that stuff?"

"It's good to mix everything together," said Maddie, sounding instructional, good humoured, a little like Jeff. "Put each thing in and then stir, stir, stir."

"*Don't* eat it, Maddie," said Pen frowning.

Maddie stopped stirring and looked at Pen. "It's not *for* eating," she said.

"Right. Well, glad you *know*. Some of the stuff you are putting in there is toxic. Really *bad* for you."

Maddie had gone back to her stirring when the house phone rang. Pen listened for the sequence of rings: one short and two longer. Long distance. She picked up and could feel the tension in the pause and knew immediately it was Keaton. After a few seconds, "Pen? You there?"

"Keaton..."

Another pause.

"Where are you?" she asked.

"Still out here."

"Where?"

"It doesn't matter." Then, "I shouldn't call you."

"Keaton, tell me where you are."

"I'll call again, Pen. I'll let ya' know."

When Jeff came in, she was holding the receiver in a death grip. He pressed his hands into the tense spots at the top of her back. Jeff has broad, strong hands, not elegant but expressive.

"Hey, it's good you heard from him. That he can use a phone, remember your number. It means he's not that bad off, right?"

She stood there, numb. "I don't know what it means. I don't know anything."

When she tells Andy about the call now, he stares into his coffee cup, his index finger occasionally tracing a circle around its rim as if to try and erase something there. He asks her if she tried to find out where the call had come from.

"Sure. I found out. A bar some place in the interior of BC. When I called back and asked to speak to Keaton, they said they'd never heard of Keaton Beau."

Andy is sitting back in his seat, slouching, considering what she has said. "Probably wouldn't be that hard to find him."

"I think he moves around a lot." She sounds sarcastic.

Andy laughs and the tension breaks. "He *ever* stay still?"

She smiles at him and then crosses her arms. "I've thought about trying to find him. Talk him into coming back."

Andy sits up and lifts one shoulder, as if to release some tension there. "It's hard to go back to things. Especially if when you saw them last, everything was so messed up."

Her coffee has cooled now and it looks unappetizing. She can feel Andy watching her, the hooded eye giving him an air of studied patience.

"Feel like walking off dinner?"

Pen sighs and then nods, grateful not to have to talk about Keaton anymore.

"You're going to have to walk half the night to deal with what you just tidied away, Andy."

"Ah, you underestimate me," he says playfully. He has said this before. His success comes naturally to him.

Andy pays with his credit card and then takes a handful of pink-striped mints from a bowl. There is a webbing of scars there, on the top of his hand. "Something for Maddie," he says. It had always been Andy who ordered her an extra packet of fries, given her his gloves on a raw day.

They walk down the main street, toward the beach.

"You were really good, Andy," Pen says suddenly.

"No doubt. At what?"

"Hockey, you idiot."

"How would you know?" he asks, laughing into the dark.

"Never mind. I don't believe in turning down compliments."

It's true. Pen knows nothing about hockey. Jeff is interested in it. At least he *watches* it, out of some kind of atavistic loyalty. Jeff says up north, where he's from, you're drowned at the age of two if you don't love watching hockey. Mothers, he says, have an instinct for who is a closet hater. It's why he had to go underground, he told her: the graphic novels, the sci-fi. He hadn't been outed the way he would have been if he'd turned out to be a tennis star or a drama kid.

"Everyone knew," she says simply of Andy's talent.

"Had to let go of a scholarship, that's all," he says lightly. "Canadian sports scholarships aren't what they are in the States anyways."

"Sorry," she says.

"I don't know. I wasn't as broken up about it as people

thought I should be. When the time rolled around, I found I was kind of glad not to be doing it."

"Glad?"

"Maybe. Maybe the want for it was never there to begin with. If you are good at something, it's easy to just do it." He doesn't look distressed about the unexpected sea-change in his life but then it is hard to tell with a man whose face is half-buried in scar tissue.

"Miss it?"

"Ol'timers' league. That's enough of a beating these days."

"Must have been painful." She motions to his hand, avoiding his face.

"It's all healed nicely," he says. "Just skin and bone."

As they get closer to the harbour, they can see the lights from the boats on the inky-black surface of the water. A few voices carry in the still air. Pen can smell the lake, moist air mixed with decay, the persistence of water, repulsive and attractive all at once. Nothing about this lake, Pen muses, is false. People are afraid of the contaminants in the fish, suspicious of the lake's murky colour, the sad horizon even on the brightest day. She thinks of the cheery "Welcome to Port Horner" sign that graces the highway on the way into town: blue water, white sails, long sandy beach. Not the lake she is looking out at now.

On the east side of the harbour, next to the dock, the fishing tugs sit low and patient. The boats are dark, their bulky hulls outlined against a watery blue-black. She is still moved by the daily departure and return of the tugs, although she can't understand why people persist in tying their fortunes to this lake. A life of hardship and disappointment. She hadn't always wanted to be apart from it, the fishing life. When she was little, she followed Keaton down to the docks, to the spot where Rod pulled in the *Isobel*, the hold full if it had been a good day.

"Tie that down," or "be okay if you stowed that, Keaton." They didn't need to talk in full sentences to understand one another. Keaton knew what to do because Rod had taught him. They had spent that kind of time together.

Pen's eyes had followed Rod's every move, the efficiency in the movements, the practiced care with the equipment, energy securely chained beneath the surface of him. Seeing her, waiting, his face would surrender to a grin. "Hey, Pea. You wanna help out the old man, eh? Good girl." He might throw her a small job, like taking a scrub pail and filling it with water. When they were done and the *Isobel* put to bed for the night, he would lift her up on his shoulders and walk with them back through town.

For him she remained the child, the little girl. It was different with Keaton, who was already Rod's designate. She supposes now it had been a relationship approaching partnership, complex and already burdened.

Pirates is still open, lights spilling from its tired windows, a flashing Budweiser sign over the screen door. Inside, men are bent down over a pool table, measuring their shots carefully, shifting around the table with surprising fluidity. Men lean against the railing of the front porch, puffing on cigarettes, bottles or cans resting in curled fists. One of them has his back slightly turned to Pen, and from the outline of the shoulders, the way his thin ponytail slides down over the glistening black vest, she knows it is T. He is just part of the larger group now, lounging with the others, their voices cutting through the thick night air. She makes out swearing, their laughter. She hears T's voice barking out a remark, and another man, a man with a shaved and gleaming head, laughs and says, "You're such an asshole, T."

When Pen stops and watches the men, Andy turns to look at her, puzzled. "Pen? You're staring at those guys. Look, I can still do some damage, but I'd rather leave bikers well enough alone."

"Sorry. One of them was on the beach the other day. T. He was the one who jumped in first..."

Andy glances at the bar, still relaxed, hands in his pockets. "T? You know his name?"

"The one with the ponytail. He has his back to us."

"Doubt he's gone in and given a statement," Andy says. "Probably has an interesting relationship with the cops already."

Just then, T turns to throw away a cigarette butt. He slides his eyes to the street. In the dark and with the distance between them, at first Pen can't tell if he recognizes her.

But then T tips his bottle at her and nods. She raises up a hand.

"When I gave my statement the other day, I should have said it was him that went in first," she says, drawing her jean jacket closer around her shoulders, walking again.

"Why does that matter?" Andy asks.

"I don't know. Because it's true. Because Ben Vasco was alone out there and he needed help. T went into that water without thinking."

They walk together, Andy looking over his shoulder at Pirates, then easing into a cantered stride.

"The drowning all seemed kind of inevitable, watching it from up on the sand. I knew he was gone before anyone else did."

They are at the beach now, the music from the packed beach bar spilling out over the sand. Andy is slipping off his loafers, rolling up his pants. "Maybe it's what you have come to expect. That people don't come back," he said quietly. "Your friend there, the others, the Search and Rescue, they might have got to him. Rescues happen."

Andy carries his shoes in one hand and points his face instinctively toward the lake, like Pen always does when she comes here. They pad along for a time, Pen liking the gentleness, the sweet mood of the water tonight. As they walk past a row of small wooden cottages, he stops.

"Keaton and I broke into number 134 one winter. Pried off the boards from the window and got in. We made a fire, scrounged around for some cans of food, heated them up over the fire the way they do in cowboy movies." Pen can visualize them doing it. Keaton, of course, the instigator, ripping away the boards with intense determination, his strength more kinetic and surprising in his small frame.

"Later we found a locked cabinet and Keaton took a knife and jimmied it open. Rye whisky. Canadian Club, I believe."

"You get caught?" Asks Pen.

"We didn't get caught most of the time, Pen," he laughs.

She is hugging herself against the damp, her feet chilled by the wet sand.

"Except once," she says softly.

He looks around and finds a log for them to sit on. It rocks a little under his weight, and then settles. Pen sits down next to him.

"That was different," he says. "Keaton was mad. More mad than I'd ever seen him. I guess he burned up Spar's boat for a reason."

Pen says nothing, instead slapping a stone with her foot.

"Sure must have been mad. He almost kills someone, wrecks his friend's chances at a hockey career…"

"And takes off, leaving his little sister behind in a pretty bad situation." He has finished the sentence for her. "I don't know. But Keaton would have *had* his reasons."

"So why not stay, face the trial? Why run?"

"Maybe he didn't want to take the chance that they'd lock him up. Maybe he didn't want you and your mom dragged through it. Like I said, he *was* a little shit."

Pen sits looking at the water, her arms still wrapped around herself. She remembers Spar only vaguely; stained teeth, a thin body, skin and eyes leaning toward yellow. A lizard, she thinks now. Spar was a drinker, but so many of the men around the docks had been in those days. Still, Keaton had really hurt him. After the fire, he hadn't returned to Port. He'd lost his livelihood. His scarring would be worse that Andy's.

"The guy had horrible burns," she goes on now. "And you," she looks at Andy. "That's gotta be one hell of a reason."

"Not saying it's a reason you or I would agree with Pen. Just saying it's a reason."

"Jeff thinks maybe Keaton was ill. Mentally disturbed, to do what he did."

Andy blows out some air, drums his fingers on the wide trunk of his thigh.

"I don't know, Pen. I don't know about that."

"Jeff says some people fall off the edge of the world because they can't take being in it the way that it is." She suddenly laughs. "Jeff also reads too much sci-fi."

"Maybe he's right. Maybe Keaton wasn't coping. Maybe I wouldn't have either. Anyways, it doesn't change it though, does it?" says Andy. He shrugs his shoulders, slides up off the log, and she senses a darker tension in him.

"You tried, Andy. You got him and that guy off that boat, made Keaton talk to the police."

"Yup. And maybe he never forgave me for it. It would explain the long silence."

From the street behind the beach, there is a brash burst of pulsating music, as if a door has suddenly opened, followed by raised voices that tangle in the dark. Soon after, the growl of a motorcycle eating up the silence and then fading above the bluffs of Port.

"There's your hero for you, Pen. A regular Easy Rider."

Andy is slapping off the sand from his pants. He presents his arm to Pen and grins half-way.

9.

IT'S HOT. T'S STANDING BESIDE a mud hole on a laneway that is mostly crabgrass and rock. A deer fly dive-bombs his head and he swats at the air, his fist closing as if to convince himself he caught it this time. When he opens his fist and looks, it's empty.

This farm leaves him feeling nothing but irritation. For days he's been waiting for the final orders, the go-ahead. Standing the way he is, squarely under the sun, he feels like a zucchini plant in a vegetable patch; small rivers of sweat collect at his hairline and snake down his cheeks.

Delays aren't unusual in this work. He squints up at the blue sky and remembers, with some effort, that he's spent a good portion of his life waiting, in parking garages, strip malls, industrial wastelands on the outskirts of cities.

Waiting for orders isn't as effortless for T as it once was. Lately, T's world has started to contract. He's being squeezed dead centre. There are coughing spells and greenish muck that rockets into his hand. At night, an evil beast plants itself on his chest-cage; he feels like a Harley has been parked there. He sweats and shivers like he's coming off something bad.

The cell phone in his pocket, silent and ominous now, has only vibrated twice today. The first was a call from Justin who wanted to know about food for later. Twenty-three years old and he acts like he's just out of diapers. Should he go over to Big John's, he asked, and lay in some grub?

"Look, dumb-ass, we're not throwing a goddamn dinner party."

"Sorry, T. Just thought we might get hungry."

Even at twenty-three, T wasn't that clueless. Not even close. He was twenty when he'd made his first real connection to outlaw culture through a trucker named George, a teamster, close to fifty, who delivered loads of shingles. T was swinging a hammer for a roofing company by then. He thinks back to the interest George showed in him. Not *kindness* exactly, but an appreciation of T's youth, his agility up on the roof. Maybe he liked T because T was part-Indian and so was he. George took T along with him when he made after-hour deliveries. Weapons, drugs, George did it all and most of it between the hours of eleven p.m. and five a.m. All through the night, T would soak up George's stories about biker-life, the crazy stuff that went on, the money, the girls. T remembers the warmth of the truck's cab, the smell of coffee and rolled-cigarettes. George made introductions to some of the leadership and that's where it started. They called him *kid,* opened tabs for him in a couple of the bars, gave him a living allowance. The organization even took care of his car repairs. T laughs, thinking of that now. For the first time in his life, T *knew* who he was. Part of the brotherhood. He looks over at the corner of the field where, decades ago, a couple of old cars had been junked. The paint is mostly gone and the seats have been hauled out. He guesses they could stay like that for a century or more, slowly turning to rust.

Last winter, he had been sick for more than a month and his doctor put him on an extra-strong dose of antibiotics. "Probably bronchitis, Tom. You might want to slow down the smoking. Maybe think about quitting." T wasn't going to *stop* smoking. T is resigned about where his life will take him, almost fatalistic. He lights a cigarette and takes the smoke deep into himself, feels a jolt of alertness.

The second call had been from Winnipeg. "Make sure you

got lots of ammunition down there, in case things go sideways. We'll be in touch with instructions."

He grimaces, looking over at the shed where the guns and ammo are stored. They've got a Mauser, a Kombat K, a Lee Enfield, a couple of Tec 99 mm pistols. And then there is the Taurus-410 — "The Judge." This isn't supposed to be a mega-operation. The way he understands it, the Toronto chapter is getting greedy. Guys he knew, guys he had done business with over the last few years, are getting ideas of grandeur, issuing orders, skimming. The direction from Winnipeg is to strip them of their patches, humiliate them, persuade them with fire power if necessary. T assumed he was supposed to rap their knuckles, deliver them a good swat in their collective butt. Now, a shadow crosses his mind; maybe he's going into this job blind.

T looks up at the sky, featureless except for a couple of scrawny jet contrails. Nothing in the drug and prostitution business is as secure as it once was. In recent years, competition has crept in from all quarters. The business is getting crowded with South Americans, Mexicans, Asian kids driving BMWs and Audi's. The Hells Angels are the real threat, having swallowed up almost every small club in this province. A few years back, while he was riding with another small gang (now defunct), the Angels shot and almost killed him. Two of the guys riding with him had died. T drops his cigarette butt and smears it into the dry, grey earth with his boot. He hates the Angels. His cold and certain hatred is, in part, like a homing device, directing his loyalty to the club whose colours he now wears, demanding of him an attachment to an outlaw lifestyle that frankly, he's grown bored with.

For T, there is a natural pecking order, a chain of command that has to do with respect, obedience. Do what's required and the club will give you the nod. Not in rewards exactly, but in approval, in a transfer of confidence. In time, the credit accumulates, can be relied upon, can be taken to the bank.

All of that vanishes once the Angels ride in. The Angels are like the Atom bomb, the great levelling machine. No shred of his former self would be allowed to survive. Thinking of that kind of future, T encounters a void, black, and terrifying. A nothingness worse than taking a bullet or coughing up a lung. The shooting incident had simply sealed the deal; everything he does now he sees as turf protection.

It now seems to T that he has only ever had two choices: to be or not to be, an Angel. Other possibilities have receded so far from him they are no longer possible to imagine, although sometimes he is visited by fragments of other lives. But he's here. Still waiting for the goddamn call from Winnipeg.

He'll need to prepare for all eventualities. He surveys the farm: ten acres of leased land, scrubby-looking, but he's no farmer. The house is close to derelict. Clearly some efforts were made to fix it up, maybe twenty years ago or more. T has worked on and off in construction over the years because outlaw earnings alone don't pay the bills. In the nineties, he had his own renovation business. Just a small crew of three or four guys. During the day, he worked alongside of them and, in the off-hours, he drew up estimates for customers, returned phone calls.

Bikers started wearing pagers in the nineties; it wasn't possible to conduct biker business while conducting his own. His business folded, and for a few years he contracted himself out as an insulation specialist. He's getting too old to crawl around in attics. Besides, breathing in fiberglass is probably what screwed up his lungs in the first place.

There is a red bathtub and toilet combo in the farmhouse — someone must have got a deal — and an air-tight wood stove on the main floor. The bedrooms have indoor-outdoor carpeting, green like Astro turf. The roof is bad and the doors to the kitchen cupboards have been ripped off the wall, leaving only the dusty shelving, thick with mouse turds.

Back in February, Winnipeg had contacted him and told him

they wanted the site to be away from Toronto, but not too far. Somewhere off the highway, where the neighbours weren't close. T suggested Erie because the area is teaming with outlaw traffic. He'd leased the place over the Internet from a guy who owned another farm fifty kilometers away and didn't much care what they did with it as long as the rent was paid up.

There isn't much around them. To the west, an old couple live in the granny-flat from hell, a brick structure the size of a shitter with not enough room to swing a cat. Their kid's idea of generosity after Dad passed on the family farm, T suspects. The old man likes to hang out at the fence line, where the land wrinkles a little, and there is a pile of stones and a view. When they drive by in their ancient Olds the pair of them stare up the lane like a pair of owls. T's had the guys shoot off ammo in the night, light bonfires close to the property line, but the old couple keeps coming out to look.

He touches his pocket, reminds himself that things need to be set up right. Privacy might be even more important than he first thought. If things get a little crazy, he'll have to decide between the farmhouse and the shed. The drive-shed's bigger but the door is half-broken, making it not quite as secure as he would like. The house has two front rooms and the kitchen. Not a lot of room for eight big boys and his own crew, if they have to get close and sweaty.

The deer fly is back at it. This time he nails the little bastard with one decisive slap and it falls into the dust. He'll be glad when this job is done. He thinks almost longingly of his house in the city, the place empty now that the girl, Eva, and the kid are gone. When he thinks of Eva, he feels a tiny pinch of his insides and he wants to hit something. It's been years since they were together, and the kid must be almost ten by now. T tries to imagine the boy at ten and all he can come up with are smart-talking TV kids who wear ball caps, their T-shirts down to their knees. Kids who say things like: *Cripes, Dad, why can't I have a BMX?* T laughs when he thinks of it. A world that never was, as far as T was concerned. Disney Land all the way.

He doesn't know what the kid would look like now but he has no difficulty thinking of Eva. He carries the image of her in his head the way some guys carry around a rabbit foot in their pocket or a St. Christopher around their neck.

He'd met her working at one of the clubs, barely nineteen and small for the average dancer except she was well-endowed, the kind of girl who could easily be taken for a doll. She'd been marked for a promotion, to the floor where she would have to learn to dance, take her clothes off, shake her tight little butt in front of a bunch of ugly mugs. Her parents had been strict. "Bible-thumpers," she said.

T said, "Like in a freakin' cult, eh?"

The girl laughed, hugging herself, her head thrown back. "Now that's funny coming from a guy wearing colours," she said. Then she was suddenly serious. "They loved me, I'm sure about that."

T was given the task of paying her, cash or eight balls of coke (her choice). She had developed a nasty coke habit since coming down to the city, but T had encountered that before. Dozens of girls came in and out of the clubs every year, hungry and scoured-out, thinking they were purchasing safety, protection, when nothing was further from the truth. *You guys are like my family.* How often had T heard that? "And what kind of twisted family *did* you come from, little girl?" They always looked stung when he asked.

There was something different about Eva. At least for T there was, though nobody else could understand it. A freshness, maybe because she had been raised by Jesus-freaks, or it was just *in* her, unique, like a thumb print.

He'd *diverted* her. (He likes to think of it as that: diversion.) He set her up waitressing in another place, a little further from the drugs and all the action. She was not entirely trusting of T, but she was grateful. She thought he had done a selfless thing, but T doesn't believe in selflessness. At least, he's never seen it.

That girl, Eva, was so pretty, T got lost in her. T conjures up a vision of her, preferring it to the idea of himself in this sullen landscape, a pasty biker, sweating and wheezing in the heat. Eva's face was shaped like a heart, hair that was the colour of a penny. He could put his middle finger and thumb around her upper arm and they'd touch.

Before long, he moved her in with him, into his little house, and she started doing things to it, painting the living room and putting in a flower garden against the chain link. She got him to build a deck off the back. "I'm gonna sit out here in my bathing suit in the hot weather," she told T. "You'll be able to barbecue steaks."

When she told him she was pregnant, he didn't ask what she would do. They went out and bought stuff for the baby: furniture, an entire stack of tiny undershirts, stuffed toys, a night light. It turned out to be a boy.

Once the kid arrived, she was taken over with caring for him, a natural, endless energy for night feedings, changing shitty diapers. T discovered that he didn't mind doing things for the kid; in fact he liked it. He liked schlepping up and down the hall at night. He liked lying next to her in their bed, the kid nuzzled in, sleepy and content.

But the demands of the lifestyle didn't just stop because he was playing daddy. The calls still came in at two a.m., the pager going off when they were watching a movie, the kid asleep and making mewing sounds in her arms. "I gotta go up to Kingston for a job tonight." She never asked a lot about it but he knew she was resentful, lonely. Once, she took the pager and put it in the fridge, mischievous, like a kid.

"A stupid stunt like that could get us killed."

"We could move away from here, T," she said. "Out west. I don't care where."

He sighed. His tone was condescending and he knew it. "This isn't the 4-H club or the bloody cadets. *Sir, I am resigning my position.* Christ."

They started to fight, the girl whipped-up, sharp, the words she launched like a shank in his gut. "You must be stupid, T, to keep going out on those jobs. Only a loser gives himself over to them, to the horrible things they do. Or a candy-ass, sucking up like that." She wasn't taunting him, though he thought so at the time. She was changing, something passing over her, like age or judgment, or just the growing want of something better. He didn't pay it any attention because in his world, people got used to bad situations. People didn't necessarily count on change.

One weekend, a bunch of the brothers came by and parked at the house, music too loud, a lot of drugs, and someone broke the Ikea glass-top coffee table she'd just bought. Eva was upset, found a cardboard box for the bigger pieces of glass and then she pulled out the vacuum for T.

"We've got a kid now, you ape. You want him to eat glass?"

T had cursed a little and then run the vacuum around the room, tossing the machine into the kitchen when he was done.

The guys were sneering, hooting with laughter.

"That chick got you pussy-whipped, T."

"Piss off," he barked back. In that moment, all he wanted was for her to disappear. Her and the kid. Not because he wanted her gone forever but because he couldn't sustain the idea of her, the truth about what he felt for her, while being who he was in that room.

The kid cried non-stop for hours after that until finally T couldn't take it any longer. He found them in their bed, the girl holding the kid, all cuddled up, rocking him.

"Shut him up or take him outside," he told her. It was rough, a lot rougher than he had ever been with her before. She looked at him with the calm, hard look of recognition.

She got the kid to stop and to finally go to sleep. When the brothers took off the next morning, leaving the place looking like a bottle depot, she packed up some clothes for her and the kid, took the keys to T's car, and stood in the doorway, frowning. He thought he saw something in her expression, a tenderness. He thought: *I'll never see her again.*

He'd thrown a thousand dollars in cash at her and told her to get lost. He heard that she went back to her born-again parents in Timmins and she was going to college for a medical job. She was learning to operate a machine that takes pictures of a body's inside chambers. He thinks of her standing vigil as the machine's cold white arm sweeps over the surfaces of a stranger's body.

She was the only time he'd really lost it for a woman, and there sure as hell wasn't going to be a repeat. Still, something sly steals up on him when he thinks of her, holding and rocking that kid. He tries to hold on to it but it is made of vapour.

There is a vibration in his pocket that reminds him of a sex toy and he sighs and pulls it out of his pants. The voice on the other end is cold and flat and very direct:

"Change of plan," the voice says.

10.

THE DROWNING HAS TURNED OVER ancient soil, and with it, the bones of Pen's past. Last night, unable to sleep, she had reimagined the scene over and over. What does she remember? What does she know to be true? Finally, she slept and dreamed of Ben Vasco emerging from the lake like a swimming champion. He was upright, confident, not limited, not delayed, as she knew that Ben had been in life. He was a man restored, a man striding away from his death.

When she wakes up, she feels vaguely cheated by the dream. She told Keaton once that if Rod came back, things would be better. They would eat better food and Keaton wouldn't have to work so much on the boats. By then, Keaton had become chained to Terry Spar and the *Dolly*.

"No one comes back from the fucking lake, Pen."

It was cruel of Keaton to say it. Recrimination for her dogged attachment to him after Rod disappeared. In those early months, Pen was Keaton's shadow, asking him for money, for food. It wasn't that she needed these things; Irene was managing to work her shifts at the Fish and Fry. Ed had moved in and was paying room and board. What Pen needed was for Keaton to make space for her, for him to at least tolerate her; to know that she wouldn't be forgotten.

She should get up. Maddie was already out of bed. It's late enough that she can hear the voices of people as they stroll past, chatting together on the street. She slides her feet onto the floor and stretches, a residue of tension still lurking in her body, nestled in her spine, clinging to her neck. When she goes into the kitchen, Ed wordlessly rises to get her coffee, his movements hushed and tentative, his slippers making a slight *swish* as he pads across the floor. Semi-retired now, Ed maintains part-ownership in one of the boats. A tug he's called *Irene*. The name was not a surprise but Ed's devotion to her mother is baffling; Pen can't help but see it as weakness in him. He has given up the daily trips on the lake now, except on the days when he cares to go. *Irene* is crewed with a succession of men Ed has met through AA, middle-aged men down on their luck, young men poised on the brink.

"I'm ready to eat, now that Mommy's up," says Maddie. Maddie is uncharacteristically quiet with Ed, but companionable. Ed slides off his reading glasses and, with an air of solemnity, delivers her a cereal box, the milk, and a bowl and spoon so that she can fix her breakfast the way she likes. Pen looks at her coffee and then decides to put it in the microwave for a few seconds, though it doesn't need it.

"You'll want to look at this, Pen," Ed is saying. He folds back the pages to find the story, and points with the arm of his glasses at a column near the bottom of the page. It reads:

LOCAL MAN'S FAMILY WON'T HAVE GROUP HOME STAFF AT FUNERAL. The family of a man who drowned last Sunday at the main beach at Port Horner, say that they will not allow staff of Woodside Group Homes to attend his funeral. The drowning victim, identified as Mr. Benjamin Vasco, 42 years of age, had Down 's syndrome and lived in the Woodside group home for the past twenty years.

Woodside staff say that they are deeply saddened by the events of last weekend, and are awaiting the results of an ongoing investigation into Mr. Vasco's death. Executive Director of Woodside Homes, Brian

Turnbull, says, "We all loved Ben. He was part of our Woodside family for many years. We would like the opportunity to celebrate his life and share our sense of loss, particularly with our residents, some of whom regarded Ben as a brother."

The Vasco family has refused to comment except to say that funeral arrangements have not yet been determined.

The day before, Irene and Pen were on the small deck, Irene watering her pink geraniums, caressing the leaves, turning the pots toward a more advantageous angle of light. "Ben Vasco's got a sister is in the States. Maybe Illinois." Irene had learned some things about Ben Vasco from Helen, a co-worker at the Fish whose sister-in-law was the cook at Woodside.

"Did the sister just leave him up here? With no one?" Pen was ambushed by a feeling of outrage, beneath which was a plummeting sorrow. She blinked and frowned into the river, not wanting Irene to see.

Irene thought for a moment and put down her watering can. "Helen said everyone liked him."

Now, Pen reads the article once more. She decides to shower, to wash away the hovering ghosts, the melancholy. She is dressing when Ed knocks on the door to her room.

"Phone's for you, Pen."

"Jeff?"

"Nope. Some other fella."

The voice that comes over the receiver is youthful, too friendly. The speaker identifies himself as Brent Barber, of the Great Concourse Insurance Company.

"Ms. Beau, we got your name from the police statement you gave the other day, concerning Ben Vasco's drowning?"

Pen feels her stomach harden into a knot. "I'm sorry, whose insurance company are you?"

"Oh, didn't I say? Sorry!" He doesn't pause. "We are representing Woodside Group Homes. Just a question of getting the details down early, before memories become muddled. You know?"

"I pretty much said everything I could remember about it to the police."

"Oh, yes. For sure. I know you gave a good and thorough statement. Just a couple of points for clarification.

"I thought you people had access to all the police reports. I don't think I can add much."

"Won't take a minute," he says.

Pen says nothing.

"Good. Well, in your statement to the police, you said that first you saw Ben Vasco in the shallows, right?"

"Yes."

"Great. Then you got busy with your, er, your daughter is it?"

"Yes."

"Wonderful. And when you looked out again, Ben Vasco was out further in the lake, his head bobbing on the surface."

"Sure. Yes."

"Okay, great. Then he came up and down a couple times until he didn't come up anymore?"

"Yes."

"Okay, well the thing is, you said you heard the Woodside staff call out to him."

"They did. Or at least, one of them did."

"Yes, and did they call out to him before he got out into the lake or after?"

"The detective asked me that. I'm not sure. I don't know when they started calling his name. There was a lot of noise from the gulls, and my daughter was crying."

"Yes, I know. I have a two-year-old myself. Kids are a lot of work, aren't they?" He laughs, breathes, rushes toward more questions.

"See, the thing is, this is kind of important. If you can nail this one down for me, boy, would it ever be helpful."

"Sorry, I'm not going to make something up."

"No, of course not. Not 'make something up,' that's for sure. We don't *want* to ask you to do that. Just sometimes, details disappear for a while, and then they come back, right?"

"Why is this so important, Mr. Barber?"

"Well, we just want to make sure that the staff's reputations are not unfairly impacted by this, you know? If they tried to warn Mr. Vasco early, well then that shows diligence..."

"I guess if they didn't, then it's negligence, right?"

"Well, it might not be so black-and-white as that."

"So, I can't remember anyway. Sorry."

"Well if you do happen to remember, you mind giving me a call? I'd really appreciate it."

"I'll do that."

"Thanks. Great. And one more thing. Has anyone from another insurance company been in touch with you? Anybody else asking some of these questions?"

"You're thinking about the Vasco family, aren't you?" Her throat had tightened around the word "family." She feels surprisingly protective but she isn't sure of whom. The family might benefit if the Woodside people are at fault. She wonders again if Ben had been abandoned by them, left in the care of Woodside for their convenience. Still, when she thinks of Ben and his sister, separated by hundreds of miles when he drowned, all she feels is sad.

"Look," she says. "Anyone who contacts me is going to hear exactly what I just told you. And I realize that isn't much. So, is there anything else?"

"No. Thanks Ms. Beau. That's all. That's all for now, anyway."

An hour later, Maddie is sitting on the edge of Pen's bed with her hands cupped over her ears, her face screwed into a grimace. Pen is trying to force a comb through Maddie's cloud of hair, but the comb is ensnared in knots. She tries to fish it out, her face red with the effort.

"You're hurting me, Mommy." Her voice is plaintive.

"I know. I'm sorry. Your hair is all fraggly from being in the sun and wind so much. It should be trimmed up a bit."

"Don't YOU cut it," says Maddie. "PLEASE, Mommy." Maddie's limbs are still baby-round, her height unchanged for the last few months. People are surprised when she talks, by how she enunciates each letter, gathering the sounds and parceling them so neatly.

"I wouldn't dare," says Pen, laughing.

Irene, just back from the beach and looking contented, watches them from the doorway. She is wearing a white Indian cotton blouse and indigo-blue drop earrings. Her feet are sandy; Irene has taken up Tai-Chi, and now practices barefoot at sunrise with a small group of retirees from the city.

She holds out a spray bottle of cream-rinse and Maddie looks over at her hopefully.

"Will that help, Nan?" asks Maddie, pointing.

"Surely it will," says Irene, sitting next to Maddie, lifting the tangled knots of hair and spraying them down, then pulling the comb through with gentle, sure movements. Until Maddie arrived, Pen had not recognized Irene's capacity for love.

"Nan, the boy who downed didn't have hair." Maddie is saying, clutching a handful of her own wispy hair, pulling on it.

"Sometimes when men get older, their hair falls right out of their heads. Like Papa Ed's hair did."

Talk of Papa Ed makes Maddie giggle. "Will my hair fall out when I am old?"

Irene laughs. "Not likely."

Maddie is thoughtful, her body suddenly still. "Maybe the boy's hair will grow back. Maybe someone will cut it for him so it won't get in his eyes when he swims."

"No, pet, his hair won't grow back." Irene says. "But *your* hair is silky-smooth, just like the pretty girls on TV. Except their hair isn't golden-coloured, like yours is. My hair was dark as a kid. Like your mom's."

Maddie's hand reaches up and she strokes Pen's hair. She peers into Pen's eyes and then she kisses her mouth.

"I *like* black hair," Maddie pronounces. She puts a foot up on the edge of the bed, wiggling her toes, cocking her head.

"I want polish on my toes. Like yours, Nan. Mommy should have some on hers too."

"Well, that's an easy fix," Irene says.

Irene disappears for a few moments and comes back with a shoebox filled with nail polish. Maddie chooses a shell pink for herself and a cardinal red for Pen. Irene nods her approval, uncaps the pink bottle and carefully, tenderly paints Maddie's toes. And then, without asking, she takes out the red and paints Pen's.

Pen feels Maddie watching her. "Thanks," she says awkwardly to Irene.

"Princess toes!" says Maddie, delighted.

Irene gives Maddie a kiss on the head and Maddie holds her legs admiringly off to the side of the bed. The day is shaping up to be sunny, although Ed says that later in the day, "weather" will move in. "Time to test these toes in the water," says Pen, tossing Maddie her bathing suit. "We'll go to the little beach today," the small crescent beach that to sits to the east of town, beneath the bluffs; the water is shallow there and especially warm.

"Will Daddy come? You could ask him. Use your phone and tell him to."

"He's in Toronto, Maddie. That's hours away."

"You always say no to things,"

Pen sighs. "I can say *yes,* you will see Daddy soon. Maybe this weekend."

Maddie stops. She has worn a sundress over her bathing suit and now she digs into the pocket, pulling from it jagged fragments of an egg shell.

"These are from the nest. From home." Last spring, they had found an abandoned nest in the backyard. Now, Maddie squats, plucks some loose gravel from the road, dumps the shell and the stones together into her pocket. "There," she says, as if something is completed, the shells becoming eggs again.

11.

PEN SITS, LOTUS POSITION, on a bench overlooking the harbour. The water and sky are seamless, the horizon buried by incoming rain. Nothing moves on the water except for the listless gulls, floating, diving, calling out in complaint.

The idea of going back to the city is more and more compelling. It has been six days since Ben Vasco's drowning. She should be at her desk in Toronto, nailed to her laptop and writing another chapter, getting herself into a routine of reading, making notes, drinking too much coffee, taking early morning runs. She should be writing for at least four hours a day.

Maddie has been invited to a cottage, the granddaughter of a friend of Irene's, someone from her Tai Chi group, and Irene has gone to the restaurant for a shift. Ed is driving to a coffee shop out of town to meet a young man he sponsors.

She could leave for the city that evening, after Maddie gets back. It's relieving to think so, but Maddie is looking forward to going to the docks later with Ed and Irene, to see the feral cats, to count them. Irene keeps track of the cats in a little notebook, identifying them by their sizes and colouring, recording cryptic observations like: "bad eye," or "messed up paw." Pen hasn't a clue what Irene does with the information. She's never asked.

She frowns, thinking of the flat grey day ahead. Realistically, she and Maddie won't leave before tomorrow. There is still the intention of going to Benny Vasco's memorial but she has heard nothing about the arrangements.

She's distracted by a community bulletin board not far from the bench. Tacked over the posters and ads is a laminated article that Pen has to stand up to read.

Sturgeon Miraculously Return to Erie

Despite the slow march of the zebra mussels, the consumption of aquamarine-vegetation, the mussels turning the lake back to sand, the fishing community has quietly been talking about the sturgeon. The sturgeon are in the lake again. A way back, when our grandfathers were fishing here, the lake was so thick with sturgeon, pits were dug to bury them because there were too many to sell. Everyone thought they were extinct until now. The west end of the lake is apparently jammed with sturgeon babies ripping up nets. In thirty years, these "babies" will grow to be one hundred and thirty pounds and three meters long. Eventually they will gorge themselves on the mussels, giving room for other species to make their comeback.

She stops reading. The article bears the hallmarks of a home editorial, just short of a rant. To her left, awkward and improbable and mounted on a pole, is a giant fiberglass model of a sturgeon. It is all spikes and teeth. A dinosaur. Port's great hope. She looks at the lake, pinned down by a heavy layering of cloud. Port is difficult on days like these, the lake's moods souring life in the town. A septic place to live, and yet people persist.

Rod had persisted. Pen knows how bad off the fishing industry was back then, the lake poisoned by a steady seepage of phosphorous into its tributaries. Dead fish washed up on the beach. And the algae. Wherever the water was caught up in inlets, small coves, not worried by waves and currents, a green sludge formed on its surface. In 1969, before she was born, the waters of the Cuyahoga River, a faithful tributary of the lake, became so choked by petrochemicals it caught fire. The authorities had been embarrassed by the incident, pledging a massive clean-up, but the glory days of the commercial fishery were gone. There was nothing glamorous left in that life, particularly here.

The memories of Rod that she carries are of a man who was not defeated or even worn, though she knows he must have been near exhaustion, getting himself out by five in the morning, working in all kinds of weather. When Rod tucked her in at night she wrapped her arms around his neck, his skin chafing reassuringly against hers. Although she can't recall everything, she still holds a bone deep certainty that he loved her.

Where was Irene? She might have been working shifts at the Fish. Or is it that Pen has willfully excluded Irene from her memories of Rod, keeping her idea of him safe and unspoiled, keeping it her own?

"Could he have done it?" Pen was living in Toronto, Irene already sober for years when she finally asked Irene about Rod. She meant scuttle the boat, or jump into the churning, frigid lake. What did it take for someone to *intentionally* drown?

A hint of strain or effort passed over Irene's features. Sitting, she firmly placed her hands on her spreading thighs, as if to settle an old dispute. "I don't think I knew him. Not deep down. We were married when we were still kids, and I was already pregnant with Keaton." She looked sadly at Pen. "He took over his dad's boat when he was nineteen. It didn't really suit him. He didn't *choose* me, and he didn't *choose* this." She opened her arms, embracing the whole of Port, the fishing, the lake. "He didn't want any of it. Except for you and Keaton."

It wasn't an answer.

On a whim, she decides to call Andy. Seeing him has made Port more tolerable for her this time and talking with him now might take some of the dullness off the day. The business card that he gave her on the beach is loose in her handbag, the corners already curling, the surface gritty with the remains of one of Maddie's cookies.

His voice, when he says hello, sounds as though he is speaking from the hollow end of a pipe.

"It's Pen."

"Was hoping it might be." The signature laugh.

"Up to much?"

"Kind of a downer day," he says lightly. "I'm on my third hour of monopoly, only the other players are all napping upstairs. Just me and all this real estate left. How sad is that?"

"Feel like a drive?"

"Actually, yeah."

She finds the cottage where he is staying with friends and Andy piles into the front seat of her Toyota like he is stuffing himself into a duffle bag. He has to use his hand to hoist in his weaker leg, the left one, and when he sits, his knees press against the dash. Although the rain hasn't started yet, he's wearing a jacket and no sunglasses. He looks over at her with that now-familiar lopsided grin.

"Where to?" she asks. "I get down here more than I want," she adds, "so there's nothing I'm desperate to revisit. Your call."

He looks straight out the window for a bit and then turns to her. "The old airstrip."

She has only a vague recollection of what that is. "You'll have to remind me where to go."

Andy directs her to take the road north, out of Port. The lazy sprawl of the countryside seems generous and easy after the glowering lake and sky. They turn west on a county line and drive through several hamlets, the houses huddled close to the highway, their yards melting into cornfields and scruffy wood lots. There are no other cars in the small parking lot. A square, plain map shows the outline of trails leading away from the car.

"What's this place?" asks Pen.

"You never been here?" asks Andy, looking at her now with interest. "It was an old training field for the Canadian Air force in WWII. Used to come here all the time,"

The site of the airstrip is naturalized now and covered over with lilac, silver tips, ancient apple trees. Only an exaggerated flatness in the terrain points to its past use.

Pen has tied her rain jacket around her waist because the air is too close for her to wear it. Limping and with his hands in his pockets, Andy sets a pace that is between a hike and a stroll. She falls in easily, grateful for the direction her energy can now take, happy to finally be away from Port.

"How do you know about this place, Andy?"

"Well, I brought my dates here," he says, the tone playful, ironic. She laughs and remembers that Andy had a car in high school, something he bought cheaply and fixed up himself. She wonders if Keaton ever drove into this place. Did he ever entertain a girl in the cramped back seat? But the only girl that Keaton ever showed an interest in was Annie. Pen thinks of her as an unlikely date, the thinness of her body, the pale knees, the round grey eyes that gave her a look of preoccupation. Annie came into Keaton's life sometime after their father drowned.

After Rod's disappearance, the bare bones of their existence began to disintegrate. Money was an issue. In their inquiries, the insurance investigators asked Pen and Keaton to describe their mother's behaviour, their father's reactions to her drinking, what kind of mood he was in most of the time. Keaton remained tight-lipped. Pen was young, clueless for the most part. She answered their questions with a dangerous honesty that must have made Keaton crazy. The heavy eyes of one of the investigators rested on her, taking in — she realized later — her dirty sweater, the knotted hair. What the investigators heard and saw must have been a story of neglect, of hopelessness. To conclude that Rod had taken his own life was not so great a leap.

Keaton started working seriously on the tugs when it became clear that the insurance money wasn't coming.

At first, he picked up odd jobs at the dock that required a smaller body to slide down into a bilge, or change a screw in a particularly narrow storage compartment. His size and his agility were his marketable features. Before long, he was permanent crew for Terry Spar, and when he wasn't on or around the boats, Keaton was roaming the ravines with Annie Lieb.

It confuses Pen that Keaton had been so set on taking over the responsibilities Rod left behind. As though that would bring Rod back, or at least make-up for the loss. And then Keaton simply left.

All sorts of investigations had grown up around the fire, around Keaton's escape. But she hadn't been much involved. An officer came to the house and asked her if she knew where her brother had gone. She answered she had no idea.

Pen hasn't thought of Annie Lieb for a long time. She vaguely remembers the family. They came into the Fish sometimes, Mr. and Mrs. Lieb both sullen and grey, Annie tall, round-shouldered between them.

An image of Annie comes, an impression of something slow, thin, and slightly bent, her long face pressed forward as though she were perpetually listening, a long-legged bird not comfortable on the ground. Yet, Annie had walked quickly, her hands at her sides while Keaton had his jammed into his pockets.

It was Keaton's comfort with her that made Pen jealous. She could tell by watching them that Keaton was telling Annie things: what he wanted to do after Port, the problems of the insurance claim, Irene and Ed. Keaton would wait for Annie to come down the front steps of the high school, her bag slung awkwardly over her narrow shoulder. They would disappear together, Annie striding, her head tipped toward Keaton, sometimes Keaton gesturing with his hands. Pen followed them once or twice, but then she stopped, knowing that if Keaton saw her, he would never forgive the trespass.

Pen wonders whether Andy — because of his maleness or his closeness to Keaton or both — understood Keaton's fixation with Annie. She wonders if Annie had come between he and Keaton too.

"You remember Annie Lieb? "

"Of course," Andy says. "Why?"

"What happened to her, after Keaton left?"

Andy seems to be considering this. "I heard that the family moved away, maybe to get her some help."

That would make sense. People used to put twirling fingers to their temples when they talked about Annie Lieb. *Crazy Annie,* though she doesn't remember anyone saying it outright.

"Why did he like her so much?" asks Pen.

Andy pauses. Pen waits for Andy to remember things about Keaton, about Annie. Anything. A reconstruction of events. This is what she is doing with Andy, she realizes. Gathering up bits and pieces, trying to make one thing connect with the next.

"Annie was kind of fragile," Andy says, hesitation in his voice. Pen wonders if he feels disloyal, talking about her, or perhaps he is still protective of Keaton, of what and who Keaton had loved.

"Strange, you mean, or *what*?" She doesn't want to interrogate him, but it sounds that way. She laughs a little awkwardly. "Does fragile mean she was ill?"

Andy shrugs. "Once, a bunch of us were standing around behind the school. A guy started talking about Annie Lieb, about how she used to cut-up her arms with a razor blade."

"Did she?"

"I don't know. Maybe. All I know is that Keaton punched the guy so hard in the gut he was dry-heaving." Andy smiled, remembering this. Then he looked puzzled.

"It wasn't just that he liked her. After your dad died, Keaton *relied* on her. You'd have to ask him why and for what. She eased something in him, I guess."

Pen thinks of Annie, melting into the dreary backdrop of Port, solitary, and shy. She wouldn't have cut herself for attention. Pain as distraction, then? Perhaps. She wraps her arms around herself and remembers sitting in an elementary classroom. Maybe she had been twelve or thirteen, rain streaming down the windows, the wet footwear, the boggy smell of damp hair and sodden sweaters. A boy behind Pen with red-rimmed eyes and pointy teeth had leaned forward and whispered in her ear.

"You smell. No wonder your dad offed himself. He couldn't stand the smell."

Pen hadn't known what it meant, but she felt the sense of shame, the certainty that she was flawed. If she could have disappeared into something else in that moment, something exquisite even if painful, she would have.

What had Keaton done? The stares, the smirks, the rolling eyes. The entire town had been alive with rumours about Irene and Ed, about Rod's drowning.

Andy looks at her. "He changed after Rod drowned, didn't he." More a statement that a question.

"Yeah, he did. He stopped being a brother. It was like he had to be more." And he hated me for that, she thinks. She remembers how, after Rod was gone, Keaton became tyrannical about the beachcombing, making Pen scavenge for hours in the cold, berating her for wanting to go inside, for wanting chips, hot chocolate, warmth.

For wanting it to become a game again.

She has tears in her eyes. Andy has his hands out, and his scarred face is tilted up and toward a gathering thin rain. "Here it comes," he says. When he turns back to Pen, he looks relaxed, like she has answered something for him.

"Kids need things," he says. "It's not their fault."

Pen unwraps the jacket from around her waist and puts it on, but she leaves the hood down, liking the feel of the rain on her skin, in her hair. The feel of it puts a distance between now and what she has been remembering.

"Ancient history, I guess," she says.

They walk for another half-hour or so and talk about Port, what they remember of it. He walks close to her, his arm brushing her shoulder. She holds some residue of Keaton for him, she supposes, as he does for her. He doesn't say anything about having had a bad year, about something not having worked out. Still, she thinks she sees an impression of a stain or a bruise in him.

He is smiling, drops of silver water collecting on the tight coil of his hair, dripping on to his shoulders, his cheeks, following the tracings of scar tissue.

"A treat, running into you down here," she says, hoping it doesn't sound glib.

He laughs. "I bet."

Beside them are the remnants of the old runway. She can make out the ruts from the wheels of the planes, perfectly parallel to the silvery bushes and the straight rows of trees.

"I wonder where all the planes went, after the war," she says suddenly. The place is beautiful, even a little exotic, without them.

12.

ANNIE KNOWS THAT SHE is in a room and that it has a door. From time to time, people come and go. They touch her. They ask her name. *Can you tell us who you are?* She has no wish to rise, to walk, to speak. Nor does she have a wish to die. She is in the world of *in between,* not waiting but becoming, stretched tight and light as air. Her mind races, leaping ahead of her body, beckoning to her but she can't let go. Not yet.

Annie thinks of Keaton, of how alone he must feel, how abandoned. She closes her eyes, the pain rising into her throat.

They had known one another's names since they were no more than five or six, sharing classes in some of those years, crisscrossing in school hallways, standing on the opposite ends of a school gym.

She remembers seeing Keaton and Pen sitting in a booth at the Fish, Pen wide-eyed and tiny, Keaton playing Xs and Os with her on a napkin, his fingers pressed around a pink wax crayon. Their mother came out from behind the counter with two huge chocolate sundaes. Pen was tense with excitement, her hand quavering as she held up the spoon to her mouth. A look of concentrated bliss. Irene slid in next to Pen, beaming at them both. Her children.

Keaton always said his mother was a drunk. But she wasn't a drunk that day. She was just a mother, and Annie had seen it. She had seen it *for* Keaton and she reminded him of it later, when things got bad. When Irene as much as left them.

It was easier for Keaton to name Irene's failures than it was for him to name Rod's. Rod's imperfections remained dormant. He almost drowned himself after his father disappeared. Annie saw it, the gathering panic, the tension in his limbs, a weight on his spirit that dragged him down into blackness. He fell away from school, working instead, getting odd jobs at the docks. One day, she found him waiting for her by a tree, close to the cement path that led from the school to the street. He stepped out when he saw her. He walked with her, his pace as fast as hers, although she had the sense she was leading him, that he needed this from her. They walked for more than three hours, through the ravines, along the beach road. *When you took that knife to yourself,* he asked, *did you want to die?* No, she told him. She didn't want that. But sometimes what you feel is big, even terrible. Sometimes what you feel tears at you. They walked almost every day after that. A few months later, he talked to her about Terry Spar.

A nurse comes in with a tray of food and puts it on a table next to the bed. She doesn't look at Annie. She busies herself with checking a chart at the bottom of Annie's bed.

"You should try to eat."

Annie doesn't look at her and the nurse goes away. She is thinking about Keaton and how he burned the *Dolly*. Annie knew Terry Spar to see him. Port is a small place, the fishing tugs and the fishing families a tight knot in the town's heart, a fist of people pounding against the bad luck of the lake. Annie had seen the *Dolly* go out many times, Spar at the wheel, something ravenous and child-like in his face. She had watched him at the docks mooching around other boats, his hands in his pockets. Keaton said that he worked for Spar because he *had* too. There are other boats, Annie said. Other men you could work for. Keaton gritted his teeth and said that for him, there was *only* Terry Spar.

If Rod's disappearance had left Keaton flailing, panicked,

it was Terry Spar that took Keaton down, deep into a murky bottom, his legs bound to the sand and lake weed.

Annie's eyes take in the fullness of the room, seeking out the spaces between things, around the bed, the chair, the metal tray of food she will not eat. Space is air, she thinks. Just breathe, Annie. Breathe.

She lies still, willing herself toward lightness, stretching herself thinner and thinner until she bares no weight at all.

13.

"I WON'T STAY. Waiting is *dumb*." Maddie is sitting sideways, her head resting on Pen's chest. Her legs kick spasmodically against the metal arm of a chair that is occupied by a neckless old lady. The woman indulgently pats Maddie's leg.

"Maddie, don't kick," Pen says flatly.

Maddie jerks her legs away from Pen's constraining arms and turns her head, then, she breaks into sobs, her face burrowing into Pen.

"I *know*, Maddie. I'm *sorry*. You have to be patient."

The old woman is shaking her head, her eyes rueful. "It's too bad she's gotta wait so long. If my turn comes first, she can take it."

"We'll be okay," says Pen. "But thanks."

Pen pulls out her cell to check the time. She wishes she had brought a book to read to Maddie, something to distract her from her ear that she now presses into Pen's chest.

The waiting room is under-sized and jammed with people. Maddie's appointment was for ten but it is already well past eleven.

Twisting painfully, the old woman peers down the hall to where the examination rooms are. "Getting near lunch," she says, giving Maddie's foot a squeeze. Her fingers are long and dry. "He won't see *anyone* over his lunch."

Pen still has her phone out and she thinks about calling Jeff. She talked to him once already this morning, to let him know about Maddie. He listened closely. "Call me after the doctor has had a look at her, Pen." She wonders why she wants to call him now, when there isn't anything she can tell him. She slips the phone into her coat pocket and looks down into Maddie's face. Maddie looks back at her, abject and miserable.

"My ear is hot, Mommy. Maybe the doctor went home and so we should come back tomorrow. *Please*, Mommy."

"Try to think about something else."

There is a momentary distraction when the old woman struggles to stand. She clutches her walker grimly and then calls over to the receptionist.

"This little girl isn't feeling well. She's been here almost two hours."

The receptionist's head bobs cheerily up from behind the counter. "He's running behind. Shouldn't be too much longer."

The old lady grunts. "Hope that's true," she says.

Yesterday, when Pen got back from her walk with Andy, Maddie was lying on the couch, one of the cats lazing at her feet. Irene was in the chair across, a small bowl of chocolate ice cream in her hand. "Maddie has a sore ear. Touch of fever too, I think."

Just looking at her she knew what it was. Pen put a hand on Maddie's forehead. Glassy eyes, the vermillion colour in her cheeks, the lethargy; Maddie is prone to ear trouble and the swimming had brought this on. Even though bacterial counts have been in the safe range since they've been here, Pen still thinks of Lake Erie as unclean.

"She's managed a bit of ice cream and some ginger ale, but that's about it," Irene said.

It was close to six. Pen knew that the one clinic in Port, which served as both a walk-in and the permanent office of the two family doctors in town, would now be closed. She could drag Maddie into the emergency department at St. Thomas but that would mean hours of waiting and a trip back home in the middle of the night.

"I've got kid's Tylenol for her," Pen said. "First thing in the morning, I'll call the clinic and see if I can get her in."

Irene hadn't offered to come with them this morning but then Pen hadn't asked her.

Maddie is breathing deeper now, her body heavy in Pen's lap. Maybe she is close to sleep. It would be reassuring if Jeff were here, to help.

How could she put words to it, her lack of faith in herself? Last fall, when she finally told Jeff to leave, what came out of her was shockingly simple. "I don't know how to stay together," she said.

Pen has a flash of recognition; she is alone, utterly alone with Maddie. The stillness in Maddie, the lassitude in her body, usually so tightly sprung, brings on a haunted feeling, a dread. *What if Maddie died?* It is a horrible thought, a secret thought, not normal concern.

Pen takes in a deep breath and looks around the room at the other waiting patients. Some read newspapers, other sit with their legs straight out and stare at the ceiling. There is nothing alarming here, she tells herself. Kids with sore throats, old people with shingles. Port has made her susceptible to dark thoughts. She is tired from being up most of the night, and they have been sitting for a long time. The doctor will prescribe some medication, the banana flavoured stuff that Maddie likes, and within a day or two, Maddie will be her old self. Even as she tells herself these things, the helplessness stays with her, stubborn and silent. She curls Maddie's sleeping body closer to her, wanting to feel her, to be reassured that Maddie hasn't left her, that she hasn't left Maddie.

From the end of the hall, there is a squeak as the door to the examining room opens. "Just give this to the receptionist and she'll make the referral. We'll get things going as soon as we can." A doctor's voice, calm, efficient. "Good luck," he adds.

Pen hopes that the doctor will walk into the reception area and call out Maddie's name.

But when Pen looks down the hall, the doctor has disappeared into his office. Who she sees is T, his brown boots turned out as he walks, the familiar leathers, a manila envelope in his hands. His face, grey under the florescent lights, is heavy and brutal-looking with exhaustion. There is irony in his expression, and either a lack of concern, or resignation. When their eyes meet, he stops and studies her for a moment, taking in Maddie, the uneaten cookies on the arm of the chair.

Maddie, awake now, looks up at him, her green eyes questioning. "You're the guy who went swimming in his clothes."

"That guy," he confirms. "And you're Goldilocks."

"I'm *not* Goldilocks," she corrects him. "I don't even like bears."

"Probably smart," he says.

Maddie giggles, which makes Pen smile.

Pen is acutely aware that the old woman is staring at them, her doleful eyes inspecting T, his leathers, then sliding over to Pen to take a second look.

T must feel the woman's eyes on him because he turns. "You wanna take a picture?" he says. He screws up his eyes and pushes his face in her direction.

"Not a bit," she retorts.

Maddie is studying T, her cheeks red, bright with fever. "You shouldn't be *mean* to old people."

T looks at her for a few moments, scowling. Then he nods. "There's lots of things I shouldn't do," he says. "But okay. Just for you. I'll lay off the old ladies."

Maddie holds out a cookie to T who takes it from her, then gives a half-salute. He hoists the envelope in a farewell gesture and then ambles over to the counter. The receptionist takes the envelope from him and pulls a sheet from inside.

The receptionist takes her time reading it, letting the incoming calls go to voice-mail. "I'm going to see who has the earliest opening. Do you care where you go? London? Hamilton? Maybe Toronto?"

"Don't plan on being around here for much longer. But I don't really care."

The receptionist gives him back the envelope, minus the letter that she tucks next to her phone.

"I have a cell phone number for you, don't I? And oh, Mister Valentine, did the doctor want to see you again for follow-up?"

Pen turns and looks at T who has his sunglasses on and his keys jangling in his hand.

Pen thinks of him, flying toward an already lost Ben Vasco. One of Irene's terrible sayings comes to mind. It appears on a mass-produced poster, in a flowery script, curling and yellowed on Irene's ancient refrigerator.

Find Hope Where You Least Expect It.

14.

JEFF IS MAKING GRILLED CHEESE sandwiches, open-faced, with olives for the eyes and pieces of curly bologna for the mouths. Giggling, her fingers pulling at the sides of her mouth, Maddie is stretching her own face into a semblance of the sandwich faces. She stomps and careens around his feet. While he assembles the sandwiches, Jeff is humming a song that he and Maddie like, something about pirates and treasure chests, and going to the depths of the sea. He makes his voice big and puffs out his already barrel-like chest. He puts bologna patches over the left eyes, and he and Maddie, like cannibals, eat pirate sandwiches together.

It had taken twenty-four hours for the antibiotics to kick in. As soon as Maddie felt better, Pen loaded the car and headed to Toronto. Irene was sanguine about their departure, kissing Pen, sending Maddie off with a smooth flat stone on which she had painted the words *Nan loves Maddie,* surrounded by a bright red heart. Ed gave her a piece of rope, a part of an old docking line off the *Irene.* Pen looked at him strangely when he put it on the back seat next to Maddie. He shrugged.

"She wanted it, Pen."

Maddie cried for the first twenty minutes outside of Port, saying that she was missing Nana and Papa Ed already. Pen said something vague about coming down again, before the fall, and then she pushed Maddie's favourite CD into the player. Before long, Maddie was fast asleep.

When they pulled onto their street in the city, Jeff was wagging a garden hose over the burnt grass, instantly cheerful at the sight of the car. He was wearing jeans, despite the heat, and he'd tied a bright red bandanna around his head.

"Daddy's here..." Pen reached back and touched Maddie's bare foot, tickling her into wakefulness.

Seeing them, Jeff dropped the hose and walked toward the car, so happy, Pen thought he might actually start to howl. Jeff opened Maddie's door and Maddie launched herself at him like a missile.

He stayed over, sleeping on the couch, volunteering to give Maddie breakfast so that Pen could get an early start in the morning. Now, without asking, Jeff slides a plate and a sandwich over to her. She's been out to the university and back again, bullying herself into finishing the book orders for her course. She should have stayed longer; she hasn't accomplished any writing yet today. She eats her sandwich and smiles over at Maddie, who is arranging the crusts on her plate into an oval. Jeff takes two green olives from a bowl and gives the oval eyes. He makes a spooky, eerie sound.

"Aye, Matey," he says. 'You've plundered my bologna."

Maddie giggles. "Sing!" she commands.

"Together, then," says Jeff. "On my cue."

His face is expectant, his arms raised like a well-muscled conductor holding a baton. Maddie hops off her stool and immediately opens her mouth and takes in a huge lung-full of air. Jeff's arm plunges down and Maddie starts to sing: *Row, Row, Row-Your-Boat, Gently Out To Sea...*

Jeff's voice follows, deep and resonant, and the two of them are lost in delight, in song. Pen puts a hand on Jeff's shoulder, and then slides in front of him to get to the coffee pot. He responds to her touch, his hand resting lightly in the small of her back.

When Pen checks her phone, she finds a text message from Andy asking her to call and she slips into the living room. She wants there to be several degrees of separation between her past in Port and her life in the city. She hasn't told Jeff that she ran into Keaton's best friend in Port, that somehow the connection is a vital one for her.

Maddie has been playing here, and although clutter doesn't bother Pen (Pen has always been more concerned with cleanliness than order), she busies herself with tidying Maddie's toys. There aren't many. A few scraggly Barbies, a couple of them missing their heads, a black carry case containing magic tricks, its contents pilfered and strewn across the floor, and a bent princess tiara. Maddie has a tendency to disassemble her possessions, reconfiguring them so they become something else.

Pen puts the toys into a wicker hamper, shoves them under Jeff's electric keyboard, and then surveys the room. It's a small semi-detached house, old and with a tired elegance in the high ceilings, the deep baseboards and trim. The room is crowded with plain, functional furniture — a faux-leather couch, metal bookshelves, a monochrome rug from Ikea. When he left, Jeff took some of his books and the futon from the office in the attic, a few plates, two pots and a fry pan. Just the essentials. He stored his weights and his spare bike in the basement, along with his out-of-season clothes. Neither of them has mentioned a desire to separate their possessions and so the house remains in stasis, reflecting a life half-occupied, an unresolved end.

Andy picks up after three rings. He's in his car. She can hear the whoosh of highway noise in the background. The sound of distance being consumed.

"You read the paper this morning, right?"

She hasn't. She got up and left for the subway, grabbing a coffee and a bagel at the coffee shop en route. She is pleased to hear his voice. It's like talking to Keaton, but before everything became broken. Before Rod disappeared and the *Dolly* burnt.

"There's been some kind of biker massacre down here. A whole pile of bodies found in a field outside of Port."

"Bodies?"

"Eight of them."

"It will be in your paper, Pen. And on the national news."

For several moments, Pen stands perfectly still, considering what she has just heard. Her mind goes to T and to the men who sat with him on the beach. They might have been involved. The idea is unnerving.

There are probably hundreds of bikers in the province, she reasons, and many in Port. Many all along the Erie shoreline. In recent years, each time a Friday the thirteenth occurs, the bikers converge on the town like a flock of black gulls. No reason to assume that T, or the others, had been involved in these killings.

Still, her mind circles around the day at the beach, T speaking to Maddie, his hand outstretched to her, Maddie pouring her treasures into his hand.

"They know who the victims were?" She asks.

Andy seems taken aback by the question. "Why does *that* matter?"

She says it doesn't. "Just curious."

"Stay in touch, Pen."

When she asks Jeff if he has heard about what happened down in Port, he says,

"Yup. All over the news."

He slides his eyes over to Maddie, then nods his head in the direction of the newspaper, which is inside of the recycling container. Pen unfolds it and sees on the front page a grainy, aerial image of a farmer's field with a scattering of vehicles, tossed over the scene like hen's teeth. The headline reads: "Lake Erie's Biker Blood Bath." The property involved was described by an elderly neighbour as "a normal kind of place." However, the same neighbour, who would not be identified, said that recently there had been an influx of "bikers in colours," who were, in his opinion, "a pretty bad bunch."

The victims are undoubtedly all bikers. Most have records

and they are all known to the authorities. They apparently had regular jobs; they were tow truck drivers, bartenders, roofers. They are young and middle-aged, their lives entangled with wives, girlfriends, kids.

But beyond those ties, they orbit in another universe. Pen imagines them on their days off, their weekends, gathered together like ants returning to a nest, their Harleys parked in a sun-scorched field.

Their stories are accompanied by photographs. Some of the photos are clearly mug shots, but others are informal and un-posed: a paunchy grey-haired man leaning against a red pick-up; a couple on a rust-coloured couch, the man's beefy arm around the woman's narrow shoulders, the tips of his fingers burrowed into her hair.

Pen pours over the pictures and wonders if she will find T, or one of the other men among the images of the victims. She doesn't. She bites on her lower lip and reads on. No group or organization has formally taken responsibility.

With her arms wrapped around herself, she watches the powerful muscles in Jeff's back flex and shift as he rinses and stacks their lunch dishes. Jeff is a strong man. He has invested years at the gym, in the dojo. He takes a washcloth and cleans Maddie's face with so much delicacy and care, he might have been taking dust from a butterfly wing.

Pen arrives early at the university where she rummages through a backlog of papers, and sorts out the mass of emails in her in-box. Over the last couple of days, she has been preoccupied with the massacre, visiting the media accounts that appear in the papers and on the web. The news has been bursting with related items. Criminologists and journalists speculate about motivation: warring clubs, retribution, internal cleansing. Pen found herself mesmerized, following the story whenever Maddie wasn't around.

Now, on campus, she launches into writing, and although at

first it is difficult to organize her thoughts, soon she is swept up in her work.

At four-thirty, satisfied with her progress, she descends into the subway, appreciating the movement of the air that is generated by the trains and nurtured into a breeze. The city's underground has its own little weather system. So did Port. It was the lake that created the microclimate, the air heating and cooling and circulating in its own idiosyncratic way.

Outside the station, people stream past her, hot, preoccupied, migrating toward sanctuary; home, the gym, a restaurant with air conditioning, a frosted glass of beer. She realizes that she relies on the anonymity of the city. Never once has she imagined seeing someone familiar, certainly not Keaton here, amidst the stream of strangers. But Keaton had found *her*, the summer before she was pregnant with Maddie.

The first call from him after years of nothing. There was a lot of background noise, music, loud voices. His voice had a careening lilt, wild, insistent, and she strained to understand him.

He didn't ask about Irene. He rambled on about a logging camp, a bar, but he didn't tell her where he was. "I don't know where all this ends," he said.

She shakes off thoughts of Keaton. It was his choice to leave Port the way he did. She thinks of him slipping out of the window of their room, one last backward glance before he was swallowed by the night. "Don't you follow me, Pen. You forget that you saw this." Sometimes, when she remembers how he left, the shock of his disappearance, his failure to reassure her he'd return, she feels a desperate fury creep up. It would be *easier*, she thinks, not to ever see Keaton again.

When she arrives home, Jeff and Maddie greet her in their bathing suits. Jeff has filled up the plastic wade-pool and the two of them have been soaking in the tepid water, Jeff with a beer and Maddie sucking on a dripping orange popsicle.

"Care for a swim?" Jeff smiles hopefully at her and she goes inside to get on her bathing suit. In their bedroom, she turns on the news network and recognizes the same clips that have been circulating for days: the field, the bodies, the victims' faces. She watches for a couple of minutes and she feels her mood begin to spiral. She turns off the TV and, without changing, goes out to sit on the patio. The sun is behind the low-rise apartment that backs onto their yard, the shade a relief, the air still heavy. Jeff sits close, his knee resting against hers, his arm locked on to the back of her chair. She finds she wants to distract herself from him, from the puzzle of their relationship, from the contradictory impulses to draw in to him and to move further apart.

"The biker thing down in Port," she tells him. "I keep thinking about it. Those *men,* their bizarre lives, them shuffling around at night, stuffing their kill into cars. And we are supposed to believe they are just regular guys on the off hours."

Jeff has his eyes on Maddie while he rests his hand on Pen's thigh. When he turns to look at her, his face expresses a frank and straightforward love. "I want to *stay,*" he says. "Let me stay tonight. With you."

She feels a sudden wash of emotion, so dense, so insistent, she feels she might cry.

"There is a story about one of those guys changing the inner tube on the neighbour kid's bike," she continues, her hand on his. "A big ape of a guy just hanging out in the suburbs, playing Shinny after work, and cooking up burgers."

Jeff studies her, suddenly looking afflicted. "Why are you talking about this *now?*"

"It's just hard to get," she goes on, frowning into the late afternoon. "They must have been capable of a different life; it didn't have to end up like that."

Jeff takes his hand from Pen's leg, looks back at Maddie, and rubs at his head. He says nothing but she can hear his breathing, steady and careful. She realizes that there is no one in the world that she trusts more than she trusts him. At the same time, she wonders whether it's possible to really know anyone.

She thinks of Rod, his lean ruddy face and how one bitingly cold day, when she was standing at the docks shivering, he took her zipper in his clumsy fingers and did up her coat.

"You are my lucky penny; you are my heart."

And then he had vanished. Perhaps he had taken his own life, perpetrating a murder, tearing himself away violently, finally. How can she make sense of that?

"Go back to your place, Jeff," she says. "I'm not good company. The heat, maybe. I don't know."

Jeff's eyes drop for a moment. He stands, frustrated, his arms knotted at his chest.

"I don't get this, Pen. What do you want? *Nothing* has changed for me. Not one thing."

That night, Pen dreams again of Ben Vasco and his return from the lake. He is wet and gleaming. This time, he walks toward her with a smile because he knows her, his look insistent, wise. Pen wakes up and feels she must *do* something but she can't think what it is.

She decides to check in with Detective Sinclair. She hopes she hasn't missed Ben Vasco's memorial service, although she knows, even as she is pushing the numbers into the phone, that probably she would have heard, either from Detective Sinclair or even Irene.

When he answers, Detective Sinclair's voice sounds breezy and detached.

"It's Pen Beau," she explains.

There is a pause.

"I was on the beach the day Ben Vasco drowned."

"Of course, I remember. What can I do for you?" He is polite but only half-interested. She imagines the drowning is already filed away somewhere, left like a car in long-term parking.

"I've been thinking about the memorial service. Is there any news? Have the family and the residence come to an understanding?"

It's a moment before he gathers his thoughts.

"I can't say, really. Still kind of a mess. Now there's talk of a law suit. Everyone's still trying to establish blame."

Two days later, Jeff calls to say that his senior colleague and mentor, Bill Carlyle, has invited them up to a cottage for a few days, a place where they have visited before and been happy. Jeff tells Pen he thinks they should go.

"Bring up some work if you want to," he says. "No pressure, and if you want me and Maddie to disappear for a few hours, no problem." He is assiduously avoiding saying *we need to spend some time together.* Pen's brain feels log-jammed. The work is piling up at the university. At night, she lies in the heat with her sheets tangled around her toes, thinking about Ben Vasco, Port, the blank flat lake. She thinks of Rod's remains, buried in the sandy bottom. And the scene of the biker massacre, torn and ugly and banal.

She sorts the images and tries to find some meaning. Maybe she is becoming unstable, the way she was after Maddie was born, although this feels different, less like defeat and more like a pressing desire to *know.* She is wrung-out, indecisive, preoccupied with her thoughts, her dreams. Ultimately Maddie is the resolution. Maddie drags a snorkeling mask, an alligator hair comb and a bag of seashells into Pen's room.

"When are you, me and Daddy going to Bill and Lea's cottage?"

15.

THE NIGHT ISN'T STILL and quiet like you would think it should be in the country. There are bugs or frogs screaming at him from the trees and a little while back, he heard something like barking. A fox maybe. Music is thudding from inside the house. No one thought to turn it off once all the shooting started.

He feels tired and too fucking old for this. Maybe if things get wrapped up here, he'll ride down to Port and bang on Big John's door. T knows that B.J. won't ask him questions and he can chill there, away from this farm.

His crew is somewhere on the property, probably self-medicating to manage the adrenaline drop. It's been a long night, particularly with the clean-up. Until a few hours ago, T hadn't thought he would need to deal with eight bodies. He came up with a temporary solution; the tractor and the cars would do for now, but in this heat, he'd have to come up with something more permanent soon.

After the call from Winnipeg, T had gone to the drive shed himself and checked on the ammo. Plenty there, and he stashed more in other spots: the grass by the driveway, and under a bed in the house. He had to admit, the new orders surprised him. He couldn't see the sense in them; he couldn't see the gain.

When he told the crew about the change of plan he said they should wait for his go-ahead. He still didn't know exactly where it would happen, he said, but he figured the house would be too tight.

It had been a tense few hours, waiting. Justin was yammering on, telling stupid stories, giggling like a girl and Solham was wearing a weird psycho-grin, something T had seen on him before, particularly when situations were about to get messy. For a scrawny crack-head, Solham can do damage, but he's also a loose cannon. Then there was Hornet, shoulders the width of an aircraft carrier, looking pale and sweaty. T had expected more of him. Hornet sure liked to talk up his talents but so far, there was not much evidence to support all the talk. As for Blue, T knew that Blue would be okay.

The cars rolled in around six. The Toronto guys had been ordered down for "business reasons," and they arrived already wired, like they'd been tipped off about getting booted out of the organization. But T doesn't think they expected what they got.

They pulled chairs out back and cracked a case of beer. One of their guys — Boomer — talked and talked and The Beef, a guy T had personally always respected, sat there like a bull moose on a yoga mat, too serious, the others drinking and watching, probably trying to figure out what was going to happen next.

After a couple of hours, T gave the nod and Solham drew on them, Blue and the others taking their cue and drawing too. Boomer actually laughed when he saw what they were doing.

"What the F? You guys for real?"

"Shut-it," T said.

They'd taken them out to the shed, a raggedy line-up if ever there was one, Justin looking like he was going to pee his pants. Jesus. He was going to lose that kid.

"What's this about, T?" The Beef had his arms spread out by his sides, palms up. He didn't look scared.

T did The Beef himself using the Taurus-410. It only seemed right. The Beef was still looking at him, when he took it, falling real slow, almost graceful. Beef wouldn't have been surprised to end up like he did. This business ends badly, any which way.

Solham starting shooting next. He took out at least four, crazy bastard, that grin plastered on his face the entire time. Hornet, Justin, Blue, all shooting too, but after a while, it's hard to know whose bullet actually brings a guy down. T thinks of how the men fell, some silent, like the Beef, others swearing, punching the air. The guy he knew as Boomer didn't stop jabbering until he was hit. Now that's denial, thinks T.

He's got a disposal problem now. Eight ripe bodies in those vehicles and he might have to wait until tomorrow night to get them out of here. The night is panting heat on him like a dog. Once the sun comes up tomorrow and hits that metal, it's going to be a mess.

T checks himself, making sure he's not too rattled, that he is still thinking straight. He's wheezing a little, his chest tight as a stretched fan belt. He sucks in air and as soon as it hits his lungs, he's taken over with coughing, deep and painful, an all-over spasm that brings the world down to whether or not he'll croak before he can take in air again.

The spasm subsides and he expels a great yellow-red glob of stuff into the pool of light at his feet. There is a lot of pain after the coughing spells now. He'd gone to the clinic the other day to get some more antibiotics and maybe some pain killers. The doctor took a listen to his chest and then ordered an x-ray. Two hours after T went down the hall to get the picture done, the doctor called him on his cell.

"We have something of concern here, Mister Valentine. Come in as soon as you can." The next morning, when the doctor put the x-ray against the light and showed T the white blob in his chest, T could only think of Eva, how she takes pictures of people now, how badly he wishes she had taken this one. T would need a referral to an oncologist and a referral would be made for him right away. In the hall, the doctor stuck out his hand to T and told him *good luck*.

So that was it. And then that girl from the beach, with sick little Goldilocks, they were there, in the clinic, and that was strange, because for a minute, seeing them, he thought it was *his* girl and *his* kid, and that they were sitting there, waiting for him. A pair of angels. T snorts, then coughs wildly; he's never thought of angels in a good way, a *ministering* way, until now.

He takes out a cigarette. He realizes he hasn't an ounce of feeling about the killing, except a little about The Beef. T's not one to get excited on a job. Never gets jazzed or even nervous. It's never been his way.

T can be counted on to do what is required.

Though for the first time the calm seems wrong. He's looking at himself as if from a distance, from the crest of a hill maybe, and he sees that something is missing. The strangeness of it, seeing the holes in himself, like he's been shot through the chest.

Something is rattling him, creating a tingling in his spine. His cell is vibrating. He puts his hand in his pocket and pulls out the phone. Winnipeg calling. Time to report in, tell the big boys that he's delivered.

16.

THE DRIVE OUT OF THE CITY, north, toward cottage country, is like stepping onto an over-crowded escalator two days before Christmas. Pen finds the trip vaguely surreal. She cannot comprehend how the ugly, flat hinterlands of the city just stop, and the magic of the near North begins.

Maddie sits in the back, wearing a pair of pink sunglasses and lime-green flannel pajama bottoms in a polar bear print. Jeff had been in charge of Maddie this morning, while Pen had packed and organized the bags.

"Why did you put her in a pair of winter pjs on the hottest day of the year?"

Jeff has music on in the car and he appears at first not to have heard her. Then he shrugs. "Just let her pick out what she wanted, Pen. Couldn't imagine it would matter."

"What she *wanted* to wear? Kind of negligent, Jeff. She's four."

Jeff looks over at her and raises his eyebrows.

"It's *okay*, Jeff. You just have to help her pick stuff out, give her the choice between three outfits. That's how it works with four-year-olds."

"I'll remember that next time. So don't call the child protection services."

He disappears into his music and Pen feels as though she's been dropped somewhere on a polar ice field. It is that abrupt, the abandonment she sometimes feels. She flips down the mirror on the visor, finding Maddie's reflection there. "Why," Pen asks, "do you want to be so *hot*?"

"I don't wanna be hot."

"So, why are you wearing those?"

"I wanna wear them."

"They make you hot, Maddie."

"No. This car makes me hot. And the sun."

Jeff laughs appreciatively.

Maddie stares out of the window, kicking the back of Pen's seat. "How long before we get there?"

"Maddie *don't* ask that again." Pen feels a dark shadow descend, a sense of inevitability.

Maddie continues to kick, with more gusto in her foot-strikes now. *Deliberately* kicking, thinks Pen. She twists around to face Maddie whose head rests against the car seat, her pink sunglasses tilted up like a movie star. Behind the glasses, Pen thinks that her face is almost contemptuous.

"Quit it, Maddie." Her tone is cutting, abrasive. "*Soon*, is the answer. And *stop* kicking. I *mean* it." Pen grasps Maddie's ankle and firmly pins it to the back seat.

Maddie breaks into a series of dramatized high-pitched shouts. "You're *hurting* me. Take your hand *off!*"

Jeff has the turn-signal on and he yanks the wheel to the right, pulling the car into a truck weigh station, abruptly stepping on the break. He slams the steering wheel with an open hand. Surprised, Pen lets go of Maddie and looks at him. His hands are back on the wheel, holding it tight, his face white, his expression pained.

"For just a couple of days, can you *stop* being so miserable? Can you make an *effort*?" He glares straight ahead, not looking at her. Pen is stung, ashamed. The car is idling, cars swooshing past. It crosses her mind that he will tell her to get out and walk.

"Alright. I'm sorry. I'm sorry, Maddie." She feels stunned by what has just cracked open in Jeff, almost frightened by it, as though she were a child. Maddie sulks and Pen says nothing. Jeff pulls back onto the highway and for the moment, they travel like three strangers on a bus. She imagines them arriving at the cottage, a family of three, a little pod of humans, presenting as though the ties between them are sure, and certain. She has no idea what family means.

"I shouldn't be up here, with you, Jeff. Bill's your friend," she says, looking out her window.

"You've got that wrong." The anger has gone from his voice but he sounds exasperated, beleaguered. "This is going to be good. A break from the thesis, from thinking about sad stuff you haven't got any control over." He sighs. "These people care for you, Pen. Just try and appreciate them."

Pen has her eyes closed behind her sunglasses, trees, rocks, imprinting themselves like chromatic aberrations. She opens them again and before long, Jeff begins to sing.

They finally pull into the drive, which winds attractively under clumps of white birch. Bill stands by the door, not much taller than Pen, tanned, a middle-aged bulge pushing out the front of his frayed golf shirt. He wears a sloppy pair of leather sandals and a pair of light-coloured denim jeans, a couple of days' worth of stubble on his face. His grin is disarming and confident. He saunters over and gives Pen a kiss on the cheek. Lea steps out of the screen door, tall and poised, her white hair gathered neatly into a black tortoise-shell clip. She wears a white linen shirt over a pair of black jeans. A beautiful woman, thinks Pen, even at sixty-eight. She beams when her eyes rest on Maddie. Pen *does* love Bill and Lea in her way, appreciates their attachment to Maddie, their friendship with Jeff, their acceptance of her, their warmth. She suspects that she and Jeff and Maddie are like family for Bill and Lea. They've never had a family of their own and even before Maddie came along, they regarded Jeff and Pen as surrogates. But she hasn't spent time with them since she and Jeff separated last fall, though Lea has been in touch through email, and a card and a present for Maddie arrived in December.

They are comfortable people and completely gracious. Lea leads them into the house and Maddie immediately disappears into her room to change into a suit for a swim. "Hot, hot, hot..." she chants. The men slide out toward the back and Lea sets down two wine glasses on the stone counter, and opens a chilled bottle of Chablis. Pen knows that after she told him to leave, Jeff would have confided in Bill. If asked, Jeff wouldn't have been able to provide an explanation for why they separated, and Pen feels certain that Lea and Bill believe she initiated it. Although they aren't people to jump to conclusions about other people's lives, she has wondered whether they have told Jeff to cut his losses.

Through the large glass doors, Pen can see Jeff and Bill standing over the barbecue, Jeff with a look of intense interest on his face, tossing out a comment to Bill who is nodding his head in agreement. Jeff has opened up two beers for them, taken from the fridge in the garden shed. Bill looks mellow, vaguely patrician, while Jeff is muscled and eager.

Maddie emerges draped in her beach towel, her bare toes splayed open on the tiled floor. Lea bows to her and calls her "Your Highness." Maddie giggles and takes pointed, princess steps over the lawn, and Pen and Lea follow..

"Water wings, Maddie. And see the rock? You go no further than that."

The sun is low and it sparks and flits though the filigreed leaves on the trees that ring the lake. There are cheery little waves on its surface, the water a uniform deep green. Pen slides down into the deep Muskoka chair, slips off her sandals, and watches Maddie jerkily ease her way into the shallow water.

"Maddie? No further." Maddie looks up at her for a few moments and then belly flops back into water that is no more than a foot deep.

"She's a prize, Pen. We are so glad you brought her up."

Pen feels herself stiffen slightly against the hard back of the chair, as if against a cooling breeze. "Things have been kind of chaotic, with the living arrangements and schedules being what they are."

Lea looks pensive, one hand floating up as if to shield her eyes from the glitter off the water. "Bill and I separated once. Years ago, now. It's hard to remember why."

Pen feels stunned by the disclosure. "I had no idea," she says.

"Of course not," Lea says. "We don't talk about it because it doesn't matter. It's different now. All that's in the past."

"It just happened for us," Pen says suddenly, "It kind of had to. It was my idea. I pushed for it. I think you are supposed to bring out the best in your spouse but I haven't been all that wonderful with Jeff."

Lea is thinking about this, nodding her head. "There are cycles to relationships," she says. "Are you better without him, I wonder?"

Pen wants to answer but she has no idea how. "I really don't know."

Maddie has come up the grassy rise and is holding up her towel so she can be rolled up and toweled off. "Hey, little beetle," Lea murmurs, enfolding Maddie in her arms, rubbing her back through the towel to warm her. "If you run in and put on some clothes, we'll eat soon. And don't forget to rinse your feet off before you go into the house." There are rules here, firm and distinct like the upright but graceful backbone of a dancer. Table manners, social graces, the undeniable loveliness of a well-worked thank you note. Maddie thrives on the thoughtful arrangement of activities, the predictability of what will come next. She is charging up the lawn, skin cool from the water, singing something jaunty. She opens the screen door and hurls herself inside.

"You can't know what it means to have you here. All of you," says Lea, her eyes on the still swinging screen door. "You will figure this out, Pen. Your instincts are good. You'll see. You will get back to it, what's important for you, I mean."

Pen says nothing. And then, "I wish I believed that were true."

Lea lightly touches Pen's arm as if to reassure her. "Just a couple of things to do in the kitchen and I want you to sit and enjoy this perfect time of the day. There's still fifteen or twenty minutes before dinner."

Taking a sip from her glass Pen scans the pretty waterfront: a new dock with an outboard boat tied up that bobs congenially against two white bumpers, a small crescent beach, clean with an upturned canoe and sailboat that are tidily paired under a wide-limbed pine tree. Pen had never been canoeing until she came up here

"How is that possible? You, a water girl, born and raised on the shores of Lake Erie?" Bill had asked.

"We didn't canoe in the lake. Some people had canoes, cottagers mostly. They would canoe the river, I guess. But we didn't do that." And then she said, "My father fished for a living," as if that should explain everything. It would be hard for people to understand, she supposes. The lake was their industry. They studied the lake, dared to plunge into it on occasion, but there was instinctual distance, a desire not to domesticate it.

It is different here. No disharmony between the small lake, and the desires and intentions of the residents.

Jeff is beside her. He sits down next to her, on the cooling grass, his arms wrapped around his knees. They say nothing at first. He rubs his hands over his face and sighs. "I know you didn't want to come up here, Pen. It means a lot to me that you did."

She puts a hand on his arm, glad for the moment to know what to do for him. She thinks about what Lea asked: is she better without him?

"I *want* more," he says, "and I know that makes me sound like a kid."

He pulls at some grass between his bare toes and looks up at her. "I want more of you than you have ever given to me."

Something in her stomach contracts. She sees now that he won't wait for her. Not infinitely, at least. She strokes the back of his neck and they sit together and watch the light disappear.

They sit down to dinner in the screened-in porch, Lea and Bill at either ends of a long pine table, candles in a wrought-iron candelabra flicking overhead. Pen doesn't have any more wine. She is more than afraid of losing her social bearings here. Maddie grazes a little on her barbecued chicken and salad, and then goes into the den, where Lea has stocked DVDs for her.

As they sit at the table, Pen feels herself bobbing on the surface of the conversation, her attention wandering, her thoughts restless. It surprises her when Bill puts down his dessert spoon and asks, "Pen, what about that drowning, down in Port? They find out what happened?"

"I don't know for sure," she says. "There still seems to be some investigation going on."

Lea slides up from the table and starts to clear the plates, and Jeff pushes himself up to help.

"Coffee anyone?" Lea calls in from the kitchen.

"Please," says Bill.

"Me too," adds Pen.

Bill leans back in his chair, his face contented. She imagines the gesture is the same, no matter who the guests are that sit at Bill's table.

"It's a dangerous lake," he says. "Could have been an undertow."

"Maybe" she says.

"Likely just a freak accident. They have proper lifeguards on that beach?"

"I don't know, Bill. I don't know much about the beach in Port. It's not my home anymore."

She looks out at the lake, and then shifts her gaze to Bill who now has his hands behind his head.

"People can drown anywhere," she says. "In their pools, a

pond, even their own bathtub." Her eyes go back to the pool of soft velvet that is night time. "It could happen even here."

Bill tactfully drops the conversation about Port and its inadequacies in life-saving. He talks instead about the up-coming federal election, about the absence of strong leadership, how the country has lost its cultural bearings. Pen is carried along by the conversation, relieved to be on safer ground.

17.

PEN HAS BEEN SUNNING HERSELF on the wide, flat rock that juts out over the water, just beyond the dock and the beach. She is on her back, arms open, eyes shut behind sunglasses. Jeff and Maddie have taken out the canoe. For a long time their voices bounce off the pink striated rocks, returning to her in fragments that are crystal clear.

Bill left early for a golf game, and Lea is inside the house. Lea often rests in the middle of the afternoon. Pen recognizes in Lea a thirst for social contact and a need for retreat, a pendulum-like swing in her energy. Perhaps Lea lives with something inescapable, like hindsight, or regret. The children she never had.

Pen's body feels weighted and drowsy while her mind floats over the surface of random objects and events, finding the faces of people who have no apparent connection: Lea, Ben Vasco, Maddie, T. And Keaton. Keaton drops in and out of her thoughts like a bird circling, diving, flying away from her until he is nothing but a dark speck.

It has been only nine days since the drowning but it seems much longer. Time sits differently when she is away from Port. Time in Port is flattened down and has no edges, the usual markers for navigation, missing or unrecognizable. She had careened between one disorienting event and the next in Port, stunned but still moving forward and away, or so she has always thought.

But she is beginning to see that the lake has its influence over her still. *Sweet dreams, my Sweet Pea. See you in the morning.* Rod said goodnight to her the night before the *Isobel* went out and she never saw him again. The lake had simply swallowed him whole. If he had scuttled the *Isobel*, she thinks now, if he had deliberately sabotaged her, it was his life in Port, on the lake, that had brought him to it.

It seems to have made a mark on them all. She thinks of Keaton, his hands bound up in bandages, slipping into the night, and Irene with her props, the AA slogans, the beach stones. And Andy. She thinks of Andy, driving down a highway in a high-end car, jacket off, shirt sleeves rolled, the landscape swimming past him, the place where he is from carved into his skin.

She wonders how the lake tracks Keaton now. Maybe he thought of the fire he set as a kind of escape.

She surveys what she recollects about the burning tug, about Terry Spar and thinks again of Andy. Andy knows something. She can sense him doing some kind of balancing act, still protecting Keaton. Or maybe he just has faith in Keaton, though Pen can't see why.

Pen has never understood the reason for the fire. Terry Spar, *Dolly's* owner, had paid Keaton good money. It was March, early spring and Port was at its emptiest, like a tomb. Keaton had been working on *Dolly* for eighteen months.

He didn't mind the long hours, and by that time he had stopped going to school, except to meet up with Annie Lieb, to walk or sit with her someplace where there were no other people.

But at home, Keaton was becoming more aloof. He was contracted and hard, something unbearable at his centre.

When Keaton set the *Dolly* on fire, from their windows and porches, people all up and down the bluffs witnessed the jerking, stabbing flashes of light. It was hours before the desiccated *Dolly* settled into an innocuous, smoking mass. Keaton was taken to the hospital at first, in St. Thomas. But he hadn't been hurt the way Terry Spar was. Or Andy. Keaton had just burned his hands.

The next day, they took Keaton from the hospital to the OPP station. Emerging from the fragile beginnings of his recovery, Ed raised the bail, signing over a cheque for fifty thousand dollars. Pen knows now that he must have taken it out against his boat.

Keaton took off and Ed lost the money. Ed didn't drink again, at least not that Pen knows. A *turning point*, Irene called it. Enough to make her put her own life in perspective and go with Ed to AA. Years later, Pen asked Irene why Ed would take the risk of losing his boat. Irene only said that once he hit the bottom, Ed wasn't afraid of the worst happening anymore.

Pen lies still for what seems like a long time, and then falls into a light sleep. She wakes when too much sun has made her head throb; her skin is frail-feeling, like parchment. She is uncomfortable but strangely unconcerned, liking the momentary sensation of being separate from herself. She stands on the rock, swinging her arms back and forth, a feeling of anticipation, and then she dives, shocking herself with the cool water. She stays under a long time, pulling herself along with wide, greedy strokes. When she breaks the surface, she tilts her face to the sun, eyes closed. She whirls her legs into the gently resistant water, and through her eyelids she senses the changes in light.

Jeff and Maddie are returning, the canoe cutting through the water, the paddle causing a demure swoosh each time it slips into the water. Maddie is chattering away and Jeff is encouraging her as he guides the canoe. He brings the canoe close to where Pen is treading water.

"Hey there, Lady of the Lake."

Maddie giggles.

"You two go far?"

"All the way around the lake," Jeff says, as proud of Maddie as he might have been if they had made it around Cape Horn and back.

"Find anything interesting?"

Always the right question for Maddie. She solemnly holds up a soggy stick, a broken stem of a weed, a piece of string.

Pen smiles. "Good work, Maddie!"

"I want something to eat," she says earnestly.

"Canoeing makes you hungry," says Pen. "*And* collecting. Sometimes you forget to eat."

Maddie studies Pen and then nods her head in agreement.

Pen watches them paddle back to the dock, Maddie sitting low and obedient, waiting for Jeff's instructions. She has on a life-vest that comes up to her ears and her head is tucked up under a powder-blue Micky Mouse baseball cap. From a distance, cradled in the canoe the way she is, she looks like any little kid, patient and waiting as her dad steers them closer to shore.

18.

BEING AT THE COTTAGE with Bill and Lea had been a good idea. Pen feels as though her limbs have been elongated, her heart slowed.

The first night back in the city, Jeff rests his chin at her shoulder, his tattooed arms, sinewy and graceful, encircling her from behind.

"I feel happy," he says simply.

"I know." She closes her eyes and leans into the plate of bone that covers his heart. They sway together for a long while, poised between an ending and a beginning. She takes his hand and they move up the stairs to her room, *their* room, because their separation is not official.

Their love-making is gentle and slow, with the windows wide open, a chorus of frogs in the trees. The tension has drained: Port, Ben Vasco, the biker massacre. She falls asleep with her arms around him, her forehead pressed against his muscled back.

It is a transitory feeling, being loved, a rare indulgence, and in the morning, still warm, and relaxed, she wakes to the familiar pull of restraint. A small, sad voice warns of the moment when love will simply vanish. There is no smoke signal, no alarm, only this small echo. A memory. A drowning occurs at the beach on the finest sunny day. A man goes out in a fishing tug, as he does every morning, and doesn't return. A brother slips out a window. She cannot rest in someone else's care. She hugs Jeff, loving the mass of him, the loyal intention of his bones, his tissues; still, the voice inside whispers to her, *he is made of sand.*

Three days later, Jeff and Maddie are outside watering the tiny garden that Pen has planted around the deck. It is the first year she has attempted to grow flowers and they have withered terribly in the heat.

"Your flowers are thirsty, Mommy," Maddie observes, her tone instructive. "Nan says that flowers need water or they go back into the earth." Maddie gives attention to each plant, watering the ground to the point of saturation. When she is satisfied, she makes the stream of water into erratic swirls. The neighbour's cat, Sniffy, dives for cover under a bush. Maddie points the hose at Jeff who feigns outrage. They circle around and around the yard, shrieking with laughter, wet splotches spreading on their clothes.

Pen thoroughly scours the kitchen and then makes a second pot of coffee. She sits at the table with the windows open, reading the paper and listening to Jeff and Maddie. Sniffy has crept from under the bush and Maddie, down on all fours, is attempting cat sounds, lifting an open palm as a means of enticement. Maddie would like to have a cat. Pen has always said no, cats are a commitment; cats are messy. They need *care*, she has said to Maddie. Maddie will turn five in October. Pen wonders if it might be time to bring a kitten into the house, to give Maddie, who has no siblings, something to love that is her own.

She finishes the paper and goes outside. Although he has been playing coy with Maddie, Sniffy now saunters over to Pen, his quivering tail held high.

"Cats always go to the person least sympathetic to their cause," observes Jeff wryly. "Don't take it personally, Maddie. Sniffy's fickle."

Pen laughs and strokes Sniffy's orange fur. "Sniffy's allowed to have preferences," she says. "And I *am* sympathetic."

Maddie stands beside Pen, one hand on Pen's thigh and the

other stroking Sniffy under the chin. The cat winds around and around Maddie's legs and Maddie increases her caresses, stroking the whole length of him. For the moment, a mutually gratifying arrangement.

It's getting close to eleven when the department administration assistant calls for Pen.

"There was a message left on the general voice mail for you last night. Someone looking for you. Regarding your brother."

The administrator quickly adds that apparently, it isn't an urgent matter. Pen says thank you and writes down the relevant information: Doctor Lynne McTeer, from Victoria Hospital, Prince George, BC.

At first, Pen is completely still. The sun is streaming into the kitchen and the room is suddenly stifling hot, the air laced with the smell of cleaning fluid, suntan lotion, the garbage under the sink waiting to be taken out. Wanting movement, she gets up and paces.

Her hand is shaking when eventually she pushes the numbers into the phone. She has to wait for Doctor McTeer to get on the line. There is nothing but muffled noise, static on the other end. And then a young woman's voice, high and brightly chiming.

"Sorry to have to track you down that way," she says. "Your brother didn't have your home number so I Googled you and your university contact information came up."

Pen thinks of the two phone calls she has had from Keaton, one only a few months before. Something happened for him to lose the number. The possibilities parade in front her, grim, obdurate.

"I don't like to have to explain his situation to you over the phone. He's close by and he's okay. While he's here, I'll be the psychiatrist in charge of his care."

Pen lets this register.

"Is Keaton hurt?"

"The physical injuries are pretty minor. But the incident that caused them is a concern. He's been admitted to hospital on an involuntary basis. He'll likely stay here with us until he's stabilized and can put in a court appearance."

Court. What happened in Port will finally catch up with him. Pen closes her eyes and forces herself to open them again.

"What are the charges?"

"I don't know all the details, actually. I'm still waiting for a police report. And he isn't telling us much about his circumstances. For instance, what he is doing here. The only thing he would tell us is that he has a sister in Ontario. It was a while before he would give us your name."

Pen says nothing and after a few moments, Doctor McTeer goes on. "It would be helpful to know whether there is a history of mental illness, substance abuse, serious medical problems, anything we should be aware of in making an assessment of what's going on now."

Pen takes in a breath. For a moment she is mute, afraid she will be unable to say or do anything but frown into the carpet. She looks at her bare feet, rigid and turning blue. At the same time, an energy stirs, impatient, demanding. *Where did you go, Keaton?*

"I haven't seen him in several years. I've probably missed a lot. There are some things in his past, part of our life here, when we were kids. For the rest, I wouldn't know."

Then, "If I leave in the morning, I can be out there tomorrow afternoon."

"Good. Yes, dealing with some of that might help him to find his way back. Maybe you would like to have a couple of words with him now? I can get him for you. It will help with the first meeting."

His voice is guarded when he comes on the line. "You don't need to come out, Pen."

"Really? They went to the effort to call me, Keaton. For a *reason.*"

"Just forget the call. Don't come."

There is a sound of swallowed emotion. The effort of holding back makes his words seem laboured. Or it is just the bad line? She presses the receiver closer to her ear.

"I'm going to come, Keaton." Her voice is full of sideways panic, an anger that seems wild and unexplainable. He won't tell her what to do this time. He won't tell her to stay behind.

She goes to the patio door and tells Jeff that she needs to talk to him. When he steps inside his face searches hers. "I have to go to Prince George. It's in British Columbia. Something with Keaton."

"I *know* where Prince George is, Pen."

"Well, he's in the hospital there. Under psychiatric care."

"I'm coming with you," he says frowning, his head shaking off her response.

"No, Jeff."

"You have to let me come. You haven't seen him in years. You have no idea what kind of messed-up state he could be in. Irene and Ed will come up and get Maddie." He's reaching for the phone now, all that kinetic energy focused on a single predetermined task.

She sits and stares at the same spot in the carpet she focused on when talking with Keaton.

"He might have done something really bad." She's thinking of the bikers, of her own father. People whose actions are not comprehensible.

"Maybe. Maybe he has."

She studies Jeff. A man taking the measure of a car wreck, a battlefield. In a fraction of a second, she decides that whatever is in Keaton, whatever craziness, it is hers to deal with.

Pen takes the phone from him. "I don't think so, Jeff," she says gently.

He looks at her, surprised, and she reaches out, touches the hard knot of muscle on the top of his shoulder. "I don't want you to *see* it."

Jeff is rubbing at his shaved head, one hand drumming insistently on his knee. "Christ, Pen. He's not you."

She sighs and looks behind her to where Maddie is now sitting on the deck, tearing petals from a flower, a garden trowel, a branch, a piece of a bird's nest lined up beside her. She looks completely engrossed in her creation, this collection of objects, this small and very particular world of hers. "You can't help, Jeff. Not with this."

The old frustration has come back into his face. He heads in the direction of Maddie and then he turns. "You can't keep doing this to me, Pen. You have to make a choice."

The study is on the third floor and Pen goes up the narrow stairs like a sleepwalker. It doesn't take long to book her ticket. She will fly out the next day, first thing. She begins to make a mental list of what she has to do before leaving. There are still some loose ends with her course. She opens her email and types in a message to the administrative assistant, asking her to confirm her book orders, and send off a course outline to the Chair of the department. Then she answers some inquiries from students, a request for a response from one of the department support staff. She decides to email the Chair, explaining that she has a family emergency, and that she will try and keep up with all departmental communications. Last, she emails her thesis supervisor, who is away at a cottage for the summer and probably doesn't care what she does.

She suddenly thinks of Keaton as he was when she last saw him, awkwardly cramming clothes into a hockey bag, his hands still in bandages. In the morning, when Ed discovered that Keaton was gone, he took off his cap. "Goddamn," he said, shaking his head. "Goddamn boy."

What followed was a somber acceptance of Keaton's disappearance, Ed and Irene not talking about him, in time, Irene going to AA meetings every day. Had Irene thought that, if she was good enough, it would bring them all back? Keaton, Rod, Terry Spar's wrecked boat?

Pen thinks about calling Irene, imagines her picking up the phone and hearing the news that Keaton has been located, that he's hurt. Irene would say the Serenity Prayer, adopting an attitude of acceptance for whatever is to come. Her calm, so different from how Pen feels now, will leave Pen feeling utterly alone.

Before she shuts down the computer, she types in a message to Andy, his address from the card he gave her in Port. "Going to Keaton tomorrow, at a hospital in Prince George, BC. I want to talk to you before I go, so I'll call in the morning. Leave your cell phone on."

19.

T IS SITTING IN HIS TRUCK, the windows down, inhaling deeply on a cigarette. In front of him is the Sadie and Ivan Rolstein Pavilion, the lettering plain above the smoky glass doors. The sun glints off the dark polished façade, a granite aggregate, T supposes, a strange choice, like a mausoleum. People walk past the old, the frail and the weary.

A few minutes ago, his hands were shaking. That was a surprise. He can't remember shaking since he was a kid, alone in a yard full of other kids, his head pushed up against the chain link. "You're a dirty Indian who fucks his sister." On the far side of the yard, the Indian kids watched with that slow and steady look they had, a tempered patience that offered no help. T was no more than six, and the kid throttling him was probably already twelve or thirteen. He was white with an eruption of angry-looking pimples and his teeth were brown with scale. T especially remembers his mouth, twisted and ugly, betraying a special hatred, not the routine animus of biker gangs, but personal. He'd seen that kind of hatred before, in the men his mother brought home, white men, losers, who called her Bucky Bride. She had a contract with those men, a kind of pact with the devil.

T finds that the cigarette makes him feel a rush of strength again, of courage, which is crazy because the cigarettes are going to kill him. He is as sure now as Moose must have been when he was staring into the barrel of T's Taurus-410.

A couple of days ago, T had come to the Rolstein Pavilion for a consultation and the biopsy. A short time after, there was a call to arrange an appointment for him to discuss the results.

"You can't just tell me over the phone?" T asked the receptionist.

"Oh, you will want to talk to the doctor, Mister Valentine. Actually, we require that you come in."

T looks around the parking lot, half-expecting a swat team to pull in at any moment. Most of the cars are Grand Marquis and Sebrings with old people climbing out stiffly from the driver's seat, but there is the odd mini-van. Christ, do people with kids get sick like this too? His mother died, hadn't she? And she did *that* to herself, just like he'd done *this* to himself. T hisses out smoke through closed teeth and thinks about kids who get dropped, who get orphaned, a world full of lost kids. His kid has Eva and probably her Jesus parents to help out. There's a stab of pain in his chest, a hot insistent squeeze that makes him hold his breath. For a moment his eyes go blurry. It's a new sort of pain and it shoots right through him.

There will be the house, some money he's got tucked away; all of it will go to Eva and his kid. It suddenly becomes very important that he arrange for that, that he talks to someone who can make it official. The parking lot is more than three-quarters full with not a police van in site. The idea of cruising around the Ontario highway system, parking in a public lot in broad daylight is a stupid one. Well, if it's just the cops who find him, let them have at it. He'll hold out his wrists and ask them to lock up the truck.

The morning after the shootings, with the bodies still in the cars in the field, B.J had called T on his cell. "You been suckered, T. Get the hell outta there."

"Christ." T had disconnected and looked at the crew who were sprawled around the farmhouse like a pack of sleeping dogs. Someone had ratted them out, either in this crew or higher up the chain, but he wouldn't make that assessment, not then.

For the moment, there was a beautiful simplicity to what had to be done. He doesn't like to overthink, a trait that has protected him from his other self, that self with sentiments. He went to Jason first who was crashed on the floor, his arms spread over his head, a little pink glow in his cheeks. With the first blow of T's boot to the kid's side, Jason yelped and curled into a ball.

"Shit, T! You're gonna break a rib!"

"Don't be an idiot. Get your ass up and wake everyone."

It took only a couple of minutes, and the crew were standing in the kitchen, bleary-eyed, wary. T told them what B.J. said. He told them they should keep their heads down for a while and contact no one, not even him. They cleared off, riding in all directions, no last-ditch attempt to shift bodies or clean up the site. He watched them go and then he left too, heading north on the secondary roads, up to Bruce County where he could find a safe house with an old buddy.

The cops must have blown into the farm later that morning because by noon, the biker massacre, as they called it, was all over the news.

When T rented the farm, he'd followed procedure: no names and a cheque that was issued to the landlord by a business in the city, a front. Still, if they hadn't already done so, it wouldn't take the cops long to put it together. There's enough evidence at the site to put T and the rest of them away for eternity, but that doesn't matter to T. Not anymore.

He could have skipped the appointment and just turned himself in, but he needed to hear what was in store for him. In his lifetime, T has spent too much time waiting for orders, waiting for payback, not *knowing* shit. Now, he wants to know what's around the next bend in the road, even if it's bad.

Going to the appointment would make him a target; it was far better to drive his buddy's old contracting truck, wear a hat, keep the windows up and avoid going in to any coffee shops. T is marked now. His own organization might take him out, just to keep things tidy. Or the Angels would, for the certainty of having no obstacles remaining between themselves and an otherwise wide open territory. T doesn't want to be taken out by a squad of Angels. He thinks of them as part of the great faceless machine. He prefers to take his chances with the cancer. *His* cancer.

Stage four, the doctor told him. T didn't know exactly what it meant but he didn't need to ask for clarification either. The doctor had given it anyway, perhaps for his own comfort more than T's; the cancer was advanced, terminal. If T had been planning something, a big trip, a celebration, he should do it now. Tie up any loose ends, the doctor suggested helpfully, take care so as not to have any *regrets.*

"You're kidding, right?" T hadn't meant it to sound sarcastic.

"This *will* happen," the doctor said. "I'm very sorry there isn't more we can do."

"I get it," said T.

"There are ways of managing things," the doctor went on, "such as dealing with discomfort, perhaps even slowing down the progress of the disease with palliative chemo. There is pain management as needed."

"We'll have to see," said T. He nodded to the doctor. "Thanks."

He won't go as far as to say he was expecting to hear this news, this foretelling, but he wasn't surprised by it.

As he left the office, he began to sweat. He was trembling, and his bowels began to twist.

As he walked out into the daylight, something besides fear hit him. A thrill. The kind he had jumping into the lake when he was a kid, everything hanging in the balance until it didn't anymore. Nothing left to do but swim.

20.

SOMEWHERE OVER THE PRAIRIES, Pen slips into a light sleep. She dreams about the lake, the cycling of species, the extinctions and resurrections, constant unstoppable erosion. In two hundred years, the scientists say, the lake will become so silted-up that it will be no more than a wide and slow-moving river. Images flit through her mind of super-accelerated topographical changes, flashes of landscape now unrecognizable, a lake erased by time.

"Hey, there's a piece in here about the bikers, Pen." She opens her eyes with a start. Andy is leaning into her, holding out the paper, wearing a stretched expression of excitement.

She hadn't expected to find Andy waiting for her at the airport. It was still early when Jeff dropped her off at the kiss-and-fly. Maddie, who had been dragged out of bed at five, was half-dozing in the back seat, sullen and grumpy. Pen hugged her.

"We could come *too*, with you, on the plane," Maddie said, her tone between complaint and hurt. She scowled and then wrapped her arms around Pen's neck.

Out of the car, wearing one of his many black T-shirts, this one faded with Def Leopard in gothic writing on the front, Jeff's hug was fierce, unequivocal. When he finally let go of her, there were tears in his eyes. He swept a thick arm across his cheeks so Maddie wouldn't see.

Pen pulled her bag out of the trunk and set it on the sidewalk.

"I didn't think I would have to go and retrieve my brother like this." It sounded like an excuse, for leaving, just when things were better between them.

"You can call me, Pen. Every day if you want."

She busied herself, pulling out her e-ticket, checking the zippers on her bag. He crossed his arms and studied the massive terminal building beside them. When he looked back at her, the look was weighted. "You'll *want* to talk to Maddie."

She straightened. "Of course, Jeff. I'll call."

She stepped toward the terminal doors, turning to wave, but he had already pulled away from the curb. She watched him jockeying his way through the tide of taxis and shuttles, and then disappear from view.

Inside the terminal, early morning travellers strode across the concourse with rolling-cases, messenger bags. A business crowd for the most part. With her back to the line-up of people forming at the check-in counter, she pushed Andy's number into her phone. It took three rings for him to pick up. She had just started to tell him about Keaton when she felt a touch at her elbow. Andy was beside her, his phone still in his ear, and wearing a half-apologetic grin.

She must have looked baffled, seeing him there. She had no idea what to say. Andy put an arm around her shoulders and gave her a quick reassuring squeeze.

"Couldn't resist finding out what the old boy has been up to, Pen."

An hour later they were taxiing down the runway, the plane clattering and shuddering. Pen's jaws clenched against the upward thrust, her hands locked onto her knees.

"What will it be like when I see him?" she asked suddenly.

Andy had slipped the morning paper into the space between his thigh and the armrest. "Chances are, he won't look the same, Pen, or even act the same. But it's still him."

The plane levelled off and Pen felt herself disappear into the thrumming sound of the engines, an in-flight magazine closed on her lap. And then she slept and dreamed that she was standing in a river that was once a lake, knowing and not knowing where she was.

"This story," Andy says now, leaning into Pen with the morning paper, "is crazy. If this is right, these guys did this to *themselves*." He taps her arm with the paper. "Your guy is right at the centre of it, blood all over his hands."

The fury about the massacre has died down. Pen has to rustle through several sheets of newsprint before she finds the article. In the far bottom left is a photograph of a fiftyish man, with a broad forehead, wide nose, a face that looks worn, the skin chaffed, colourless. His hair is pulled back off his face and he is glowering, as if he is looking into the sun. She sees right away that it is T. Underneath his picture, the article says that Mr. Valentine had recently rented the farmhouse which later became the site of the murders.

...Evidence suggests an "inside job." Apparently, the victims were all members of a particular club, the Banditos, which had been attempting an expansion. Despite enjoying only a small presence in Canada, the club was attempting to go head to head with the Hell's Angels, who are the preeminent outlaw gang in Quebec, and the far western part of the country. It is likely that the victims had been ordered to take on the Angels for the purpose of establishing a greater western foothold. Having surmised that their chances of dethroning the Angels were poor, the victims apparently refused the directive. Insubordination in Biker culture can be fatal...

Pen reads detailed descriptions of the bodies, their placement in the cars and the tractor, the kinds of weapons that were used for the killings. The possibility that this was an inside job makes the whole mess more sordid; that T is implicated in the killings makes her profoundly sad.

She imagines T as she last saw him in the clinic, grey-faced, drained. Another image comes to mind. She thinks of T Valentine hurling himself into the water, propelled by some interior force, free as a bird.

It is still afternoon when they land. The rental car is clean and smells of plastic. They travel a highway that winds through acres of rock and dusty-grey trees. An inky lake appears and then disappears, and the smell of a paper mill finds its way into the car through the vents. She asks Andy to stop.

"I feel sick," she says. "Car sick," she adds because she feels like she should explain. The sun overhead seems very yellow and everything around her looks brittle and dry.

"Just walk a bit. Get some oxygen." Andy climbs out of the car and languorously stretches his arms and rests them on the hood. He gazes at the scenery, detached from it but not unappreciative. "Not easy country, but beautiful."

She turns away and walks along the shoulder. A truck roars past. She takes her hair in her fist and feels her forehead, which is clammy and damp. Her stomach cramps. Beside the road, there is some long grass. She steps into it and bends over, bringing her focus down to the few square inches around her sneakered feet. She is sick, and then endures one or two dry heaves. After, there is an empty feeling, not precisely relief. She breathes deeply and then walks back to the car on shaky legs. Andy is leaning against the car door with his cell phone in his hand.

"You okay?"

"Yeah. I think I'm good to go," she says, not looking at him, pulling the hair back from her face.

"No rush," he says, turning off the phone. "Your colour is a little off."

She opens the car door. "I feel like we should get there," she says, frowning.

Andy shrugs and then gets in the car, turns on the ignition. "You want me to stop in somewhere? A pharmacy?"

"We should just go."

He turns the car off again and looks at her, his expression earnest. "He's not going anywhere. The two of us, *we* have already had to wait a long time to see him."

In profile, she can see only the good side of his face, but for an instant she is sure that she can see the slightest tracing of a long white scar there, or perhaps it is the unexpected tightening of his mouth, a hardening of his features. He starts the car and as soon as it moves, the light shifts and what she saw before is gone.

"Are you angry with Keaton?" she asks, opening her water bottle, taking a few sips.

"Sure," he says. "Little tool." The tone is amiable.

Pen pauses. "It was a serious question."

He shrugs. "I probably was. It seems like a long time ago."

They drive on in silence.

"Andy? Do you think the biker guy, T, knew that his life would end up the way it has? I mean, why live that kind of lifestyle if the cost is a dead end?"

Andy tilts his head.

"He probably knew the risks." He shrugs. "People don't always recognize their options."

She stares out at the road in front of them, trying to imagine why it is that people choose the things that they do. If T had chosen to kill all those people, he had also chosen to dive into the lake after Ben Vasco. She thinks about what Keaton has done, the parts of his life that are hidden from her. When she imagines Keaton, he is bitter, impatient, the person he became after Rod disappeared. The person who burned the *Dolly* and then ran away. She pushes back a wave of fear about seeing him. One thought remains clear, anchored in memory, undeniably true. Keaton was her brother once. They had cared for one another.

"I've changed my mind, Andy. Pull off at the next coffee place you see."

When Andy gets out of the car, she tells him she'll be right back. She goes into the coffee shop, orders two bottles of water, and takes them around the back of the building. She places a call to Detective Sinclair.

"Yes. I think there's something you should know," she says, taking in a deep draw of air. "About T Valentine."

Another long pause.

"Sorry. I'm not clear about the connection. What about Tom Valentine?"

"Tom Valentine is the man connected with all those murders, right?"

"Allegedly one of them, yes."

"Did you know he was there the day of the drowning?"

"He didn't exactly come in and give a statement, if that's what you mean."

"Well, he was. I recognized his picture," says Pen.

"Okay. Maybe so. Well, the Valentine arrest and everything around that whole situation is being handled by the RCMP."

"Sure. I know. I just thought that it might be important…"

"Bikers go to the beach too. It doesn't change that they are bikers."

She thinks of the insurance investigators, the steady, knowing look in their eyes when they asked about her father, his money troubles, and the problems with Irene. Eyes steady because minds were already made up.

"I'm just saying he had a role to play. That day on the beach. He was the first one in. T Valentine dove into the water before anyone else. He tried to save Ben Vasco. Do you see what I mean?"

"Do you mean he did a good thing that day?"

"I just thought someone should know what he did, that's all."

There is a long sigh. Detective Sinclair is thinking, but not really wanting to think about this too hard. "Okay. Well. I'll add it to the file. Anyone else see him go?"

Pen pulls up the memory of the line of people at the water's edge, human forms joined at the hands like a string of paper cut-outs. "Yes. Probably a few."

"I don't think anyone has mentioned a biker in their account of what happened," he says patiently.

"Maybe people didn't think of him like that. Like a biker."

The detective clears his throat. "Kind of hard to miss, don't you think?"

"Look, he was in the water. Up to his chin."

"I see."

She doesn't think he does. "Well, it should be considered, right?"

"I'll make that note and I'll mention it to one of the investigators on the federal end. But they've got their hands full. I doubt this is going to mean very much to them."

"Thanks for that."

She hears him mumble something.

They check in to their hotel and once they have put their luggage into their adjoining rooms, opened the heavy curtains, adjusted the ventilation systems, they meet in Pen's room, Andy sitting in the small club chair with an ankle crossed over his knee. Pen has changed her shirt and brushed her teeth.

"I think we should eat something," he says, watching her come out of the washroom.

"I need to see him, Andy."

"Yeah. And you need to do it with some fuel in the tank," he says. "At least I do. I'm not going into any hospital feeling like I might pass out and eat the floor. Generally not a good policy."

The woman at the desk shows no curiosity when they ask for directions. The hospital, she says, is on the north hill of the city. She hands them a photocopied map from under the counter and puts a big "X" where the hospital is. Looking at it, Pen tries to imagine Keaton as a single fixed point on a map. She concentrates on it, willing herself to put faith there, the way sailors had to set their faith on the stars. But Pen thinks about the earth turning, and how much time has passed, and how nothing is ever what it seems.

21.

THE HOSPITAL SQUATS AGAINST a scrubby hill on the north side of town. It is boxy, with low outcropping additions and a covered, multi-tiered parking arcade. A fortress adapted for northern weather. She imagines that here, the winter buries people, the snow coming in like an invading army each fall, silent and cunning. It would claim every last inch of open ground. Even under the trees, in all the gullies, ravines and hollows.

When Keaton and Pen were kids in Port, winter was just another of the lake's moods. Sometimes in a temper, the lake spat out snow squalls and winds that closed the schools. Winter could be crashing waves, rolling skies, the beach swept clear of any sign of snow. Other days were downright balmy. It was the water that changed everything.

"Do you think he's been living here, all these years?" she asks Andy, trying to imagine Keaton in this unfamiliar place: it is a young Keaton she thinks of now, the Keaton she knew before Rod disappeared. It is somehow both easier and more sad to think of him that way. A small figure engulfed in infinite snowfalls, wave upon wave.

Andy doesn't answer. He tucks the parking pass into the visor, and navigates the rental car into a tight spot between two SUVs.

They sit in the cave-like dark.

"You want me to come into the room with you, Pen?" Andy asks. There is a rare tightness in his tone. It tugs her back to what she must do: get out of the car and walk to a brown metal door marked entrance. And then she must find Keaton. She studies Andy and wonders if maybe he is looking for a way out.

"You don't have to..." she says. "I'm not looking for help."

Andy is swinging himself out of the car, stretching a little, tilting his head from side to side as if to crack his neck. From outside of the car, he says,

"Of course not. The Beaus don't ask for help. Besides, that's not why I came here. I have reasons of my own." His tone is neutral. He says it as a matter of fact.

She says nothing. There had been stories about Andy, tales that circulated through the halls of the elementary school long after Andy and Keaton moved on to high school. He wasn't always an athletic star, the school darling. At eleven years of age, Andy weighed one hundred and sixty pounds and was close to five foot, eleven inches. He moved slowly, his child-brain unsure of how to maneuver his adult body. He was better on skates, but his peers didn't know that about him then. His easygoing manner was taken to be a sign of stupidity. "A retard." He was taunted, bullied, except by Keaton, something Pen guesses that Andy has never forgotten.

Andy bends down and puts his face into the car and grins the lop-sided grin.

"Guess we could drive around for a bit and come back..."

"No. It's fine. I'm coming." She gathers up her bag and hurries away from the car.

On the floor designated *psychiatry*, a nurse perches in a chair behind the counter, a pen tucked neatly behind one ear. She shifts a stack of charts.

"And what can we do for you?" For a moment, her eyes rest on the piercing in Pen's eyebrow.

"I'm looking for my brother. Keaton Beau."

The nurse pulls a chart from a file holder and scans it. "Right. You must be the sister from Ontario."

"I am. Can you tell us how he is?"

She flips through a few pages in the chart. "Minor cuts, broken ribs. And some burns to his hands."

"How did he get all of that?"

The nurse shrugs. "Well, when they live that kind of life, they are prone to risk — accidents, other things."

Pen feels herself redden, thinking about the investigators after Rod's disappearance, about the police after Keaton broke his bail. Her family under scrutiny. A family of runners, of drunks.

"You can wait in the family room," the nurse goes on. "We have to page Doctor McTeer." There is a pause. "She'll definitely want to chat with you."

Andy is leaning against the counter. "Thanks," he says, tapping the counter's surface with his fingertips. "Don't trouble yourself. We'll find it on our own."

She has directed them to a small room that is over-stuffed with two sagging sofas and three armchairs, a TV, and a bookshelf filled with ancient paperbacks. The air is stale and dry and the lighting is a penetrating cold blue. Pen is suddenly and desperately in need of a washroom and finds one close by. She lets the cold water run for a long time and then splashes her face twice, avoiding meeting her own eyes in the mirror. She would like nothing more than to bolt.

Back in the family room, Andy has two paper cups of take-out coffee from the cafeteria. He puts one down on the arm of the chair next to Pen. They don't speak, though Andy finds it in himself to flip through an outdated *Sports Illustrated* magazine.

They hear Doctor McTeer before she enters: a brisk determined step, light and unmistakably feminine. She is pretty, and about the same age as Pen.

"Hi," she reaches out a neat hand, and smiles. "I'm Doctor McTeer."

"Pen Beau." Doctor McTeer shifts her eyes to Andy and nods her head.

"And this is Andy, Keaton's closest friend," Pen adds. "I'd like him to stay."

They are all seated, Doctor McTeer on the edge of the armchair, a folder resting in her lap. "I'm really glad you made the trip. Family support means everything. And friends. All the difference." Her words are rushed. "Your brother will meet with you soon. I just thought that first, you should know his situation."

"On the phone, you mentioned charges."

"Yes. That's right. He's been charged in connection with a fire that was set in an old mission school outside of town. It hasn't been used since the late nineteen-sixties. Probably should have been demolished long ago."

Pen had read about mission schools. She thinks of bare feet on freezing floor boards, nuns wielding straps if children spoke in their native tongue.

"What was Keaton doing there?"

Doctor McTeer cocks her head and considers this. "We don't really know, but it's likely that he was living there. People have, over the years. There are dorms, old mattresses, even a fireplace."

"So he was living like some kind of indigent," says Pen darkly.

Doctor McTeer looks at Andy. "Lots of people here live a sort of, hmmm, free-style life. It's a sort of *choice*, you see..."

"Was he trying to hurt himself?" Pen interjects.

"It's possible. At least, we know it was deliberate. There were gas cans, lighters, the whole thing."

"My God."

"Doctor McTeer crosses her arms, drums her small, light fingers against the upper flesh of her arms. "And there is something that makes it more serious. Someone else was with him. A woman. She was sleeping in one of the rooms upstairs when the emergency people got there. It isn't clear what he was trying to do... "

"So he's been charged with trying to hurt her?"

"Yes." The Doctor's eyes slip away and then hold Pen's again. "And she isn't speaking. She isn't talking to anyone, and neither is he."

"Who is she? Do you know who?"

Doctor McTeer is shaking her head. "No. Probably someone he hooked up with along the way. We see that a lot. People drift together for a time and then they part ways. This time, something went very wrong. I know I asked you about some of this. It's very important. Do you know if your brother had any addictions, or history of psychiatric problems?"

Pen is frowning into her cold cup of coffee. She decides in the moment to not say anything about Keaton setting fire to the *Dolly*.

"I haven't seen my brother in years. He's probably a very different person now." Doctor McTeer is waiting for her to say more. She thinks about biting her fingernail but instead, puts her hands firmly between her knees.

"What will happen?" she asks.

"We have to complete a psych. assessment, and the police will want to finish their investigation." Doctor McTeer's voice becomes quieter, almost apologetic. "As part of that, they will want to speak to you."

Pen is silent for a moment;

"Does he know I'm here?"

"Yes, he knows. I think he's glad." Doctor McTeer's voice is kind, encouraging.

"I'd like to meet with you again, before you leave. People in his situation don't always know what they should and shouldn't say."

She thinks of Keaton, running from Port, leaving nothing but questions behind him. All that silence hadn't helped any of them.

"I'll give you a full history," she says, "after I've seen him."

"Fair enough," Doctor McTeer says, rising from her chair.

Andy gives the name of their hotel, their cell numbers, and says that they haven't confirmed a return flight.

"I'll go and get Keaton for you. I think meeting with him here is as good a place as any."

After she leaves, Pen looks over at Andy.

"There is no way he was trying to hurt anyone, Andy. No way. It must have been an accident."

Andy isn't saying anything, but Pen knows that the gas cans, the matches, probably even more evidence than they know about, all point to the fire being intentional. She watches Andy as he gets up heavily, his face tired, the scars white against the tanned skin. He puts a hand on the door. "You better talk to him first on your own, Pen."

"Andy. Stay. Please?"

He pauses for a moment. "He hasn't seen me in a long time," he says, hesitating. He is thinking of how Keaton will react, seeing him with his scars. He shrugs. "What the hell...."

It isn't long before Keaton comes into the room. The recognition Pen feels is instantaneous. He has the look of a man in early middle age, the features less sharp than they were, the head thicker, the frame softer. But his face is gaunt, and there are shadows and lines where there weren't before. Despite the crescents of purplish-grey beneath them, the dark eyes are the same. There is an unnatural stillness around his body, a particular slowness in his limbs that doesn't seem to belong to him; she imagines that she sees the old restlessness, a tension in his deepest layers. She stands for a moment and then goes to him, wraps her arms around his neck and Keaton pulls an arm up and rests it on her shoulder. After a few moments, he puts both of his arms around her and squeezes tight.

When Keaton sees Andy, his body straightens a little, the energy climbing up into his neck and shoulders. Pen pulls away, and Keaton stares at his friend, who is on his feet now, a smile engulfing the entire right side of his face, the left side straining.

"Oh, Andy."

Keaton has tears in his eyes. Real tears. Pen can't remember ever seeing him cry.

Andy takes him first by the arm and then folds him in a bear hug. "You little jerk," he says. "Sit down and tell us what you've done this time."

Pen can't take her eyes off him.

22.

KEATON TELLS PEN AND ANDY how it is that the mission school burned with Annie Lieb in an upstairs room. At first, Pen shakes her head at the mention of Annie, as if to correct him, pull him back on a truer course, but he insists on using her name when talking about his life: "Me and Annie…" he says, and finally Pen begins to let belief take shape. Annie it seems, has been a part of this all along, and there is an unexpected relief in the discovery that Keaton has never been completely alone.

An image of Annie and Keaton comes, their hands clasped together, spirits roaming over the beach, the town. After he fled from Port, Keaton called Annie's house, disguising his voice when her mother answered. Annie's parents had never liked that he was her only friend.

Keaton takes in a breath, and rests his head on the back of the couch. His words are strained, dry. "People in Port had opinions about the Beaus. What happened to our dad," he says, "Irene and her carrying on with Ed… But everything turned really dark after the fire." Pen remembers the talk about Keaton then, that he was disturbed to do something like he did. "Annie's parents would have called the police if they saw me anywhere near her."

He had to stay under cover. It would have been too risky to come back into Port. He would have been caught, locked away. He looks at Pen when he says this. "I thought about trying it, coming to see you, after dark, but I didn't know what Irene would do if she found out. We weren't on the best of terms when I left."

For the first few months, he stayed close by, working in the barns for a dairy farmer too deaf and too ornery to care much about burned-up fishing boats or young men who jump bail. Keaton slept in a small outbuilding with a cot and a heater, and in this way, by early winter, he had enough money to leave completely and take Annie with him.

He talks about Annie as though for him, she had some irresistible pull, as though she was his only direction. Annie had simply met him on the outside of town. The walk into St. Thomas wasn't hard for them. After all, they had walked for hours together, all over Port. Keaton had the money saved up for bus tickets; they were gone before anyone thought to look. The Greyhound took them as far as Winnipeg, where they stayed at a Sally Ann shelter, and then Keaton found work in the rail yard.

They always managed to find a room somewhere, a place with a hot plate or the use of a kitchen and bath. Annie didn't like how cold it was on the prairies. She said if he was trying to hide out, it was like hiding in a fish bowl with all that flat land and sky. It was her idea to go further, find a different place. She had always been restless, even in Port, roaming the ravines, walking beyond the public boundaries of the beach. Strangely the restlessness made him feel safe. "An energy," he says, "that is bigger than you."

Pen remembers how he was after Rod disappeared, his wire-tight tension, how he looked like he might have jumped out of his own skin. She imagines that the energy Annie and Keaton fed on in one another was disturbing and vast, as essential to them as air.

By the first spring, they had made it all the way to the west coast. Annie loved the size of the trees, the clean, salty breeze. It was the sight of the water that Keaton liked, the lines of fishing boats lashed to the docks, the strong pacific blue spanning out to the clusters of dark green islands in the distance.

The salmon run was expected to be poor again that season, as it had been for some time. Owner-operators of fishing vessels weren't looking to pick up extra crew unless they had to.

Keaton just happened upon a boat where one of the men had fallen and broken a foot the week before. The boat's captain was eager to get the boat out, and so he signed up Keaton on the spot.

Keaton worked hard, and anyone could see how at home he was on a boat. And the Pacific Ocean was surprisingly docile compared to Erie — the rain, the occasional fog — more a backdrop to a Hollywood film, when he remembered the storms on the lake. Sometimes, he told them, it was like he was dreaming.

In the meantime, Annie found a job making beds in a motel. Soon they had enough to rent a little apartment in a low-rise apartment building with a balcony, tucked into the cedars. It was like being in a kid's tree house.

They would have stayed living that way, with him fishing and her working for the motel. He was happy on the coast. As it was, they were there for more than three years, and then something started to change with Annie. When he was away on the boats, Annie didn't eat. She had always been thin, but now her hip bones protruded and her arms were like sticks. He tried. He left her packages of food — cheese strings, granola bars, cans of soup — and notes on the fridge reminding her to fix herself something. It didn't seem to make a difference. The skin under her eyes, on the inside of her arms, began to go a grey-blue, and she slept all the time. Keaton came to the conclusion that Annie was starving herself to death.

He took her to a clinic and the doctor there ordered hospitalization. She needed re-hydration, and then a slow regime of reintroducing foods.

The hospital kept her for six weeks, until her weight stabilized, and the medication had a chance to work. And then, when she got out, Annie said she wanted to leave Vancouver.

She loved it there, she told him. She really did. But she also said that the place felt like a lie. The water made her think about Port, except it wasn't Port. She didn't know what was real and what wasn't anymore.

He didn't ask her if she wanted to go home. When he says this, his face clouds over. "I could have sent her back, on her own, and she would have been looked after." He rubs at his forehead with the knob of his wrist. They had been away from Port for a long time by then. Annie had called her parents once, years before. They knew she was with him, though she told them no, they were wrong. They were dogged, pragmatic people and they would have been determined to find her, thinks Pen.

"They must have put a call in to the police," Keaton says, looking at Pen, reading her thoughts. Pen knows that the police would have contacted Irene, told them that Annie and Keaton were probably together. Pen stares back at him blankly. "Irene never told me that Annie was with you, Keaton."

Keaton shrugs. "Irene must have decided to leave it alone."

They started moving from one small town in the interior to the next. As much as he hated to, he worked in hotels and taverns mostly. They were horrible places, Keaton tells them. He began to drink on the job to make the shifts go faster. A couple of times he got into fights and was fired, but he was careful not to get charged. He didn't want there to be any way that he could be traced back to Port. "Christ Pen, I know I called you from one of those dumps. I don't know what I said." The first call, she thinks.

Annie went off her medication. She said the pills erased her, made her stop seeing things, feeling things. Going off them didn't matter at first. Keaton had been suspicious of the drug's sedating effects, and now she was Annie, like she had been before.

But then the change came. It wasn't that he turned a blind eye to it. Maybe it was a year or more, but he couldn't be sure.

"It's how she is. You have to know her," he tells them.

He came home one night after a shift at the tavern; minus thirty-two below Celsius and the air as sharp as a blade. Annie's coat was hanging on the back door, and her boots were in the corner, but the door was open. He found her wandering around the streets wearing just a pair of jeans and a sweatshirt.

Keaton had to carry her back to the room. He made her strong tea and put her to bed. Then he drank a lot of whiskey and wondered what the hell they were going to do. It's when it first occurred to him that she might die. Go off into the woods like something wounded, or stop eating and die in her bed.

He drank more; to keep her from drifting off, he yelled, broke some of the crummy furniture that was in the rooms where they lived. But he wouldn't leave her. And he was afraid of taking her to a hospital. His chin sinks down into his chest as he tells them this, and he raises his hands as if to shut out something he doesn't want to hear. "I was afraid of *this*," he says.

Andy stands up, still looking at Keaton. "Let's take a break," he says. "I'll get us some coffee."

Just like when they left Vancouver, Annie was always better when they made a change. She would say that she wanted to move, that she didn't like the town, or the place, or that the people made her sad, and Keaton would jump on it. He would throw their few belongings into a couple of hockey bags and they would head out of town, feeling suddenly free, but knowing it wasn't forever. They went on like that for years, even spent some time in Alberta. There was hardly a place in BC. they hadn't seen. "We moved around like there were no borders, no seasons, no clocks or calendars. No one else. She must have been lonely sometimes." He looks at them both. "Christ, I was lonely sometimes."

They had been in Quenelle for nine months when she started talking about the mission school. She'd heard about it from an ex-Jesuit, a regular in the coffee shop where she was working. He was older than Annie. Old enough to be her father, and he offered her a sad kind of friendship for a time. Annie liked him, Keaton could see that.

It was the Jesuit who told her about the old school on the outskirts of Prince George, about how he had taught there as a young priest. "It wasn't all bad, what we did," he'd told Annie. "We taught them how to read and write, to make themselves understood." And what use was that? Annie asked Keaton later, the sorrow pressed onto her face. All those children. Where had all the books, the classroom lessons taken them?

She told Keaton she wanted to go there, to the mission school, so that she could see it for herself. Keaton said sure. Sure, he would find it for her. It was well into spring by then, and it wasn't so hard to move on.

They took a bus to Prince George and then hitch-hiked out of town, to where they picked up the old gravel road that took them down to the school. The school was in the middle of a large meadow, thick with yellow daisies, corn flowers, purple thistle. It was a simple three-story frame building, with an old-man tiredness about it, said Keaton, but it wasn't creepy or evil looking. Some of the windows had been smashed, but not all, and the paint was peeling. There was a sagging porch that extended across the front, a simple cross still nailed to an oversized plank door. The school looked like a husk, he said, that would soon just vanish beneath the meadow.

Annie found them a room on the second floor, a place where it was clear other transients had been before. She swept out the leaves and put down two of the narrow mattresses, side by side. They used their coats for blankets, and when it got cold, Keaton made them a fire in a pit outside. Not far behind the main building, there was a little stream where they could wash and get water. It wasn't a hard life, but they still needed food.

Behind the main building, Keaton found a shed half strangled by vines. Inside, there were gardening tools, rusted-out mowers, a couple of cans of gas. He also found an old bike hanging from the rafters. The next day, he walked into town and bought patches and a hand pump. When he got back, he made the necessary repairs.

Every few days, he rode the bike into town for supplies. Annie seemed better for a time. Keaton said he would see her, with her long bare legs thigh-deep in the stream, watching her toes, touching the tall grass that grew up on the bank with the tips of her fingers. She wanted to know every part of the place. It was like the old school was speaking to her.

And then Annie opened the door on a storage room full of boxes, stacked against the walls and left behind when the Jesuits finally abandoned the place. The files inside were a coffee-coloured brown, with the names of students printed on their covers in a fine, precise hand. Keaton found Annie there, legs crossed, head bent over the yellowed pages.

Inside were reports, written by the nuns mostly. Words like "liar" and "slow," "belligerent" and "primitive," cropped up a lot. Pen imagines the nuns' words: comments about deportment, estimations of relative intelligence, capacity for language. The kids were put in rooms by themselves, beaten, says Keaton. Pen has seen such accounts. The nuns would have been clinical, detached. Words like "isolation" and "corporal punishment" would have been used. In other files there was just a straight-forward recording of grades, illness, dates of leaving for home visits, and the dates of return. Annie found a beautiful beaded leather necklace in one.

She never removed anything from the boxes or the folders. They don't belong to me, she told him. They belonged to *him*, or *her*, Annie's long finger tracing the letters of the child's name like she was a ghostwriter.

Keaton knew the names might not really have belonged to the children. The priests would have taken their real names away, choosing more suitable Christian names like Charles or Rose.

They were running out of money. Keaton saw that he needed to find some work, save up for rent, and maybe he could get Annie to move into town by the fall. He took the old bike from the garage and went to town, where he found a job pumping gas at the corner of the highway. It was only a forty-minute ride each way, he said. And by the time the snow came, he was sure that Annie would want to move again.

They lived like that for maybe a few weeks, with Keaton going into the town, bringing back food in plastic bags that he hung from the handlebars of the bike. Annie spent most of her time with the boxes, with the children, the little Indian kids who had lived there before them. It was different this time, he tells them. She wasn't shutting down or starving herself.

Instead, it was like she was burning up with something. Could they understand that? Something so big, so terrible, it devours you and so you have to devour it.

He hadn't burnt down the mission school. It was Annie who did that.

He came home one evening and the building was already burning. The stairs were on fire. He looked up at the second floor, at the broken windows, the window frames already black with smoke. Annie was up there, he knew that much. He could feel her watching the flames, him down below; she wouldn't have come out on her own.

He doesn't remember burning his hands, although he knows he tried to punch his way through whatever was in his way, and all of it was on fire. The stairs collapsed. His arms make a tilting motion as he tells them this. Everything just falling away.

When the fire people got there they put a ladder up to the second floor and pulled Annie out. They must have thought Keaton was crazy, because by then he was smashing up everything in sight. He pulled the door from the building and hurled it at the flames. He cracked his ribs when three of the firefighters threw him on the ground and pinned him there. He didn't know what he was thinking then. Probably just that Annie was dead.

Pen has not taken her eyes off Keaton. Not once. He doesn't look like a person who tried to fight his way into a burning building. All she sees is in him now is defeat.

"I was sure she was dead. I *knew* it." His elbow comes up and jabs at his sternum, like he would punch himself if he could. Pen winces, thinking of his ribs.

He drops the elbow and fiddles idly with the edge of a bandage, and although the fight seems to have gone out of him, he says, "But she isn't." He looks at them with a hint of the old defiance. "Annie just hasn't woken up yet, that's all."

23.

KEATON'S STORY HAD UNFOLDED differently than Pen imagined. She hadn't understood his attachment to Annie Lieb.
Everything has a history, she tells herself now: Rod's drowning, Irene's drinking, the fire, Keaton's flight. Even Irene's recovery. She positions the events the way she has seen Maddie position her assortment of treasures, arranging them like they are continents on a map.

As Keaton speaks, he keeps his bandaged hands crossed over his chest, his eyes on her. They are sitting close enough for their knees to touch. At points his face changes, anger tightening the features, and then yielding to something sorrowful, deeper than regret. She finally sees Keaton as he really was after Rod went out on the *Isobel* and never came back; still a boy after all, his jacket pulled up around his ears, tossing a stone across the hard, impassive surface of the November lake.

It takes Keaton two visits to get through it. It is probably the most he has ever said to her. At the end of the second visit, Pen lightly touches his arm. "We have to tell the police everything, Keaton. All this has to come out or they'll think you did it."

He pushes himself back into his chair, a jerking reactive motion as if he's been stung. "You've never been locked up, either of you."

Pen looks at Andy. He hasn't said much throughout Keaton's telling of the story. Now, Andy shifts his weight, leans in toward Keaton.

"They'll put her away," Keaton goes on. "For good maybe. I won't do that to her."

"She's already in pretty deep, Keaton," Andy says. "I mean with her medical history, everything she's been through..." As Andy speaks, he remains completely still, the stillness in such a large man, the self-possession at once reassuring and unnerving. "Maybe they won't see it as a criminal thing."

Keaton is shaking his head. "You don't get it. They'll see it like she was trying to hurt herself."

Andy pauses and takes a breath. "And if she was?"

"There's more to it than just that. I won't give her up."

Pen sighs with impatience. "It isn't like you are *abandoning* her, Keaton," she says. "She's not *talking*. She's obviously sick. You aren't making any sense."

"I won't do it. And if you don't get that, then you can't help me. Go back home, Pen," he says. "Get the hell away."

Pen looks away from him, her eyes swimming. It's hopeless, trying to hang on to him, just like it was back in Port, Keaton climbing out of the window of their room, his face already taken up by the dark. A rising line of resentment moves through her, making her voice suddenly whiny, like it must have been when he left. "Not fair, Keaton. You took off, with Annie, and you never looked back. Well, I've been *waiting*."

"Not fair. No. I guess not. Never figured you could see any of it as fair. I sure never did."

They are looking at each other now, same eyes, same jutting chin.

Andy shifts a little in his seat and clears his throat. He looks at Pen, and then back at Keaton. "Nobody's making the mistake of trying to push you to do anything you don't want, Keaton." He shakes his head, as if remembering all the times he'd come up against Keaton in the past. "I'd have to be pretty dumb..." His hand has been resting on his thigh and now he stretches it wide, looking down at it as if he is considering his scars for the first time.

"I know how you are. You haven't changed all that much. Course you don't want to do anything bad to Annie. Why would you? The two of you have been so tight, eh? The thing is Keaton, if you take the rap for this, if you don't set the story straight, you will probably go away for a while. Don't think they won't find out about what happened in Port. They put two and two together, and then, BAM, you are at least an arsonist, and maybe worse. Yeah, I see you shrugging like you couldn't care less about that. But you gotta think, Keaton. With you away like that, in a cell someplace, how will that be for Annie? Keaton, that sounds pretty lonely. That sounds like an awful price for Annie to pay."

Pen is struck by the logic of it and knows that Keaton sees it too. He shifts his body, straightens. "There are outstanding charges. I'll go away anyway."

Andy's hooded gaze is penetrating, compelling. "A lot of damage was done on that boat. By you, and you have to face that." He shrugs, a kind of release. "Never had your day in court, did you Keaton? You never did tell the whole story."

Keaton looks at Andy and something passes between them. A piece of shared knowledge, or forgiveness, Pen cannot tell.

A doctor is paged, and there is the clatter of stainless steel trays on a cart. There is a buzz in the room and Pen doesn't know if it is from the overhead lights or whether her thoughts are revving into some kind of overload.

"Then I'd have to go back. Not happening. I'm not going back without her."

"Who's saying she can't go back? Maybe there's a way for you to pick up your lives again."

Keaton is quiet, his eyes on the table, his features unreadable.

"I'm not saying anything until I see Annie. They won't *let* me see her. I won't say yes or no until then."

A silence comes into the room. It holds both tension and relief. Andy nods his head, and then cracks a sideways smile. He is the consummate negotiator now. "I'd say that's a definite maybe, and we can work with that. How about you leave things with us, Keaton."

Keaton walks with them to the elevator and, while they wait, he shifts his weight from one foot to another. He frowns at the up-down button until the doors slide open and they step inside. The final look that Pen has is him pushing the button with his elbow to close the door.

Andy says, "First, we tell Dr. McTeer what he said. Give her the full background. The *Dolly*, the charges." He looks at her. "Your dad… See if it meshes with what she has figured out so far. Then we go to the police and convince them to give him an escorted visit with Annie. Once he sees her, he'll want to stay out of jail for her, and we can see about getting him home."

Pen smooths her hair back from her face. She feels suddenly exhausted from the visits, emptied out from Keaton's story. She wants to slide down the wall and close her eyes. "But he's got to deal with the charges back in Port," she says, her eyes stinging. "Those haven't gone away."

Andy isn't looking at her. Instead, he's striding out of the hospital, urging her on with a grin.

"Have a little faith, Pen," he says.

24.

THE SOLES OF HER FEET are sweaty and cold underneath the thin hospital sheet. She is lying on her back, rigid, because something in her says *don't move.* She can smell antiseptic and beneath that, something else. Something more human. It makes her want to cry. They mean well. But they don't know. They don't know what it is to be pressed down like this, a moth pressed beneath the stretched white sheets. Sounds come from outside her door and she knows that people are there and although they are kind, they are beyond her.

Earlier, the doctor had come to see her. She is pretty, light-filled. "Annie, isn't it?" Her voice is soft.

Annie closes her eyes and listens.

"Keaton is here. Did you know that? He wants very badly to talk to you, to see you."

Annie takes a breath in and holds it.

"Perhaps you could tell us what happened, Annie."

She can't explain what she knows.

They have seen so much, she and Keaton. The day they left Port they walked along the highway, away from the lake. She felt like the first mammal crawling out of the sea. It was painful, of course. There had been a great tearing away at first, the vibration of cloth ripping along a seam, and she had thought of her parents who would now be living a kind of hell. She has anguished over this, what she has done to them.

Her sense of time has collapsed, but there remains for her

a continuity, a rhythm to her experience that she wouldn't know how to describe. There were days, perhaps weeks, of what she believes must have been happiness: joyful outbursts, like punctuation marks, short flights into ecstasy, inevitably followed by a kind descent. She would feel herself spreading out, elongating, disappearing into a vast terrain of ancient trees and mountains, into a world of exquisite loneliness. The loneliness wasn't for people. She had Keaton with her most of the time and she needed no one else. The loneliness was more longing; she was yearning for the end of one thing to become the beginning of something else. Pain into beauty. Anger into ease.

They will want to know if she was trying to kill herself. *Dust to dust, ashes to ashes ... but ashes are born of fire, fire from sparks, sparks from friction and friction from energy, and on and on and on.* Her mind races, even here in this white room, her tongue thick and lethargic because of the pills. But she doesn't need to speak. She comforts herself with this. She doesn't need to struggle with the awkwardness of words.

Keaton couldn't understand this obsession of hers with transformation. He fought to keep her tied to him. They shifted from one place to another, Annie the catalyst, Keaton complicit in the decision to move, a perfect synchronicity of longing and restlessness. And all the while, Keaton's anger, his guilt, rode beside them, half-strangled like a chained-up beast.

One night, back in Port, the two of them huddled beneath a porch high up on the ravine, a thin rain falling, Keaton told her that he hated Irene. Earlier, he'd fought with Irene about her drinking; he'd shoved her hard against a door. His voice was a whisper, telling Annie this: he had wished that it was *Irene* who'd went away. He told his mother that he wished that she had drowned.

What Keaton wanted was some kind of absolution. What Annie wanted was a knitting together of all the wounds, a release, a kind of reinstatement. They are one another's source, each the slipstream of the other's existence. But there is more, she knows. There is more than their strange love to be reckoned with now.

They'll ask her what she feels. What makes her so silent. She curls her toes and squeezes them painfully.

It isn't the what. It is the size. The weight of it. The depth. What she found in those boxes, the voices, the lingering wood smoke, the smell of those children. All of it, beyond what she can tell.

When she found the room in the mission school, she felt them stirring, heard them murmuring to her, pleading. The words in the files were hard, unforgiving, at times laced with a bitterness she believed to be the self-loathing of the nuns. She found only fragments of the children there.

Lie still, Annie. Lie still and just cease, just cease.

Another thought comes, but it is more like a feeling than pictures in her head. They have pinned down Keaton, too. Captured him.

From the window, she had watched Keaton try to get into the mission. He hadn't understood that she wasn't frightened, that it was *good*, what she was doing. Good to let the boxes go to ash, blown by a west wind to where the commingling of rain and earth and sun would bring the children home. She hadn't wanted to go with them, really. She hadn't thought about herself at all.

Keaton wouldn't see it that way. He would think she was taking herself away from him. He would see it as punishment. He would feel responsible, and for Keaton that would be too much.

Annie lies in the hospital bed and aches. They will believe he has done this; he will believe he has done this.

The doctor has been sitting next to her all of this time, her small hand on Annie's arm. Annie can feel her get up lightly from her chair. "It will help him, Annie, if you speak."

She closes her eyes as if to shut off everything outside of herself. She is caught in her silence. She is caught in those boxes, holding the silence inside.

25.

IT TOOK ANDY THREE CALLS and a visit to the RCMP detachment before he could convince someone that Keaton should be allowed a supervised visit to Annie's hospital room.

There was some doubt as to what really happened at the mission school, enough that it was believed that a discussion between Annie and Keaton might be enlightening, particularly as neither of them had given a full account of the fire.

"He didn't have any reason to torch the place, Pen," Andy told her when they met for coffee earlier. "Besides," he said, "the RCMP investigators found out that Annie had a history of mental illness, so now they get that she might have had something to do with setting that fire."

By ten-thirty a.m., Pen and Andy stand against a shiny wall in Annie Lieb's hospital room. Under the white hospital blanket, Annie is laid out like a corpse, her long face slightly angled against the pillow, her eyes huge and grey. Her chin is tipped up and her mouth is slightly open. She barely blinks. Maybe it is the medication that has left her so cataleptic, though there has always been something in Annie, Pen remembers, of both the kinetic and the still.

A young female RCMP officer sits almost demurely on a hardbacked chair beside the door. She looks Native, Pen thinks, her wide face yielding to a soft, kind chin. The investigators told them that the officer would not be engaging either party in questions. The RCMP was solely there for security reasons.

It was imperative, the investigators had explained, that Keaton understand the limits placed upon him. He mustn't try and leave without an escort. And he mustn't try and remove Annie Lieb from the room. Finally, a representative from the Crown Attorney's Office would be present; Keaton would not be permitted to coerce or influence Annie's statements about the fire. If that were to happen, then the visit would be promptly terminated.

The Crown Attorney, a puffy man with a glistening forehead leans against the opposite wall and picks at his nails in a distracted way. Every so often he breathes in heavily as though to stave off boredom. He isn't looking at Keaton, who holds his bandaged hands at his chest, like a boxer, his face fixed on Annie.

There is a long stretch of time when nothing is said. The sweating lawyer from the Crown's Office is getting impatient. He checks his watch with heavy eyes and shifts his bulk in his chair. "Can we get started?"

Keaton looks at him, then at all the faces around the room. He is taut and restless, moving to the end of Annie's bed and then away from her. A flash of the old fierceness comes over his features.

"Annie."

He doesn't touch her at first. It's as if he is willing her to come back, challenging her not to break the pact. The lawyer clears his throat and the RCMP officer's features remain expressionless.

"Annie," Keaton says again in a low voice. "Annie, I know you can hear me."

Annie slides her eyes over to Keaton. They rest there, Annie saying nothing.

Keaton is shaking his head now, back and forth, his jaw still clenched.

"I gotta ask, Annie. You know I do. Why would you try a stupid...? "

"Mr. Beau? Don't be suggestive with your questions, please."
It is the lawyer, his arms draped lazily over the sides of the chair.

"Okay." Keaton takes in a breath and seems to hold it.
"Look. I'm glad you aren't hurt bad, Annie. I'm glad you ...
the fire didn't do damage." A look passes between them, and
Pen sees Annie bite down hard on her lower lip, the way she
has seen Annie do years ago, in Port.

"If you don't want to talk to me, that's okay. I wish you would
talk, though. I wish you wouldn't just let yourself float away."

"Mr. Beau..."

"If I caused any of this by dragging you with me, by *running*,
then I am sorry beyond anything."

Annie's eyes fill slowly but they hold.

The lawyer is about to intervene again, to stop Keaton from
suggesting anything more. But before he can, Annie speaks.
"You didn't do this."

Her voice is deeper than Pen remembers it. But then, Annie
had still been just a girl back then. Annie has grown into a
woman.

"It should have burnt down a long time ago," she whispers.
"All those children. Someone needed to let them go."

Keaton groans, more pained than frustrated.

"They deserved better," she says.

Keaton reaches down and takes her hand, clutching it through
the lumpy bandages.

Her eyes glitter, vast and grey and watery. "It doesn't matter that I'm here. It doesn't matter at all." Annie looks at the
policewoman, whose face is quiet, unchanged.

"I'll tell."

Her voice is soft but the words are clear. She will speak
about what happened, she says. She will talk about all the
lives in the files, each weighted down by the next, an endless
pillar of boxes.

The lawyer sighs a little and snaps open his brief case.

"You'll have to leave," he tells them. "All of you."

Out in the corridor, two nurses are laughing together. An elderly woman sleeps, mouth sagging, her spine curled into a wheelchair.

Pen touches Keaton's arm. "This is good. They'll know now. Maybe they'll do something for her."

Keaton brushes his foot against the floor and stares down at the beige, glossy tiles.

"Maybe," he says. "I've thought that before. Lots of times."

Waiting for the parking elevator, they run into Dr. McTeer, a soft indigo-blue messenger bag slung across her shoulder, her car keys in her hand. She stops and smiles when she sees them.

The day before, Pen had spent over an hour in Dr. McTeer's office talking about Keaton's history. She asked Pen to be particularly clear about Keaton's age when their father drowned, and she asked about what had changed for Keaton, for all of them, after. Pen said, "I don't know. I don't think of *how* it changed, but Keaton wasn't the same. He was harder." She stopped for a moment. "The money problems, Mom's drinking, and then all the questions about Dad's disappearance…. There wasn't anyone left in charge. No help for us, really. But he did try."

Dr. McTeer looked thoughtfully at the carpeted floor between them. Her gaze lifted to Pen, her keen eyes holding something sharper, truer than simple kindness.

"Well, he found Annie, I guess. But I don't think you had anyone, did you, after Keaton left."

It was like being swept up in a gigantic swell, nothing but an utter loss of control, water streaming from her eyes, and a panic about breathing. Dr. McTeer gently handed her a box of tissues, then poured her a long cold glass of water from a jug.

After a long while, Pen was able to find the words. "I didn't know what else to do but wait. Wait for him to come back." She thinks of all the moments of paralysis in her life, in her marriage, in her mothering of Maddie; that same gripping fear there with her, in Port on the beach, the day Ben Vasco had drowned.

Now, Dr. McTeer pockets her keys. "How did it go? Are you holding up, Pen?"

Pen nods dully. "Sure," she says, thinking now that she has found Keaton, the anguish of waiting should be over, but it's not.

"Did Annie say anything?"

When Pen tells her what happened, she doesn't seem surprised. "I'm still going to have to complete that assessment for the Crown's Office. I'd like to get started tomorrow, and I'll have some more questions."

"Just call. And in the meantime, what about Keaton? How do we make sure he's okay?" There can be no simple answer to this. "Come in and see him," she says. "Talk. Listen. The contact helps to bring him back." She pauses. "He's been away a long time."

"And Annie?" Pen asks.

"Annie's situation is a little more complicated. I'll want some information about her family, who we can contact. I'm sure you can help me with some of that. Now that we have a name, the police can check to see if there is a missing person's report on file."

When Pen and Andy leave the hospital, it is still afternoon. Pen blinks into the harsh dry light and reaches in her bag for her sunglasses. She is hollowed-out and jittery, exhaustion making her head throb.

"*That* was unbearably sad," she says.

Andy shrugs. "That was a beginning."

Pen looks over her shoulder at the hospital where Keaton and Annie are, separated from one another again. Then she looks at Andy.

"Well, whatever. I'm done for today. I don't want to think about it. What I could use is a long shower and a drink."

"Or a short shower and a long drink. In either case, I can

fix the drinking part real easy," he says, looking pleased with himself.

"I guess I'm in your hands, then."

"Oh, I doubt you put yourself in anyone's hands much," Andy says, throwing her a winning, crooked smile.

He drives them back to the hotel, where they shower and change. Pen puts in a call to Irene, but gets Ed instead, who doesn't ask any questions at first. He explains that Irene is working the evening shift. Once she gets in, he says, he'll pass on the news about Keaton.

"Well, when you do talk to her, ask her if she knows where Annie Lieb's parents are. Ask her if she knows where we can get in touch with them." Her tone is accusatory. Irene had known that Annie was with Keaton all along. Irene had been playing God, withholding information, deciding what was important and what wasn't.

Ed's voice is steady. "Sure. Pen? He okay?"

"Yeah, Ed. He's okay."

"You?"

"Yeah. Think so."

After she hangs up from Ed, she calls home. Jeff picks up after the third ring. She talks about Keaton, about Annie, careful not to make mention of Andy; she's almost hopeful about Keaton, she tells him.

Jeff is uncharacteristically quiet. She imagines him rubbing his head, taking the measure of things. "That's hard to understand," he says, "the two of them living that way."

"I don't really get it either," she says. "He doesn't *seem* like he's crazy. I just don't see why he'd run for all of these years. Sure, he didn't want to face the charges in Port, but Keaton's not a coward. If he'd plead guilty, the sentence wouldn't have been too bad. I mean, he was still just a kid when he left."

"I guess there's more to it," says Jeff.

There is a pause. She can hear his breathing.

"I could still come out there, Pen. Irene could be in Toronto by midday and I could be on an afternoon flight out."

"It's okay. I'm okay, Jeff."

Jeff goes on to talk about how Maddie has been blathering on about a party. "Some random characters to be invited," he says, "and weird party games involving people running around, waving their arms in the air, like birds."

"Seagulls" she says, thinking of Maddie on the beach at Port. "Who's on the invite list?"

"Seagulls? That fits. Well, apart from the cats she knows, Irene and Ed, us, of course. And Bill and Lea. Some of the neighbours. And a man with a ponytail. Someone she gave some beach glass too? But the weirdest one is that guy who drowned."

"Ben Vasco? She call him by name?"

"Just 'the boy on the beach.'"

Pen holds the phone and stares into an empty wastepaper basket, her foot jammed against base of her swivel chair. Maddie has found a way for Ben Vasco to come back from the lake after all. "A collection of *people*," she says. "That's something new."

Maddie comes on the phone next, her voice babyish, sweet, like she has just woken up from a nap. Pen wants to reach through the phone and touch the tangle of bright hair. She struggles to keep her tone right, to swim up from the familiar wash of love and sadness and constraint.

There is a knock on the door, and when she opens it, she finds Andy carrying a large tray with a bottle of wine, two plastic glasses, purple grapes, a box of crackers, herb cheese in a vacuum-sealed package. "Brought to you by the fine folks at Safe Way," he says to Pen, handing her the tray. "And your local wine store."

Pen clears off the small round table in the corner of the room and sets the tray down. She has dumped her clothes on one of the chairs and now she bundles them self-consciously at the foot of the bed.

Andy unscrews the cap from the bottle and pours wine into the glasses. After she takes a sip, she deliberately puts the glass down on the table. *Slow down,* she tells herself. It would be so easy to drink too greedily, to numb herself, to cut herself adrift.

Andy is watching her. "So what are you thinking?" she asks, levelling her gaze at him.

Andy grins, eases his legs out into the room and takes a sip from his own glass. "That you don't look comfortable anyplace I've seen you. It's like you're wrapped too tight in your skin."

She looks around and frowns a little. "It's a hotel room, Andy. And a pretty mediocre one."

"You've always been like that, Pen. Even in Port."

"I don't feel completely comfortable in Port. And for good reason."

"And I guess you do in Toronto," says Andy, popping some grapes into his mouth, pouring out more wine. "Don't be shy about the wine," he says. "I've got another bottle chilling in the fridge in my room."

She doesn't know how to reply to the remark about Toronto. *He* should be bound up in all those scars, made smaller because of them, but he isn't and she can't understand.

"What about you, Andy? You seem to live in your car. Or an airplane. Where do you feel at home?"

He lifts his eyes to her. Her question doesn't seem to have jarred him in the least.

"I liked living in Port, when we were all young. I liked my life; the hockey, me and Keaton, knowing everyone there, the way we did. I felt a part of it. Until Keaton and Spar's boat, Keaton leaving. And I guess, if I'm really honest, the way my future seemed to just disappear. Things changed for me, Pen, when that boat lit up. And so, even though everything *had* changed, when I left Port I kind of had to make myself comfortable some other way."

"And that's what you did."

He opens the box of crackers. "It was different for you. Different because things went bad for you so early. Your dad, Irene, then Keaton. Maybe you came to expect that things would always just turn over on you." His giant's hand makes a turtling motion, miming a boat rolling over in the waves.

Pen is quiet. She gets up, looks for a knife for the cheese but doesn't find one. Her glass is empty and she pours herself more. It's true of course, what he is saying. Painfully obvious.

"Port was a strange place to grow up," she says. "A kind of exception. Just tell someone you're from a long line of South Western Ontario fishers, and they look at you like you are putting one over on them. And then say you come from Lake Erie, and they stop smiling and start looking a little disgusted, and a little sorry for you too."

"You mean, it's like the place has a bad smell," says Andy, grinning.

Pen laughs. "Yeah. I mean it does sometimes, right?"

Andy shrugs, the smile fading. "Finding Keaton going to help you with that, Pen? Help you know where you should be?"

She feels a lump rising and she swallows down on it hard. "Dunno. He's so beat-up. I don't know if he's ever going to be okay."

"That's not what I'm talking about. He's going to do what he's going to do. Hell, did you ever know him to be any different? It's you I'm talking about now."

When she looks at Andy across the table, the easygoing charm, the denial of pain has disappeared and she sees him as older now, scarred and changed. The desire to touch him is intense. She takes her fingers to the back of his hand, to the light spider web of burnt tissue, and then to his face, tracing his mouth, venturing up to the smooth ridges of scars on his cheek. Sitting on his lap, her own face close to his, they kiss and she folds herself into him, feeling the certainty of his hands on her hair, her back.

After a time, Andy takes her face between his palms and

looks at her with the same look of honesty she saw before. "This isn't going to help, Pen. It's not what changes things."

Pen pulls away and brushes back her hair with the ends of her fingers. She is both furious and embarrassed. "You were sending me signals."

"Probably," he says. "Look, I came here to support you, yes, but I came for my own reasons."

"What would those be?"

He's got his arms around her, like he's content that way, just feeling her weight against him. "I told you it was a bad year. I lost something. Someone. Doesn't matter, really."

"It does matter. It matters to me."

Andy sighs. "After I left Port and the hockey future was gone, it was like I was that useless kid again — a freak. The thing is I had to prove myself, working all the time, *winning* whenever I could. And I won a lot. So I kept working. Really hard. I became more and more confident and the better I did, the more all of *this*—," he spreads out his hand, nods at the mass of scars, "just disappeared." He tips back his head and closes his eyes. "This someone I had in my life was a person I really cared for. But so much of the time, I was travelling, caught up in the job. Last November, she told me she didn't want to be alone so much. That I had to make a choice."

"So, have you?"

He is quiet. "Yes. I believe I have. Just now, finding Keaton. Hearing about him and Annie, what it is to belong to someone like that."

Pen takes a hold of his chin. "So, why did you come here, with me? You didn't know Annie was with him. You haven't told me what your *reasons* were."

Andy pauses. "Seeing Keaton again is like seeing the whole of me. That part that needed Keaton to come charging out onto the ball field, to cut me free from that damn fishing line, to rescue me. The part of me that isn't good at anything much but was good enough for him."

"I haven't a clue what you mean," she says.

"I know you don't," he laughs.

He is looking at her, thoughtfully, carefully. "What about your marriage, Pen?"

She starts to feel her spine stiffen and she slides herself away from him, her feet on the floor. He makes no attempt to stop her.

"Don't go feeling all embarrassed or anything. We both kind of fell into this."

But Pen has her back to him now, and she's stuffing her feet into her shoes.

26.

NEW WORLD INSURANCE
November 25, 1984

Re: Policy #RW1680-9

Dear Mrs. Irene Beau:

Thank you for filing for a reassessment of your entitlement status for death benefits. We appreciate that under the circumstances, you would of course, wish to have the case re-examined.

Unfortunately, I must inform you that the appeals board has denied your claim. Although I am not at liberty to disclose to you the full body of evidence that has led to this decision, I am able to provide a brief summary.

In the case law associated with life-insurance claims, the party applying for benefits bears the burden of responsibility for demonstrating that the requirements for eligibility have been met. As you know, in Mr. Beau's case, it is unclear whether his death was accidental. This does not mean that, in our view, his drowning was a suicide. Simply there is a significant probability that, under the circumstances, it was. The appeals board was swayed by several undeniable facts in the case. First, that a seasoned and experienced commercial vessel owner/operator, as was Mr. Beau, chose to ignore gale warnings in favour of voyaging out on the lake, despite knowing the risk to himself and to his vessel. Second, that he did not follow his usual and sound practice of crewing the vessel, choosing instead to be alone on M/V *Isobel*. Third, there was no evidence that he made an attempt to save himself, either by customary distress communications or by using the safety equipment on board. Fourth, there was no evidence that M/V *Isobel* was mechanically or functionally compromised and therefore we have no explanation for M/V's capsize.

Finally, there were many indications in Mr. Beau's circumstances of multi-factorial stressors in his life circumstances, which may have caused him to engage in despairing thoughts around ending his life. In the absence of any other clear reason for the capsizing of the M/V *Isobel,* the appeals board found that it was likely Mr. Beau took his own life by drowning.

I am genuinely sorry, Mrs. Beau and hope that you will consider community and social services when planning for your own, and your children's future. You will of course, be eligible for the Widow's Benefit, as stipulated by federal regulations.

This letter serves as a notice to you that your file will be closed. Further inquiries should be made to the Records Department, at this address.

Yours sincerely,

Mr. Everett B. Cook
Chief Investigator, Claims

27.

KEATON CHOSE THE WINDOW SEAT for the flight home. His forehead rests against the glass, his eyes half-closed; he's either exhausted or resigned, Pen can't tell. When she touches his arm, he doesn't turn from the window. "Keaton? I'm sorry…"

"It's my choice to go back."

In the seat behind, Andy works on his laptop, relaxed, his attention on the screen. He seems unperturbed by what almost happened between them in Prince George; Pen bristles, thinking about it, a scorched feeling of humiliation spreading, blooming profusely, invisibly; but she also sees Andy more clearly now, the Andy beneath the scars, the history with Keaton. He won't be held back. She imagines him gracefully rocketing toward the net, his eyes fixed on what he wants.

Before leaving, Pen had spoken by phone to Dr. McTeer, who was finishing off her assessment of Keaton. Dr. McTeer hesitated before hanging up.

"You know, what happened to you and Keaton was a huge slam to the psyche. It would have changed how you saw yourself in the world. You've heard the terms, 'flight, fight or freeze'?"

"Yeah, sure," said Pen, bracing for what sounded like it was going to be a well-meant psychology lecture.

"Some people live in one of those states, or a combination of them, for a long time."

Pen waited for her to say more but she didn't. She simply wished them all the best.

On the basis of Dr. McTeer's report and Annie's statement, a conditional release has been arranged for Keaton. The RCMP is satisfied that he is not to blame for the burning of the mission school, but they insist that he face the outstanding warrants in Ontario.

Annie will come home, but not until she is stable. No one saw them say goodbye, but somehow, Annie made it possible for Keaton to leave her. The court ordered that Annie undergo a thirty-one day forensic assessment. With undisguised indifference, the Crown Attorney told them that, likely, Annie would be flown back on probation. There would be conditions regarding on-going care, etc. Pen had thought about the sprawling psychiatric facility near Port. She imagined Annie, her face at the hospital dorm window, her luminous eyes on the abandoned orchard, the wild apple trees that grow there still. But probably people like Annie don't stay in those places anymore. She would probably take drugs and live, supervised, with her family. She would probably have to see someone like Dr. McTeer once a month.

The Crown Attorney seemed pleased to tell them that Annie's parents had been notified, and that they were greatly relieved. "But I guess Mr. Beau isn't top of their Christmas list. Probably be best if he weren't around Prince George when her parents come out to collect her." His lips had pressed together disdainfully. "And once they're both home, he shouldn't try and find her. He should keep himself on a leash."

Heat flashed over her cheeks. "He's looked after her for all of these years, hasn't he?"

"How soon can we take him?" Andy interrupted. "We just want to get him home."

"Make the arrangements and we'll prepare the conditions. He'll need to report to the local OPP within twenty-four hours of landing in Ontario."

Keaton didn't want to leave so soon. "Look," Andy explained, "her folks are coming out, Keaton. Think how hard it will be on Annie, if you're still here. It's going to be hard enough."

It meant that there would be at least a month before Annie came home. A month for Keaton to settle a little, for them to find him a lawyer, make some progress on getting his life back.

Before they land, Pen tells Keaton that he might find it hot and muggy in Ontario. He has on a long-sleeved plaid shirt and a pair of heavy jeans. "Things are going to seem strange for a while." He looked at her and smiled a little. Stupid thing for her to say, she thinks. Stupid, given how strange everything up until now had been.

At the airport, they make their way through the streams of people, Pen walking slightly ahead so she can make a space for Keaton. His eyes glance off the faces of strangers, his expression flat and unchanging. Pen has arranged a rental car at the airport. When she called Jeff, he tried to convince her that they should stay in Toronto, that they could all drive down together to Port in the morning.

"Toronto will break him," Pen said. "You don't know how he's been living, Jeff. Bush towns and taverns. He wouldn't cope."

There was quiet on the other end. "I might have *some* idea about bush towns, Pen."

"Look, I know. I didn't mean it that way."

An image of Jeff and Maddie in the kitchen came into her mind, Jeff with a spatula in his hand, chatting to Maddie, trying to keep the disappointment out of his face. There would be alternative rock blasting in the background, a definite, progressive beat; "Won't be long now, Maddie. Mommy's going to be home in a jiff."

"What's a 'jiff'?"

"Good question. Don't know. But anyway, soon. Just a few more sleeps," he'd say.

"Jeff?" she said before hanging up. "I miss you guys." He hadn't said anything. She hoped that he believed her.

Andy says goodbye to them at the car rental counter. His own car waits for him in long-term parking. She doesn't ask him where he's going.

"I've got some things to take care of over the next few days," he says, "but I'll get to Port soon as I can." He is looking at Keaton. "It'll be okay. It's all just got to work itself out." He wraps Keaton in a hug and then turns to Pen.

"Call me?"

She doesn't say she will. "Thanks for everything, Andy. Really." She watches him walk through the sliding glass doors, his stride ungainly but rhythmic, his jacket slung easily over his shoulder. She doesn't know how she feels about him now. She imagines herself in the moment: a small, tense woman wearing a frown, and behind her, a man in a frayed plaid shirt, his hair long, his hands bandaged, his expression vague.

Andy had been the connecting thread.

The day is sunny and hot, but the brightness doesn't buoy them. They drive west down the highway toward the lake, Pen gripped with foreboding, and Keaton indifferently eyeing the landscape through the tinted glass. He hadn't wanted to change into a T-shirt at the airport and now his arms are resolutely crossed over his chest. She keeps the air conditioning on low, afraid that he might actually be cold.

She pulls in at a rest stop and gets them each a steaming hot coffee, a straw for Keaton, and while she is there, she puts in a call to the university, punching in the extension for the department administrator. The message kicks in and Pen leaves a message of her own. "I have to finish some personal business down here. Please check on those book orders for me. You can call me on my cell."

After she re-engages with the traffic, she starts to tell Keaton about Irene.

"You're probably wondering what to expect," she says, trying to make her tone sound light. "She's changed, I guess.

I mean in all the obvious ways. No more drinking. She and Ed are teetotalers, all the way. Big on the Twelve Steps, and New Age stuff. But she's still all about Irene." She regrets saying that part. Keaton deserves a less complicated homecoming, and Irene, as a mother, is much improved from what she was. "She's happy you're coming, Keaton. Ed too. You know, he's turned out to be all right."

When Keaton speaks, it surprises her. She hadn't really thought he was listening. "I spoke to Irene. A few years back."

Pen's hands tighten on the wheel, her palms moistening.

"I called her. I don't know why, but I wanted to know she was still there. Her and all the rest of it — Port, the house. She knew I was with Annie but she didn't want to know where. I asked her a couple of things, like where you were living, about how Andy was. I asked her whether Spar was alive. It was a pretty short conversation but I could tell she was sober, that she'd put a lot of thought into her part in what happened. She told me she was sorry..."

Pen looks straight ahead. "And so what were you thinking? Too little too late?"

He shrugs. "I'm not mad at her. Everyone's done something they're ashamed of."

Pen pushes her back against the firmness of her seat and takes in a long ragged breath, hoping to loosen the knot in her centre.

"I'm separated from my husband Jeff. Since last fall."

Keaton doesn't seem surprised.

She takes a sip of her coffee and tries to decide what to tell Keaton about her marriage, her life.

"I have a daughter. You know that, right? She's four. I want her to meet you soon, Keaton."

"Maybe when Annie gets home," he says. "Annie loves kids." He has turned away from Pen, his thoughts on Annie. Pen decides to stop talking now, and puts the radio on instead. When she gets off the highway onto the secondary road that leads down to the lake, he lifts his head and looks. "Has it changed, Pen? The lake, Port, I mean?"

She thinks for a moment. "I thought so before, but now I'm not so sure. It's still the same old mix: fishing families, the summer people, a few more restaurants and boutiques. Oh, and bikers. Lots of them."

He laughs. Then Keaton says,

"I heard about the massacre. It was near Port, right? Close enough anyway."

Massacre: a strange word. But fitting. The senselessness of the violence had been staggering. "Yes," she says. "It was big news around here. They made some arrests. Seems it was an inside job."

"Well, loyalty is rare," he says vaguely.

Pen thinks of T. She wonders if he had put his faith in the brotherhood, if he had *assumed* that he was secure and that the ties that bound him to his brothers were sound. If so, the betrayal would have cut deep. She glances over at Keaton. *He* had broken her trust long before he left Port. Some part of him disappeared with Rod.

As they get closer to Port, the road winds and the river comes into view. Soon they see boats docked, and the first scattering of modest cottages along the riverbank. Keaton tells her to pull over for a minute. She opens the door for him and he pushes himself out of the car. They lean together against the hood, and she lights a cigarette for him, the first one he has smoked since they left BC. He doesn't look nervous, just the same resignation she has seen in him since they left.

"You okay?"

"Sure. No point running, is there? Done that. And besides, it would be pretty lonely this time."

"Keaton, we'll get a lawyer. Ed and Irene are already working on it. It might not be so bad."

"That's not it. No lawyer can fix all this." He's talking around the cigarette, looking out in the direction of Port. Pen follows his gaze, sees the tiredness in his face, and imagines everything he thinks is waiting for him.

"You're not alone," she starts to say.

He interrupts her and the cigarette drops, his boot grinding it into the black asphalt. "Let's make tracks. No time like the present."

The lake is calm, despite the breeze, and it's dotted with boats, colourful sails that make her think of confetti. Keaton is staring at it with a sly look of amusement.

"Sly bitch," he says suddenly.

"What?"

"The lake." He gestures at it with his chin. "Don't ever trust it."

Pen laughs. "Spoken like the true son of a Lake Erie fisherman."

He smiles, the first real smile she's seen, and as they drive through the main intersection of town, he watches the summer people walking aimlessly in flip-flops, clutching their ice-cream cones, lobster-red shoulders, beach-tussled hair.

"There was a drowning here," Pen tells him as she pulls up in front of Irene's house. She wants to tell him about Benny Vasco. It suddenly seems very important that he know.

"A man with some kind of disability. It was the on the nicest day of the summer. He just went out and he never came back."

He nods. "There will be lots of questions, then."

28.

PEN WAKES TO ENGINES STARTING UP in the early morning. Fishing tugs, and there isn't a hint of light yet in the sky. She has slept on the couch, jammed against a musty pile of Irene's New Age books. The door is closed to her old room, and she thinks of Keaton in there, awake too, caught in the familiarity of an early morning in Port: the departing boats, the rush of cool, heavy air coming in through the open windows. She lets herself linger in it. Her thoughts soon drift to the inescapable demands of the day ahead, namely Keaton's surrender to the OPP.

Ed shuffles out in his bathrobe. He gives her a solemn nod, and they greet each other silently like survivors of a wreck. Keaton's homecoming had been hard. The house felt too small, almost cloying. Marilyn, one of Irene's cats, had continuously wound herself around Keaton's legs. Pen felt like she was suffocating and assumed Keaton was feeling it too.

Keaton simply doled out gauzy strokes over Marilyn's back. "Don't remember us ever having cats this calm before," he said, giving Irene an unexpected smile. "They were always kind'a wild before."

Irene had held herself off, her eagerness leashed, eyes glittering and fixed on Keaton. "I still try and keep my eye on the wild ones, down by the docks. Put food out for them when it gets cold."

Keaton nodded his head thoughtfully, appreciatively and

then let his eyes travel over the house. "Things in here look mostly the same."

She came over to where Keaton was still stroking Marilyn and gently touched the back of his collar, where his dark hair grew long. "This place was pretty shabby before, Keaton. Not much of a home."

Keaton awkwardly straightened. "It's good now, Mom. Just fine."

Eyeing the bandages on Keaton's hands, Ed took hold of Keaton's bag and tossed it into his old room. "Likely nicer on the deck," Ed said over his shoulder.

Outside, Keaton had visibly relaxed. They sat in the greying resin chairs, their backs to Irene's pink geraniums, all of them drinking iced tea through straws.

"When can you start using your hands?" Irene asked.

"I'll take the bandages off them today and rewrap them with the fingers left out. The fingers aren't bad anyway."

"So you're here for a bit," said Irene.

"Never thought I'd be back."

Irene smiled, like she understood what it was to go and return. They sat there for a long time until the sun cut behind the building on the other side of the river, and the air turned suddenly cool.

"End of the season's coming," said Irene, sighing. "Bittersweet." Then Ed said that each August, the backbone of the long, hot summer would crack, and rain and wind would wrestle their way in. "Sometimes it's just for a few days, but it gives you a taste of what's comin'."

Keaton disappeared into his room, changing his bandages, showering, and then Irene produced a large bowl of steaming pasta and tomato sauce. "Go ahead and help yourselves," she said.

Pen was surprised at how much Keaton was able to put away, especially now with the use of his fingers. After they ate, he said he was tired. "I'll be ready for a good sleep," he said.

"Thanks for the meal. For everything." He was looking at Pen.

That night, she called Jeff and told him she was in Port, that Keaton seemed to be settling-in. "But I'm worried he might bolt. The charges, being here. I know how I'd feel, coming back and I don't have half the baggage." She paused. "Jeff? As soon as I get hold of something, I'm afraid I'm going to lose it."

There was a long silence, an anxious thought forming. Maybe Jeff had finally had enough of the see-saw; maybe he'd simply put down the phone, taken Maddie to the wade-pool, or to the petting-zoo to see the baby goats.

"Are you there?"

"I'm here."

"I've been that way with you." She could hear Jeff breathing, thinking about what he would say. "I'm sorry," she said.

"That's okay, Pen. I know."

She talked to Maddie for a couple of minutes. Before she hung up, Maddie said, "I think that the boy has come out now, from the lake."

"What boy, Maddie? The boy who drowned?"

Maddie was busy with something, rustling and snuffling.

"Maddie?"

"You should come home soon, Mommy." Pen promised that she would.

When it was dark, she bundled up in a fleece jacket and sat out again with Irene and Ed. The air was damp, pungent with lake-smells and diesel. "We should take turns staying up in case he tries to leave," she said.

Irene's face was in half-shadow and she seemed to be smiling. "You gonna tackle him if he goes?"

"Of course not."

Ed chuckled and cleared his throat. "That boy doesn't look like he's got anything left in him to bolt with."

Pen let her eyes stray to the water, lights from the boats playing innocently on the black surface. She wanted to believe that Keaton would stay. "If he bolts, things will be even worse. He'll try to go back for Annie."

"Must have thought coming back here was what he wanted to do. Unless you think he just came back because you wanted him to," said Irene.

"I *went* out there because he needed his family."

"I guess the rest is up to him."

The old stretched silence fell between them and then Irene and Ed went in to go to bed, Irene turning to Pen at the last. "I'm glad you're home too, Pen."

On the couch, Pen listens to the rigging in the boats, fragments of sound, at once lyrical and percussive. The room is full of shadows. If Rod had not drowned, if the *Isobel* had returned to harbour, she wonders if she would have been a different person now. A resourceful mother, a generous partner to Jeff. She feels a tightening in her limbs, a shallowness of breath that she suddenly names as *waiting*. She has spent too long waiting. What does she wait for, she wonders? She waits for what she expects will happen. She waits for the lake to open itself and swallow what her heart can't loose.

She throws off the blanket and swings her feet onto the floor. Beside the couch, on a cracked dinner plate, is an assortment of beach glass, greens and blues, fuzzy with twenty years of accumulated cat hair. She leans down and touches the blunted edges, picking up one in her hand. A memory of Irene comes: Irene on the beach, small, thinner, her dark hair loose, streaming wildly, fantastically. She bends, slips her hand into the little fretful waves that anxiously break at her feet. She straightens, turns, holds out her hand to Pen. Irene's expression is nothing short of dazzling.

Pen blinks, dropping the bit of glass onto the plate with the others. The morning light creeps over the walls and one of the cats scratches at the door to be let out. Ed is in the kitchen making coffee and Pen goes into the kitchen too and sits down with him. He doesn't look up from the paper.

"That policeman called you a couple of days ago."

"Who?" asks Pen.

"Sancton, I think. Maybe somethin' different."

"Sinclair?"

"Yup. The one handling the drowning. Wants to talk to you about some things. I told him you'd give him a call."

"I can do better. I have to go in there today with Keaton."

Ed looks at her over the top of his glasses. "I can run him in. Or Irene."

Pen is quiet. Looking into Ed's hound-dog face, she is ambushed by a feeling of love for this man.

"Of course, if you want to, that's different," says Ed, flipping the pages of the paper. "Or we can all go. 'Cept that might be a bit much for our boy in there." He nods at the closed door to the bedroom.

"How do we know he's still there?"

"He's still there," says Ed.

Pen takes a sip of coffee, rubs her eyes. She wants to check her email. It's almost September and campus life will be gearing up soon. She hasn't brought her laptop with her, just her phone.

"Anybody around here have a computer I can use?"

"Try the Inn. They might let you."

She decides to put that on her list.

"You hear any more about the biker mess, Ed?"

"Oh, sure. Town's still buzzing with it."

"One of them was on the beach the day of the drowning."

Ed looks up from his paper. "That what the OPP want to ask you about?"

"I don't know. All I know is that he was one of the first in the water. He never hesitated." Ed's still looking at her, his eyes not moving from her face. "It's more than I did," she says.

Ed eases away the mug she holds and puts his hands over hers. "It was a good thing you did, going out there for your brother, Pen."

"I think I did that for myself. To bring him back. It's what I thought I wanted."

"Good all the same," says Ed.

Pen is making a list of things she should do before the term starts. She knows she is distracting herself, determinedly pulling her thoughts away from Keaton and the visit they'll soon make to the OPP. She's still at the table, a pad of paper in front of her, when Keaton emerges from his room. "Hey," she says. "There's coffee if you want. Help yourself."

Rubbing his eyes with his wrist, Keaton goes into the kitchen and finds himself a mug. "Where's Ed?" He asks.

"Gone. Probably to the docks. I saw him earlier, but he's usually out before anyone else is up."

Keaton has his back to her, pouring coffee into a red and green coffee mug. "He still fish?"

"Mostly retired now," says Pen, "but he co-owns *Irene*."

Taking his mug over to the table, he sits beside her and pulls over a section of the paper. "Must have done okay, after I left." He is staring at the print on the page but Pen knows he isn't really reading.

"Re-mortgaged," she says simply. "Re-mortgaged the boat when he lost the bail money. Then he started to do pretty well. The yields were good over those years."

Keaton glances at the window. He looks relaxed, brighter after sleep.

"On the coast, when I said I grew up on commercial boats they thought I was from Nova Scotia or that I was a Newfie. They laughed when I told them that I came from here." He smiles at her, his expression warm, the sleep still there in the lines and creases. "Then I was crewing one year with a guy from down around Port Burwell. He went on and on about zebra mussels. How they are vacuuming up the bottom of the lake. I thought he was bull-shitting at first. Like he was talking about an alien takeover. Guys talk about a lot of crap when they are out on the boats for a long time. But then I started thinking about the lake, how it has to choke on everything that flows into it from someplace else."

"No, they're real. If you walk the beach, you see them washed up at the water-line. By the thousands." She shrugs.

Keaton is quiet. She can seem him thinking about the lake, what lives in it now, and what doesn't. He was on the tugs, Pen needs to remember, from the time he was young. He went out with Rod, and after Rod disappeared, Keaton had worked on other tugs.

"Keaton, we're going to have to take a drive, when you're ready."

"Guess I know."

Keaton gets up just as Irene opens her door. She's already dressed, and she's wearing a new-looking pair of jeans and a pink cotton sweater.

"Not working today?" asks Pen.

"Thought I might take a ride in with you and Keaton."

Pen's about to say something, but Keaton nods his head at Irene. "That would be good." Pen gives Keaton a hard look, her face fixed in frown. "You sure?" It feels to her that Irene is being given something, a privilege, she doesn't deserve.

"Let's go," he says.

It takes her a couple of minutes to gather up the documents they will need, to find her sunglasses and her keys. Keaton might have to remain in custody. She hates to think about that but she knows it's true.

"Keaton, you pack a bag?"

Keaton doesn't say anything. Instead, he swings a small carry-on bag over his shoulder and heads for the car. Pen is sorry that she is hounding him. When Irene goes to get in to the back seat of the car, Keaton slides in instead.

Pen involves herself in driving and Irene starts to talk. She starts with the restaurant. How people come from as far away as Toronto looking for a little Lake Erie perch. Her voice is bright with the affection she has for the place. "Years ago people made jokes that the fish positively glowed on your plate. Now it's served up like something gourmet."

They both laugh. "How many times has that place changed hands?" he asks.

"A few," says Irene. "But I hang in there. Pretty much name my own shifts now." Keaton is nodding, an unguarded look of appreciation in his face. Pen can sees him in the rearview mirror. She glances down at the speedometer, wanting and not wanting to make the arrival at the police station.

"Keaton?"

"Yeah?"

"Are you going to tell them what happened? On the *Dolly* I mean?"

He looks out the window, putting his bandaged hand up to the glass. "Guess I'll have to. That's sort of the deal, right?"

She glances furtively over at Irene. "Will you tell us? Sometime, I mean."

"I guess."

They drive in silence until Pen pulls into the parking lot of the OPP station. It's busier this time than it was when she was here last. A man and woman come out, clinging to one another, and from behind them, a group of grungy looking teens push past. When Pen looks over at the window in reception, she sees that it is the same flat-haired woman who was there the first time. She steps closer to the counter but Keaton moves in before she can get the words out.

"My name is Keaton Beau. I'm here about some outstanding warrants." He takes the documents from Pen's hand and places them on the counter. "I think this will pretty much clue you in."

"Mr. Beau, I believe we were notified that you would be coming. Please have a seat and an officer will be with you shortly."

Irene and Keaton walk back to the sitting area, and Pen stays at the window.

"You're here with Mr. Beau?" the woman asks.

"Yes. I'm his sister. But there's something else.... I believe Detective Sinclair called me last week about the Benny Vasco drowning. He asked me to contact him."

The woman looks at Pen, her expression unchanged. "And your name?"

"My name is Pen. Penelope Beau."

"Did you want to speak to him now, or wait until after your brother's matter has been dealt with?"

Pen pauses. The woman blinks at her over the top of her glasses.

"Oh, I'd like to be with my brother if that's all right."

"That's fine. I'll let Detective Sinclair know you're here."

Before long, two uniformed police officers come out into the waiting room. One is short and dark-haired, the other has reddish skin and a beefy look. They seem overly courteous, like they are managers at a four-star hotel.

"Mr. Beau? Would you and your family like to come this way, please?"

They escort him back, Irene and Pen following through the glass doors and down the same corridor Pen travelled before, although they stop at a different room this time. Once they are all seated, the small, dark-haired officer explains that Keaton will now be arrested. They will read him the charges, and then ask him if he would like a lawyer.

Keaton nods that he understands and the other officer reads the warrants. He reads the charges slowly and in a hushed tone, and then looks solemnly at Keaton. "Mr. Beau, do you want to talk to us now, or do you want a lawyer here."

"Keaton..." Pen jumps in, her pulse beginning to hammer.

"Mr. Beau?"

Keaton has laid both his bandaged hands on the table, the fingertips pink, the nails ragged. "I'm just going to tell you what happened. Straight up, if that's okay. That's what I came all this way for, isn't it?"

"Works for us," says the smaller of the officers. "In that

case, I'm going to ask that your family wait outside until we are done interviewing you." He singles Pen out with his look. "We'll let you know."

"He should have a lawyer," Pen says, back at reception. "You said you and Ed would line someone up for him."

"If he's going to tell the truth anyway, he doesn't need one."

Pen stares at Irene. In a matter of seconds, years of disbelief, of frustration simply slip their moorings and rage rushes in. Pen could be shouting, or wailing, she no longer hears herself:

"Don't you get it? He'll get thrown in jail — because you won't lift one of your sacred sober fingers to help."

Irene is very still, her voice kept low. "I guess you must be right, Pen. You are, usually, about most things."

It's rare for Irene to be so caustic, so sharp. Pen immediately feels its effect, as though her line on resourcefulness, on cleverness, has been utterly severed. Now, she flounders, bobs, roles, an awful bitterness rising.

"I brought him back here to have the best chance to straighten all this out."

Irene's gaze is relentless. "He didn't come back here for you. He came back to face things he's done. To take up his life honestly. Are *you* going to call Jeff, ask how he and Maddie are getting along without you? No, I guess not. Just throw yourself into the deep end with Keaton, eh? Flail around until you go under."

Pen stares in amazement. The old Irene has resurfaced after all of these years, the sweetness dissolved, hard reckoning glinting dangerously in her eyes. Only now she isn't drunk and she doesn't sound sorry. "Guess you must be an expert on quality family time," Pen says, astonished, her eyes widening.

Irene doesn't say anything at first. It's infuriating how she seldom offers up any defence.

"Far from it," she says finally, her gaze going in the direction of the interview rooms, to where Keaton now sits with the police. "That's something I never got right." With the admission, something settles in her, like sand poured into the bottom of a glass. "And I can never make up for it. Not now."

Without warning, Irene reaches out and places her hand on Pen's cheek, stroking her with the outside of her fingers. Her touch is cool, the skin rough. "You make things so hard, Pen."

Pen's centre drops like an anchor, and rests, deep down, in a trough of sadness, her eyes filling, her heart lurching madly. Her fingers follow Irene's to the piercing in her eyebrow, searching the place where metal meets flesh. Why has she done this? What had made her want to tear at herself this way?

She takes in a breath and holds it while her eyes stay on Irene's face. In some part of herself, she has imagined seeing *this* Irene. She has longed for it.

Irene takes her in her arms, a gentle, rocking embrace, and neither of them care who sees.

29.

T SHOULDN'T HAVE COME BACK to the house. He left the cancer clinic and found the road going north, retracing the route he had taken earlier that day. He got as far as the number seven and without thinking, he turned east. The highway took him to a familiar town where he picked up another highway, this time going southeast, and before long, he was on the 401, travelling toward the city, going back to the only home he has ever known.

There hasn't been much rain over the last several weeks and the patch of grass in the front of the house is almost dead. Depressed by the sight of the wretched lawn, he thinks briefly about pulling out the sprinkler and attaching the hose. But he's too drained to do more than climb the front steps. He tugs on the storm and props it open with his boot. Jammed between the doors are a dozen flyers, still rolled in their plastic sleeves. A note pokes out of his mail slot, politely telling him that his mail is being held in the postal depot, at the strip mall.

Unlocking the door, he kicks one or two of the flyers aside and steps over the rest. With the blinds drawn, the house is in semi-darkness. The air is too still. T lets the storm swing closed and leaves the front door open. No sense in worrying about dead-bolts or locks; if someone wants in, a lock won't stop them.

He slips from room to room, opening windows, checking lights, quiet and gentle as if to not wake a sleeper. The rooms are messy, the bed unmade. Just like he left them. It was neat as a pin when Eva lived here. The place is tired now, scuffs on the base-boards, burn-marks on the couch. Still, the fundamentals are the same; the spring colours on the walls, two sets of sheets and a pile of marine-blue towels in the linen closet, a kitchen equipped with fry pans and mixers. He has lived with what she left behind.

T goes into the bathroom and runs the bathtub faucet, watching the water sputter and then become a gush. There is a sponge under the sink and he takes it to the inside of the tub, wiping away the weeks of dust. T doesn't take baths, preferring the shower, the water pressure cranked up and the water hot. But he and Eva used to bathe the kid in here, the kid slipping and squirming like a shiny little fish, bubbles up to his chin.

He stares into the tub's cold white interior and thinks about how tired he is. He turns off the water, watching it drain, and then kicks off his boots, climbs in and lies down. When he sinks low enough, with his knees bent, he feels himself disappear.

A breeze sweeps through the house, rattling blinds and stirring the shower curtain. He puts his hand up as if to touch it. When Eva lived here, she asked him to buy her a washer and drier. When they were delivered, a discounted pair that was a robin's-egg blue, she ran her hands over them and said,

"We won't use the drier on sunny days." She looked at T, serious at first, something old fashioned and motherly in her. "*You* can hang the laundry out on a line for me, Tommy. Won't that be great?" Her face relaxed and she laughed, throwing her arms around him. "Scary T Valentine, hanging out laundry, a clothes peg in his mouth."

He was pissed at her for making fun. "Ball Buster," he'd snarled, but she squeezed him harder until he squeezed her back.

He would have let go of anything for her. He believed that then and he still believes it. But he had watched them go, her and the kid, Eva's face still holding on to some feeling for him, whether pity or care, and he had done *nothing* to stop them.

He couldn't have stopped them, and that's the lie he's been caught in, probably for most of his life. When he was a kid, it was true. He thinks of his mom opening her door to all kinds of losers, T parked in front of the TV like a deaf-mute kid, *pretending* he didn't know what she was doing in the back room.

T's mother had been dead for years, and he was over forty when Eva left.

He lies in the bathtub with his arms crossed loosely over his vest, his knees splayed out.

He thinks about securing the house, driving back to his buddy's after dark. No part of him wants to. This is where he wants to be, in the bathtub, in this bungalow with its violet walls and a box of the kid's toys still in the bedroom closet.

He hears a soft click.

It is a few seconds before he opens his eyes. Two RCMP officers, armed, and wearing black vests and headsets stand over him;

"Please don't move, Mister Valentine."

30.

KEATON IS IN WITH THE OFFICERS for what seems like a very long time. Uncomfortable in her chair, Pen stretches her arms, yawns nervously, and then loosens her hair from its clasp. Irene has settled back into reading her book and for the moment, the two women are quiet with one another, a new, uncertain tenderness having crept in.

A copy of the latest *Maclean's Magazine* is in a wall-mounted rack. On the cover is a photo of T, taken from some distance, looking passive but unapologetic, implacable, the broad, heavy mouth tightly shut. His hands are cuffed and there are officers on either side of him, one of them wearing a black protective jacket. T is strangely inscrutable, like a man who has been largely erased. On the four occasions when they met, Pen saw a shadow about T, a residue of relationship, of family. Perhaps it is too late for someone like T Valentine. It strikes her that people can't go through their lives without anchors. She thinks of Rod, sending her to bed with a gruff kiss, the memory incorruptible, true. She closes the magazine and then closes her eyes.

"Penelope Beau." She is startled awake. The receptionist motions to her with the slightest nod of her head. "Detective Sinclair would like to speak with you." Pen stands, awkward and waiting, until Detective Sinclair saunters in.

"Heard you called," she says, forcing lightness.

"Glad you could come down." He gestures with an open

arm for her to follow. "I just want to update you," he says walking, talking over his shoulder. "You were good enough to give us your statement about what you saw on the beach the day Ben Vasco drowned. And then, you let us know about Tom Valentine's part in the rescue attempt."

"T," she says.

"After you came in, I decided to speak to some of the other witnesses. A couple of them corroborated your story about him — Mr. Valentine — going into the water. Some of the others couldn't remember, or said they couldn't, as soon as they realized who it was we were asking about."

"He makes people nervous, I guess." Pen says, smiling a little.

Detective Sinclair nods his head. "These guys don't have many friends. For someone like Tom Valentine, personal relationships are extra freight they don't need. Still, he appears to have one friend. The owner of Pirates has known him for years, and he's not a member of any of the outlaw groups operating in the area. But he wasn't on the beach that day."

"Will what I saw make any difference?"

"I don't know, really. It doesn't change the basics of the thing. Eight bodies found on land he had leased, an operation he was clearly in charge of. But who knows, if it goes to a jury, a piece of character evidence might make some impression. I wouldn't count on it though. He has quite a history with the outlaw gangs in this province." He shrugs. "Anyway, I've passed it all on to the investigating team at the RCMP." He hesitates and looks at her.

"That's not what you called about, though. Am I right?" she asks.

Detective Sinclair sits back a little in his chair and runs his hands through his thinning hair. "No. All of that is kind of secondary to the Benny Vasco situation," he says. "It seems that when Ben was out in the water, the lifeguard in the chair closest to him was taking a short break. Their protocol is that the guard in the next chair should take over, but that lifeguard was watching a woman and a small child farther to the eastern boundary. The child was upset, crying in the water, choking, and the guard was tracking them."

Pen considers what he has told her. "It all comes down to what someone did or didn't do?"

Detective Sinclair looks apologetic. "Whenever there is a death and we don't have all the answers…"

"Then people want to place blame," she says, interrupting him.

"Look, from our perspective, this is procedural. Nothing more. It's not reasonable to think that the lifeguard could have had her attention in two places at once. Sad, but just a circumstantial tragedy. I don't think we'll ever know what happened."

Pen stares at her hands and sees Ben in his last shining moment, captivated and enthralled by the lake, his head an orb riding its glittering surface. He would not have thought about what was underneath: the writhing current, the half-lit cold. She wonders if his ankle gave out, whether the sand had shifted. Was there an irresistible distraction on the beach — a dog barking, one of his friend's calling out — had he turned and lost his footing?

Detective Sinclair leans toward her. "I doubt we'll keep the investigation open now."

"What about those women? The staff people on the beach?"

"That's a different matter," he says, his eyes on the floor. "That will be up to the family — whether or not there will be some kind of civil suit involved."

There is a lapse, the detective careful not to go too far or say too much. Then, "You asked before about a service for him."

"Yes."

"I understand that the family has agreed to allow the Woodside staff to attend a memorial service next Wednesday."

"So the family's changed how they see things?"

Detective Sinclair hesitates. "I wouldn't go that far. I don't know. But it is a positive step, I think."

Pen stands up and thanks him for the information. "I'll keep an eye out for details on the service," she says. He walks her out into the corridor and she sees him glance in the direction of where Keaton is giving his statement. "I hope things work out for your brother," he says quietly.

She stops and studies him.

"I didn't know Keaton very well, but we were at school together, in Port. I played hockey with his friend, Andy Ruddell." Pen is instantly wary, old stories about the Beau's pressing in.

"Anyway, I just wanted to say that a lot of years have gone by. He's had a tough time and he was only a kid, back then. Your family had a bad time. There might be more compassion for his situation than you think."

"He still has a lot to get through."

He's thoughtful for a moment, his hand straying to his pocket, fiddling with his keys. "I expect so. More than just the charges, I guess."

He starts to leave her and then turns, calling her back, his face well-meaning, curious. "Oh, Pen? You ever hear from Andy? He ever get back to hockey?"

"I've seen him," says Pen. "And no. He never did."

"Too bad. He was pretty good."

"Yes," says Pen. And then, as an afterthought. "But he's okay with it. Andy seems to be just fine."

It is another thirty minutes before Keaton comes out of the interview area. Only the smaller of the officers is with him.

"We will be releasing Mr. Beau on certain conditions," the officer explains to Irene and Pen. "There will be a preliminary hearing, and the Crown wants him to stay in the area until this is all cleared up. He'll have to check in with us every week until then."

"Should we get a lawyer?" asks Pen, standing. The officer nods, and casually rests one hand on the counter. "Yes, I would. There are facts involved in this case that came to light after

Mr. Beau left the area. He's just corroborated some of them in his statement. We'll need to do further investigation and then present the evidence to a judge. At that time, a decision will be made about the charges."

They wait for him to say more but he doesn't, and Irene slips her arm through Pen's, smiling brightly at Keaton. "Let's take the long way and drive home along the shore. Maybe walk a bit."

Nothing stirs on Keaton's' face, no hint of what he's just told the police. He eases his shoulders, as though a weight has been lifted, and walks with them to the car.

31.

WHEN KEATON CAME TO HER ROOM to say goodbye he looked ashamed. That was what broke Annie's heart. Not the parting. She knew they would see one another again.

They sat close on the side of her bed, her head tucked into him, his arms tight around her.

"It's good that you are going back."

He was silent, gazing at the floor, not wanting to speak. Annie took her hand and stroked his hair and he let himself fold into her, his head resting in her lap. She began to talk to him about all of the places they had been, the view from their window in Vancouver, the flower garden she planted in William's Lake: daisies and bachelor buttons, golden-eyed chrysanthemums.

"We slept on the beach in Powell River, beside a fire you made from driftwood. The water pulled at the stones and it was as if the ocean was breathing. If *we* stopped breathing, the ocean would breathe for us. Remember this Keaton. All of it."

Keaton didn't move.

"They'll want to know what happened, Annie. If I go back, I have to speak."

She prodded the back of his neck with her fingers, kneading the ruthless knots of muscle.

"What are you afraid of?"

"Of what I've done."

Outside, the sky was turning to purple. The day was dying. Tomorrow morning he would fly home with his sister and

Andy, Andy's face carved-up with love for him, and Pen's face still bright, still shiny, despite the dark layers of cloud around her. They will go on, and Keaton with them.

"Is it that you don't know how to tell it?" she murmurs into his hair.

"I'm ashamed."

Annie thinks of the stories of the children from the mission, residing in cardboard boxes, how they whispered to her to free them. Keaton's story is in a box too. She bends her head and places her cheek on his back.

"Then let me find the words for you, Keaton. Lie still and listen. We'll tell it together and then we'll let it go."

32.

THE DAY OF THE DROWNING has resurfaced in Pen's mind countless times since she came to Port with Keaton. The image is disturbingly clear: a pure blue sky, the lake innocent, playful. Benny Vasco is smiling broadly, his legs lifting in turn, his arms moving the warm air like turbines.

Now, when she looks back, she sees him poised at the moment of his intention. The image is imbued with a kind of sunny and inevitable tragedy. She reads this, mistakenly, as foreknowledge and cannot forgive herself for it. She had not stirred from her spot on the beach while Benny Vasco had drowned.

Even T managed to do better. Much better.

There is a notice in the paper:

"Memorial Service for drowning victim Benjamin Vasco will be held Thursday August 29th, at Victoria United Church, St. Thomas..."

Four days, thinks Pen. It is as though she has been waiting for years.

She spends time in the house at the kitchen table, reading articles she has downloaded at the Inn while Keaton sits on the deck, still wearing long sleeves, despite the warmth. His hands are better and he has taken off the bandages. Now he spends hours writing letters to Annie, his fingers curled awkwardly around the pen, gingerly pressing the words onto the page. Pen can tell that the effort hurts.

Sometimes, Keaton lifts his head and calls out a question.

He wants details about Port, about the fishery. She thinks of him as he was, years before, drawing quickly, ruthlessly, never finishing. Casting off his drawings to Pen. He seems determined to finish now. "I want to tell Annie what it's like."

Gloria, one of the cats, has sunk down on his lap, and he strokes her tortoiseshell ears. "It's strange, being back here," he says. "It feels like you've fallen off the edge of the earth and come up on the other side."

She thinks about how she feels about this place, a push and pull.

"You said yourself, it hasn't changed that much," says Pen.

Keaton tugs gently on the cat's ears. He doesn't look up. "Irene's different. And you."

"Irene's gone to a lot of AA meetings," Pen says equivocally.

"Irene's a miracle."

Pen tilts her head, the word *miracle* a puzzle. "I haven't been able to buy it," she says. "All the recovery stuff. It seems to me like she's only been interested in one person."

Keaton laughs. "That's a little harsh."

"I don't think she was thinking about *us* when she was drinking. And I don't think her so-called recovery was for us, either."

Keaton is quiet a moment. "It must have been tough with the old man. He didn't care for her."

He seems so certain. She's never thought about Rod not caring. "I don't know about that. I don't remember what they were like together. Anyway, it doesn't change that she bailed on us after he was gone."

"People get mixed-up about what it is to keep living. They have to go somewhere, and so they go someplace in-between." He pauses, then adds, "I guess Irene must have decided to save herself."

Pen lifts an eyebrow. "Irene's good at that." She smiles slyly at Keaton and he laughs, his shoulders shaking. They are grinning at one another, conspiratorial again. It has cost him to come back here, to face the old demons, to leave Annie behind. A single bright spot opens in her thoughts, a gathering place for her unspoken hopes, her longing. It *is* possible for people to go and to return. Keaton has. Perhaps Irene has too. She feels the rush of possibility enter in, and with it, a lightness, a tingling of anticipation, a letting go.

Keaton goes back to his writing, and the room is full with the two of them, with the purring cat, the breeze rattling the screen in the door.

A boat in the harbour passes, its slowed engine sputtering, struggling. Pen follows the sounds with her eyes. Keaton hears it too. "Dad could listen to an engine for a couple of minutes and know exactly where the problem was. Did you know that, Pen? He was smart; he'd grown up on the tugs."

A silence falls between them, fraught with their memories of Rod. The feeling is electric, alive, as if Rod has just strode into the room.

She concentrates on Keaton's words, what he is really saying. "Maybe not in a storm, Keaton," she says, shaking her head. "He wouldn't be able to hear that well and the tugs are so noisy. Think of the high wind."

"He would have figured it out," Keaton says simply, "but the solution was likely beyond him. Too difficult a repair or he didn't have the right part."

She is confused, unsure. "Keaton, we *don't* know…"

"I've thought about all of this. More than you can imagine. Look, it might have been the engine. He was flirting with neglect when it came to the *Isobel*. You wouldn't remember that about him, Pen. How headstrong he was. When it came time to renew his registration, he would get her patched together with a lick and a promise but that was only every few years. In between, he let a lot of things slide. It was a choice he made, probably to save money." He looks at Pen, his eyes dark, stormy. "He could be reckless, impatient, Pen, especially when it came to the *Isobel*. If you ask the guys who crewed for him, they'll tell you the same."

When her chin thrusts forward, his expression softens and his voice becomes less pressing. "Look, it doesn't matter, the mistakes he made. Rod would have come back, Pen. He would have come back if he could."

His words are matter-of-fact. He's involved in stroking Gloria, the hand rising a little each time and then drawing itself slowly over the soft fur. Images of Rod come, bright flashes. Smart, vital Rod, his face lighting up as he turned from the tug and saw her, waiting on the dock. More than anything she wants to have Keaton's certainty about him. "I wish I knew him like you did. I wish I knew that he wouldn't deliberately leave."

She can think of nothing else to do but throw herself into her work. For the next two days, she makes notes for her classes and checks her emails on the computer at the Inn. The department administrator has sent a couple of anxious messages.

"When can I say you will be back in the office?"

Pen responds but doesn't give a definite date. "I'm attending a memorial service and settling some personal business."

She could go back to the city now. She realizes that Keaton doesn't need her. She sees how able he is to step into his own uncertain future. If they are to have a real relationship now, Pen will have to let him go.

She calls home and talks to Maddie, who rambles on about a nest full of dead baby birds that she found on the sidewalk. She wanted to take them home. For the collection. "Daddy told me no."

"But Maddie, that happened in the spring time. You didn't find the nest now."

"There are three birds in the nest," persists Maddie. "And I don't know where the mother is."

"The mother will have gone off to have more baby birds."

"A cat might come and get the nest."

"The nest is gone now, Maddie. That was a long time ago."

"There are three babies." Maddie is emphatic.

"Those babies aren't alive anymore. You know, life ends, sometimes too early, but it ends." She knows as soon as she has said it that it is too much information for Maddie.

"You don't *know*," says Maddie, beginning to cry.

"Look, I'm sorry, Maddie. It's hard to understand, but people and animals, even flowers and trees die. Like the boy on the beach, Maddie. The boy who drowned."

"You didn't *see* them," Maddie is sobbing, persisting with the birds. "You don't know where they went. You don't know if they're gonna come back."

"You're right, Maddie. I didn't see them and so I don't really know. There are lots of things I don't know. So let's just wait and see. Okay?" She realizes that it is true that she has made assumptions about loss. What she thought of as finality in the world is really change, a vast and confounding transformation, disorienting to the point of despair.

When Jeff gets on the phone, she tells him that she is sorry about making Maddie so upset. "I wish there was something easy to tell her," she says.

She can almost see him shrug. "But it isn't easy, Pen. That's the point."

It will be Labour Day when she gets back. She feels reluctant, telling him that she'll be away longer, although he doesn't mention her staying in Port. Lea and Bill have invited them to their cottage for the long weekend. "Be great if you came, Pen."

"I'll try," she says simply. "But I want you to go anyway."

Quite suddenly, she is utterly taken up with the desire to see Maddie, to feel the lightness of Maddie's small body in her arms. And she wants her life back, her life in the city, with Jeff grounding her, his good nature feeding her like an irrepressible underground spring.

Andy leaves a message on Pen's cell. "How's everything with

you? With Keaton? Call me, if you get a chance." She wants to, but she won't.

Instead she tells Keaton that he should call Andy and update him as to what will happen now with the charges.

Ed cooks for them in the evenings, and they sit at the kitchen table, the four of them, eating together, something they have never done before. Keaton seems relaxed and quiet and Pen asks him the odd question: have you called that lawyer, yet? What about having someone check out those burns?

Irene doesn't ask anything. Instead, she tells him about the families in Port, people he probably remembers. Many have gone, moved to take up factory work, but some have stayed, still trying to make it in the fishery or picking up scraps of seasonal work with the tourists.

Ed tells Keaton about some of the tugs that are docked in the harbour. "You'll remember quite a few," says Ed, "though the names might be different. Different owner, different name. But the boat's the same boat." Ed talks about optimism on the docks, despite what he calls the doom and gloom. "Environmentalists, economists, they all say Port should be sucking wind. But we're not. Not yet, anyway." He pushes his chair back and places his big arms across the expanse of his belly. "Still lots of fish out there, and yields have been good. Lake keeps on surprising us." He looks at Keaton and smiles encouragingly. "Maybe you'd like to go out? Now that your hands are gettin' better."

Keaton wears an inward expression and he keeps his head angled over his uncovered hands. The skin is raised on his palms, small mounds of pink that will probably never fade entirely.

"I'd like that Ed. Maybe do a day run out to wherever the fish are. Maybe on your boat." he says nodding. "I'd like to get the feel of her."

Ed nods his head. "That'll be fine. I'll fix it up for tomorrow if you want. Weather's still good."

Pen gathers up the plates, scrapes them and piles them next

to the sink. Ed turns on the television in the front room, and the patio doors slide open as Keaton goes out for a walk. She washes the dishes in a mountain of suds and then looks over at Irene, who dries them silently and carefully puts them away.

33.

T OPENED HIS EYES and registered that a pair of RCMP officers stood on his bathmat. He was relieved they weren't Angels. The officers ordered him to raise his arms, which he did, and one of them frisked him for weapons. They told him to climb out of the tub, slowly, with his hands over his head. It was surprisingly difficult to lever himself out, his weight beyond him. It was not exactly weakness he felt but a surrender to gravity. He scrambled once or twice to gain leverage, using his elbows to brace himself against the sides of the tub. When he stood, he was swaying a little, like he was punch-drunk.

The first few days after he was taken into custody were an endless string of interviews. The cops like asking questions over and over, waiting for a slip or a contradiction. Although T grew tired of the inquisition, he recognized that it brought some reward; gradually it became clearer what the cops actually knew. He figured out early in the questioning that there had been an informant. It was Hornet, a police plant, self-professed, and as far as T is concerned, a candy-ass coward. T reassures himself that he always thought of Hornet as a fake. All talk. Hornet told the police about the kill orders from Winnipeg and claimed that he didn't shoot anyone himself. Hornet had participated that night, whether he claims different now or not.

And then there is the rat, Solham.

T managed to piece together that Solham is Winnipeg's lapdog. He is denying any kill orders, saying instead that T is an opportunistic lunatic, a born killer; the massacre had been T's idea and his alone. Based on Solham's statement, one of the interviewers actually asked T if he had a history of mental illness.

"No," T told them flatly, "but I *am* dying of lung cancer, *just* so you know."

Then they laughed, even T.

A crackhead like Solham might think he's got it made, now that he's under Winnipeg's protection, in good with them because he covered up. But T knows better. Solham is an organizational liability, and that won't buy him a future. None at all.

T is lying on a metal cot in a holding facility, not far from the mid-sized city where his court appearances have taken place. There is a building roar in his head, a rush of blood when he thinks of how they, the organization, simply gave him up. The betrayal, despite the years of his loyalty, claws and burrows its way inside. T thinks back to those early days, riding in the truck with George, the air in the cab sweet with tobacco, the night rushing past while George talked. He thinks of George giving him that Indian half-smile, wise, amused; right there, T felt he was where he should be.

Any loyalty he might have felt has been blown to hell. Now, he is finally free of the bonds of fucking brotherhood.

He told the cops about the call he received from Winnipeg on the day of the killings.

"Eliminate them, T. All of the them."

It was an unusual order, but not unheard of within outlaw organizations, and if T felt any surprise, he didn't express it. What happened later that night, T told the cops, was a result of that phone call. Nothing more.

He looks up at the concrete ceiling, cracks spidering out from the light fixtures, the paint a greying white. It doesn't bother him that he is in here. Most of his life on the outside has felt like nothing more than a dream.

When was the last good day? There haven't been many. An image comes into his mind of the beach in Port, the little girl darting around in her bathing suit, smiling at him impishly, playfully. The kid's mom was pretty, all caught-up in herself.

He went in for the kid, although he wasn't thinking of her as he hurled himself into the water. Somehow, and he sees this only now, she had changed the day for him. *She* was a different sort of future, one that had nothing to do with him, the life he had.

The jump in the lake was a leap of faith.

T lies there considering that maybe a person only gets one or two real moments. His mom, his beautiful screwed up mom. He guesses now he probably had loved her when he was a little kid. And Eva…. He'd like to stroke the inside of her arm again with the tip of his finger; he'd like for her to pull him in close.

He's letting himself drift to the child-leap, the total immersion in water, the water cold on his skin, his mother behind him, smiling, her face tipped up to the sun, and ahead of him, that tiny island, that bright hope.

34.

THE DAY BEFORE BENNY VASCO's memorial service is a day full of rain. Pen wakes to it; the water pounding the roof, rushing through the gutters. The sound sets up a slow small vibration that settles in her bones and in her muscles. She feels listless, unsure of how to apply herself to the hours ahead.

The last time she was in Port on a day like this, Andy had been with her. They walked around the old flight-training site and Pen had watched raindrops cascade down Andy's cheeks. Andy isn't here and despite the rain, Ed and Keaton have gone off early in the *Irene*. A solid windless rain never kept the tugs off the water.

She should be doing her work. There are still unplanned classes and a book review. She thinks about going for a bite at the Fish and Fry, where Irene is working, but decides against it. It's a relief to be outside.

She has no plan or direction.

She could go left, toward the little crescent beach where she often brought Maddie to swim. Or right, over the lift bridge, past the painted tower and down toward the wide sandy beach that stretches toward the bluff.

The idea of open water calls to her. The main beach, then.

It's a short walk really, once you cross the bridge. Why had she thought it was such a long way, when she was young? How is it that things become less than they were? She wonders if that will happen for Maddie. There is so much that must be left behind. She stops and looks at the odd assortment of houses, the squat oil tower, the tiny main street, and behind those, the water, still limitless in her imagination. Only the lake has kept its childhood dimensions for Pen. She walks again, a strange eagerness overtaking her. She is thinking of her dream, Ben Vasco stepping from the ancient lake onto land, restored. She feels light, almost giddy as though she is on her way to witness something wonderful. The lake relinquishing a small and glittering piece of itself, offering up what it has tenderly sheltered. Astonished, she smiles and thinks of how derisive she has been about this lake, its sullen nature, its contaminants.

She turns left onto the street that ends in the main beach, and the *Bud* sign in the window of Pirates blinks at her through the rain. Two of her encounters with T had happened here.

T remains a puzzle. She stands outside the bar, beside a row of dripping black Harleys and struggles to put the different pieces of T together. How is it that people can be capable of so much and so little?

She thinks of him, the moment he was almost flying over the water, his arms outstretched. Ben Vasco died that day. And on another day, most likely, T shot some of those men. One thing could be true and so could another. Actions, she is beginning to understand, can start out in one place, with a single intention, maybe a single *unknowable* impulse, and turn up someplace different.

She has numbed herself to the connections between things. Each tragedy, each joy in Pen's life has stood alone, crashing into her, over her, leaving her reeling and fighting to stand. What was the first point of impact, she wonders. When Rod was lost? Keaton leaving? For Pen, there has not been a *before* or an *after*, no continuance of hope.

It is occurs to her that for most of her life she has been both waiting for people to return to her, and expecting that they won't. Maybe it has cost her her marriage to Jeff. Maybe it hasn't. One thing is clear. She isn't waiting anymore. She decides that she can draw a circle around herself that is wide and generous. She takes one more look at Pirates and knows now what she must do next.

Drinking in the moist air, she pushes her face up to the watery sky. The beach is lost in a ghostly band of cloud. She thinks of Keaton out there, in the lake with Ed. Their voices will come back to them on a day like this. The sound has a way of going in circles in the fog. She stands, her face wet, her arms outstretched and wonders who, in this moment, she has become.

When she got back to the house, she called Detective Sinclair who immediately arranged for her to be security cleared and placed on T's visitor list. "Least we can do for you, Pen," he said. The facility where T is being held is about forty-five minutes from Port. She Googled the address so she wouldn't get lost. Now, music plays in the car from her iPod, a mix of female songwriters: Jan Arden, Sarah McLachlan.

She is clear-headed and full of purpose when she enters the building. A security guard at the front gate asks if she is Mr. Valentine's counsel. In her knee-length black raincoat, and with her hair tidily pulled back, she probably looks like a professional, and today she feels her age. No, she tells him; she is simply a friend. It takes a while for her to be cleared for entry, her ID scanned and checked, her bag emptied onto a tray for examination. She is led down a long hall to a glassed-in visiting area. A guard shows her to a small three-sided booth, where a plain beige telephone hangs on the wall.

"It will just be a few minutes," she's told. "Mr. Valentine isn't expecting visitors." If there is any humour in the remark, it doesn't show on the guard's face. The lights in the visiting area are fluorescent and unusually bright. Pen puts a hand over her eyes. She glances to her left and then to her right; none of the other booths are occupied.

T enters the room on the other side of the glass wearing an orange jump-suit that looks too large. His hands and ankles are shackled, and he shuffles to the plastic chair directly opposite her. He seems to have aged about ten years since she last saw him. He doesn't look surprised to see her. He simply nods his head.

With two hands, he picks up the receiver. Pen picks up too and then smiles. "You look thinner, T," she says.

"Yeah, I've been on a reducing diet," he says. "South Beach. And because you've been such a great role model, I've taken up running — gonna train for the Boston Marathon this year." He says this flatly. "But you know marathons — tough as shit!"

Pen laughs. "I haven't been doing much running actually."

T leans back in his chair and rests his eyes on her. If he wonders why she has come, he doesn't ask.

"Strange, I don't get many visitors," he says. "Can't think why that might be."

Pen looks at him. "You're in some serious trouble," she says.

This makes him laugh. "Yeah, well, you might say I have reason not to worry."

"I'm glad to hear that," she says. She looks away, gathering her thoughts.

"There are a couple of things I want to say."

T's eyebrows go up in his face. He looks amused.

"Let me guess. You know who shot J.R."

Pen ignores him. She folds her arms on the counter and with her shoulder presses the receiver closer to her ear.

"I saw you go into the water that day, T. I saw you jump up from your chair and throw yourself into the lake, clothes and all."

He's smiles wryly, then shrugs.

"So what?"

"It's what *you* did."

He doesn't say anything. Her eyes rest on him, willing him to take in what she has just said. Then,

"Maddie saw you do it too."

A spark of interest comes into his face.

"She knows you were trying to bring him back."

He snorts. "Yeah, and didn't that turn out well—"

"No, it's true that he drowned anyway. That doesn't change that you went in."

Everything in his face is monumental and grey except for his eyes which glitter like precious stone, Tourmaline or Agate. She thinks maybe he is remembering something. He looks squarely, indefatigably at Pen.

"Your kid's lucky to have you."

She colours, her face tensing. "She's got more than just me. But thanks." She goes to stand, but before she hangs up the phone, she puts her hand on the glass between them. "And T? Maddie knows now that people go and don't always come back. She's sad about that, but she's going to be okay with it."

"Yeah," he says, nodding. "She will. She'll be fine."

35.

PEN IS WAITING FOR THEM when they get back into the harbour. She had listened until she heard the first of the tugs return, and then she slipped on her sweater and walked down to the dock. The rain had finally stopped and the air was cooler. She kept her eyes on the lake, watching the pug-nosed boats turn toward the harbour. Once inside the protection of the little concrete pier, they go to unload their catch, empty their holds onto the weigh-scales, and then sputter up river toward the docks.

She has waited for more than half an hour. When the *Irene* gets close enough she stands ready, and Ed throws her a heavy docking line. Keaton has been lashing down equipment on the foredeck. He smiles over at her and pushes back the damp, lank hair from his face.

"Good day?" she asks.

"Oh yeah," says Keaton.

Ed looks up and nods his head.

"Get wet?"

"He won't melt," says Ed.

They busy themselves for a while tidying the boat, stowing lines and equipment, finally locking down the pilot house. Pen gives them a hand, surprised how easily she remembers what to do.

The sky over the lake has broken open into pinkish streaks and shafts of frail light fall onto the water.

"Now you decide to show your face," mutters Keaton looking at the sky.

Pen laughs. "Timing is everything."

Ed walks ahead, his form lumbering but well-directed, like a bear returning to its den. Pen watches him. Beside her, Keaton eases into motion, his pace still quick and tight but the urgency now gone.

"I want to know what you told the police the other day. All of it." She takes in a deep breath of air, not wanting her words to sound rushed. "Whatever it is, I just want to hear it, face it, move on," she says.

Keaton looks at her, his eyes steady and dark. "It's an ugly little story, Pen."

"I would assume so," she says, looking back squarely into his face, a face that in many ways, is a mirror of her own.

Keaton gestures to a bench overlooking the harbour. His features in profile look older, his skin coarsened, ruddy from a day on the water. From higher up on the street, Ed looks back at them, raises an arm and continues walking. Keaton's eyes shift to the boats, taking in each one, their lines, and the limb-like angles of their rigging.

"You remember before the drowning, I used to help the old man out on the *Isobel* a lot?"

"Of course," says Pen.

"He used to get me to do jobs on the boat that needed someone small. I was small enough, I guess."

Pen waits while Keaton lights a cigarette. "I didn't mind doing it," He takes a drag, holds it, exhales. "Everyone used their kids like that back then. One time, he seemed particularly pushed to get a job done.

"What was wrong?" Pen asks.

"Fuel line, I guess. He said the engine was acting up. The *Isobel's* engine was under the floor, the fuel line running aft. He knew what the trouble was but he couldn't get far enough down just by reaching. He didn't want to lose a day having the engine hauled. Couldn't *afford* that, he said. He'd walk me through the repair; it wouldn't be too hard. Anyway, he drew a little diagram on a piece of paper and pointed to what I'd have to loosen off. He gave me a new line to put in, told me I'd have to put a new casing on after." A look of anger and confusion clouds Keaton's face and he taps the ash from his cigarette, takes another puff. "Actually, I don't even know if the line *was* new. Maybe it wasn't a fuel line at all. He might have scrounged up an old line he had lying around. You know. Desperate times, desperate measures. Like I told you the other day, the old man was always making things do. The crew talked about the shortcuts he took but I also saw them for myself. I didn't question him. Not because I was afraid to — he would never have jumped down my throat for asking a question. I guess I *needed* to believe that he was too smart to make a serious mistake. I had faith in him, Pen." Keaton shrugs.

"Anyway, I didn't know anything about diesel fuel lines. Once I got down there, he asked me to describe what I was looking at. Hell, I didn't know. He gave me directions, like 'crank left, crank it hard, now test it by trying to loosen it off. If you can't, that's good. Not turning? Good. Go to the next....' At some point, the guy with the boat next to ours was coming over, offering his two cents worth. You know who it was, Pen?" Keaton's eyebrows rise a little when he says the name. "Terry Spar."

Keaton shifts his weight on the bench. He goes on, telling her about trying to make the repair, how he wasn't sure if he really put everything back right.

"I was down there for hours, working on my back with my arms over my head. I wanted to tell Rod I was too tired, but I didn't want to disappoint him. I thought I had the line in right. When I crawled out, I was just glad it was over."

Pen is quiet. "And Dad couldn't check it. He wouldn't be able to..."

"Yeah. Anyway, Spar was there, smirking. Called me a little grease monkey, smacked my butt." Keaton's face holds disgust, embarrassment. He looks at Pen. "Rod didn't *do* anything. Too distracted by the repair. Or maybe that's just how he was — turning a blind eye. I mean Christ, when you think of the stuff that was bringing us all down..." He's talking about Irene, Ed, the ocean of debt they were drowning in. She sees now how much Rod had disappointed him.

"The next day the storm blew in. A tug is a deathtrap, Pen. Free surface on the deck is enclosed against the weather, and the scupper drains are small. People have been caught and drowned before. That's what the investigators were looking for: if they found his body in the hold with all the hatches secured, it would have been clear it was an accident, that he had been trapped down there. But there was a hatch open and his body was gone. Like he had cut the engine, opened up the hatch to capsize her and then either jumped or just let himself get taken. But that's not what happened."

For a moment, he stops talking and they listen to the ragged sound of tugs returning to harbour.

"You know what I think?" Keaton rubs at his nose with the back of his hand, his eyes sweeping over the harbour and out to the lake. "I think that fuel line leaked. With the wind conditions, some water got into the bilge and the engine sucked water into the fuel system. That would have killed the engine and with no power, she would have laid broadside to the seas. He would have had the auto-pilot on so that he could work the nets. Once he knew the engine died, he went to look at the instruments but the *Isobel* was drifting sideways fast. Only one of the big hatches was open when they found her because he didn't have time to close them both. He went down to the engine room to try to get her going. That's what the old man would have done, Pen. He thought he could just push through the problem, figure it out. But in less than sixty seconds she is broadside to those swells. There was no time. Water piles up. She's light and shallow, with hardly any gear. No ballast to right her when she starts to roll. He drowned down there and then he got washed out through the hatch he left open."

Pen is taking in the full weight of all of this now.

"So, you think you sunk the *Isobel* with a lousy engine repair."

Keaton cocks his head and looks out at the lake. "You know different? The thing is, I might have. Then things got so messed up with Irene, the insurance claim. I began to see that they were thinking he offed himself, and that we wouldn't get the life insurance money. I knew she'd tried to appeal the decision because I'd seen the letters from the insurance company she'd dumped in the kitchen drawer." He sighs. "Along with a whole lot of unopened bills. One of the letters was from the appeals board. They listed reasons why they thought he did it. They talked about the fact that he left the Tillbury lashed to the deck, never even tried to launch it. Christ, those things are beasts to wrestle down, especially with just one set of hands. And he still would have been focused on fixing the problem. Then there was the business about the pulled antennae. They assumed he pulled it himself but it was worn, Pen. Unreliable for months. I remember one of the crew talking to him about it. And of course, his *bad circumstances* — Irene, Ed, the money — point to one fishing family in this town that *hasn't* had bad circumstances at one point or other. It was no day to go out. He knew better but maybe he thought he could outsmart the lake, the meanness of this crazy industry." He nods in the direction of the water. "I think a part of him hated this lake. We are different in that way. I have his impatience, and I can be a hot head. But the boats, a life on the water, all that suits me. I didn't want anything more." Keaton turns and looks directly at Pen. "He was more like you. He should have been something different than he was. He hated the life he was stuck with and so he always held something back. He would have been fighting the lake, the *Isobel,* until the end, Pen. He wouldn't have given up.

"Anyway, after I read that decision from the appeals board, I began to think, I should tell them that I screwed up. But I didn't. Part of me was frozen up with guilt and the other part was furious. Furious with him for being so reckless with the equipment, so stupid to trust a kid to do a repair like that, furious with Irene for being a drunk, furious with you, Pen, and this is the shitty part: furious with you for wanting me to be him."

"That's not what I wanted, Keaton. I just wanted it to be like it was," she says softly.

He looks at her for a moment and then looks back at the lake. "And then Spar came and asked me to work on his boat and the money sounded good."

Keaton runs a hand through his hair. "Thought I could fix everything by making some cash, to buy groceries, stuff we needed. Maybe I thought Spar was doin' us a favour. The problem was, he was warped. Sick." He looks down at his hands and then raises his head again. "He was always groping me, touching me from behind as soon as we were far enough from shore. Once I was aft, pulling in the nets when he called me into the pilot house. I got back there and his pants were down around his ankles. He was grinning at me like a scare crow, his cock in his hand." His words are more strained now. "Just me and him out there."

Pen feels her throat tighten and she has to force herself to speak.

"You should have quit. The very first time…"

Keaton laughs. "Oh, I would have," he says. "But he'd seen me working on the engine that day. He saw how I looked when I came out. Every time we went out on the *Dolly* together, he let me know. He'd say 'good with your hands, eh, Keaton? Real good with a socket wrench.' He had me. I don't know what I thought might happen if I told anyone about working on the engine, but I guess I thought if nobody knew, then maybe I wasn't responsible after all. Stupid, right?"

Pen is shaking her head, but finds she can say nothing.

"Anyway, it went on like that for a while. And then one day, he was walking back from the Fish when he ran into me and Annie. I could see him looking at her, that stupid grin on his face. That's when I really started hating him.

"I knew he would tell me I had to bring her along, out on the *Dolly*. That's exactly what the drunken little bastard did and I told him to fuck himself. He just laughed at me, said he was going to say I tampered with the engine. That I did it so that Dad would drown. Maybe I did it for the insurance money, he said. I know, Pen. There was no evidence that the engine failed because of me. But I guess I was scared someone would believe him. Anyway, I went back that night and torched the boat. It was the best way I knew to hurt him. I didn't know he'd be there. He was never there after dark. But he was that night. Drunk and passed out down below."

"And that's how Andy found you."

"Andy's as strong as a workhorse. If it weren't for him, that guy would be dead. I don't know if I'd have tried to save him, Pen. That's just the truth."

"Did Andy know the rest of it?"

"I think he suspected it."

She blinks, a sad long pull at her centre. "I'm so sorry, Keaton."

"I saw myself as just an evil little bastard at that point. I didn't think sticking around was going to do you any good, Pen. I didn't think I had *ever* done you any good. But even if I was responsible for the *Isobel*, there was always Annie."

"She knew?"

"Everything. No judgments." Pen looks at Keaton's face, the features sharp with memory. "If they make it too hard for me to see her, I'll just leave again."

"I know."

It isn't a threat. She sees it now as just part of everything else.

It's several moments before he speaks again. "I think they have evidence that Spar had done it before, to other kids. That, and my age when it happened, that's why the Crown thinks that they won't pursue it now."

"Spar never came back to Port," she says. "I think I heard he was living up in Cornwall, with a sister..."

"For a while. Then he got himself into trouble with his girlfriend's kids. I got the impression that he's locked up somewhere. They weren't giving me a lot of details about that." His voice has dropped. He has let the hate for Spar go. Maybe that part of Keaton was filled up long ago by Annie. She hopes that is true.

"If I knew where you were, I could have helped. Both you and Annie..."

He shakes his head. "I don't think so, Pen."

The sky is still pink and streaked but a dark blue steals over it from the east.

"Red sky in the morning, sailors take warning. Red sky at night, sailors delight," says Keaton.

They sit together for a long time, silent, watching as the last throb of pink slips behind the horizon and the sky is enveloped in a deep velvety dark. Pen looks over at him and sees that his eyes are still on the horizon, long after the light has disappeared.

36.

THERE WERE TWO BOUQUETS of yellow daisies at the front of the church, and an oversized picture of Ben wearing a baseball cap, grinning widely at the day in front of him. The service for Ben had been simple. The minister had talked about how much Ben was loved, how much joy he had brought to his many friends.

Apart from the sister, no family had come. No neighbours, teachers, or people from that larger world who would remember him. Ben had been in residential care for most of his life and so it was the Woodside people who carried his memory.

None of them spoke at the service. When the organ started with "Oh God Our Help In Ages Past," the man Pen remembers as Sal howled like a dog. One of the residents, a small cross-eyed woman with dark frazzled hair, went to the front of the church, her outstretched hands holding a folded khaki-coloured vest. The vest was covered in pins, the kind that people collect when they go to fairs or congresses or travel abroad. After she laid the vest down in front of Ben's picture, she turned and scowled triumphantly, tragically at the gathering of people.

Now, in the memorial rose garden at the back of the church, tea, coffee, and sandwiches are being served by the church volunteer ladies. The garden is laid out in a grid pattern, with slatted wooden benches placed at intervals, each with a brass plaque "in memory of...." Not all of the roses are in bloom now. But, Pen notes, the pink ones are, small delicate heads on irregular stems. They are less convincing than red roses in July might be, but undeniably lovely.

All of the benches are taken by the Woodside residents. They sit with their sandwiches piled up on their laps, the men with their shirts buttoned tight against their throats, the women disheveled-looking and exhausted by the heat.

A warm breeze blows over the garden. Pen recognizes the Woodside staff from the beach. The younger woman, Danielle, wears her sunglasses, her arms tucked bearishly around herself. Deb, whom Pen remembers as the more mature of the two, is quietly talking to the woman who, moments ago, carried Ben's vest.

Beside the church entrance is Ben's sister. Her face is pointed and wary. With her is a small slight man wearing a navy blazer, a yellow tie, his expression both bored and restless. A husband, Pen suspects.

Deb gets up from the bench and walks toward them. She steps in close to the sister and bends her head to speak. Every so often, she half-turns, extending her hand, gesturing to where other people mingle and sit in the garden — the residents, and the staff. Her message doesn't take long, and she straightens, the two women facing one another, both painfully still, their heads slightly bowed at just the same angle. There is the suggestion of movement, the briefest brush of Deb's fingertips on the sleeve of the sister's dark nylon dress, the sister's hesitant nod, and the passing of a tentative smile across her lips.

The small cluster of Woodside staff breaks apart and the Woodside Director, and some of the staff, gently tell the residents that it is time to go now. Time to go home. Some of the residents look baffled by the proceedings, and they stand blinking at the rose bushes, watching for the staff to show them to the waiting Woodside bus.

Pen steps out behind the stream of people leaving the garden. When she looks back, she sees the sister and her husband sitting together on one of the benches, the heads of the pink roses nodding all around them in the breeze, Ben Vasco's vest folded in his sister's lap. The shiny pins on the vest catch the late summer sun and send out bold flashes that catch on people as they turn to leave.

37.

THE LAKE AT SUNSET has settled into a rhythmic push against
the shore. With the close of the day, the sand has begun to
cool. There are just a handful of people on the beach at this
time of evening, particularly now, at the end of the summer.
Mostly couples, young and middle-aged, their arms entwined,
their feet leaving parallel tracks in the coarse sand. There are
the dog walkers too, of course, and further down the beach,
where the cottages are, one or two small families are picnicking.

Most of the sailboats and leisure craft have already docked
but there are still white sails beyond the pier. Pen watches a
small v-formation of late-returning motorboats sweep into the
harbour, a convoy of baby ducks.

Labour Day weekend, and although September may be warm
and bright, in the minds of the summer people, fall is at their
doorsteps. Pen remembers how she always loved the autumn
months in Port: the empty beach, the golden light, and the way
the leaves on the poplars shimmered and danced as though
attached to tambourines.

Behind her, on a large piece of driftwood, sit Keaton and
Andy. Andy, it seems, had called Keaton earlier and Keaton
told him to just come down.

Ed has brought a folding chair to the beach, which had made
Keaton laugh, and he sits not far away from the driftwood, his
hands folded across his belly, his thick legs awkwardly splayed
out over the sand. They have been talking about Port, about

all the changes in the place, how people are committing to it again. "Look at the tourism," Ed points out. "People used to come in droves," he says, "back in the thirties and forties: The Stork Club, The Fraser House Hotel. Of course, people aren't gonna come here and dance the night away like they used to, but they'll come because of the spas, the restaurants."

Ed gives a respectful nod in the direction of the lake.

"Nobody really knows about the fishery," he says, "That all just depends...."

Jeff has been sitting with the men, thoughtful, curious, clearly enjoying the company and the talk. It had been a surprise, his coming down with Maddie. When Ed saw him earlier, he'd rubbed his big hand affectionately over the dome of Jeff's head; "You better grow somethin' up there, or wear a hat. Aren't you the guy who's so afraid of the sun?" A second later, Jeff was wearing a cap with Bourne's Fisheries written on it, looking pleased.

Irene is further down the beach, her bright scarf moving a little in the breeze, bare feet planted in the sand, an oversized shirt billowing around her like a sail. She has her eyes drawn down, and every so often she takes up a piece of polished glass, a speckled, smooth stone. One or two that she gathers are fossils, thinks Pen, the history of this place imprinted on the shore.

Not far from Irene, Maddie hunches over an assortment of treasures that she has carefully arranged over the sand. She keeps her back to Pen and the others, her spine curled like the tail of a sea horse. Pen looks out toward the grey-green water, and feels at once the smallness of the lake, and the vastness of its spirit, its limitless longevity, all the various reincarnations, shape-changes, the resurrections. In two hundred years, if in fact it becomes a wide, silted river, the bluffs eroded by the relentless wind, the water marred with bull-rushes and reeds, the lake will not have devoured itself. It will simply have changed.

Jeff walks over to her and wraps his arms around her waist his chin nestled deep into her hair. She sways a little and looks over at Keaton, sees how relaxed he is and knows that once Annie comes back, he will find her and Keaton will finally be home.

Just then, Maddie stands up, a small urchin child in the sweep of the beach, and motions to them all to come. She hops a little, swirls in a semi-circle, and then races back. They all see her, and respond to the irresistible tug.

Somewhere out in the lake, a horn blows. The breeze carries the sound to them on the beach, like an offering from the past, and Pen holds it close while she enters into the magic circle of Maddie's newest collection.

ACKNOWLEDGEMENTS

Port is a fictional town, but its situation on the north shore of Lake Erie, couldn't be more real. In writing *After Drowning*, I was lucky enough to encounter many people who have lived along Erie's shoreline, and who generously provided observations about the changes in their communities, the future of their towns, and the impact of the lake on their lives. Thank you for stopping to chat with a stranger.

For sharing his expertise in all things boat related, (and in particular diesel engines), a huge and heartfelt thanks to Peter Mills. For providing guidance about commercial marine insurance, I am grateful to Doug Searle.

The Lake Erie Marine Museum in Port Burwell is a fascinating place and provided a rich historical context for the area. Many other resources were essential to the writing of *After Drowning*, including: *The London Free Press; The Great Lakes Environmental Directory*, Great Lakes Aquatic Network and Environmental Association for Great Lakes Education; The Department of Natural Resources, Cornell University, *Agriculture and Life Sciences Publications; Sea Grant Great Lakes Network Publications; Canadian National Geographic; The St. Thomas Times; The Simcoe Reformer; The Globe and Mail*. Characters portrayed as gang members in the book are of my own invention. Descriptions of gang activity are not based in fact or offered as interpretations of actual events. *The Road To Hell: How Biker Gangs Are Conquering Canada* by Julian Sher and William Marsden was helpful in understanding the internal wars within and among these organizations.

Without first drafts, subsequent drafts can never emerge. Thank you to Heather Barclay and Michael Milde, my intrepid early readers, who with kindness and diligence read a somewhat awkward early draft and helped push the book forward. Gratitude to Bethany Gibson for being stunningly perceptive, both with respect to the writing and to the writer, and for her questions, nudges, and unfailing attention to the project. Thank you to Inanna Publications, specifically editor-in-chief Luciana Ricciutelli for her careful reading, and for pushing the book further still.

Thank you to Maggie, who at the very last, dove in to help bring the book to completion.

Many friends have offered companionship and much needed encouragement. I am grateful to each and every one. And most of all, an enormous thank you to my family: to my daughters Clara and Margaret for putting up with my regular third-floor retreats and the time I've given over the years to writing; to my brother Peter for all of his help with this project, and to my sister Cec for her loyalty and support; to Donna, and to Michael Sr. and Maria for their enthusiasm and interest; and finally, to my husband Michael, who believes in me. What a gift that has been.

Valerie Mills-Milde lives, works and writes in London, Ontario. Her short fiction has appeared in Canadian literary journals across the country. When she is not writing, she is a clinical social worker in private practice. *After Drowning* is her debut novel.